NOT HER VILLAIN

IRENE BAHRD

Cover created by Love Lee Creative
Line editing by H.M. Darling
Formatting by Irene Bahrd

 Formatted with Vellum

For everyone who only watched Once Upon a Time for Killian "Hook" Jones.

CONTENT WARNINGS AND AUTHOR NOTE

By reading this book, there is a good chance you will experience the following side effects:

- Wet panties.
- Desire to move to England in search of your own morally gray billionaire.
- The urge to get a piercing to ensure you don't have sexy on a second date. (Don't do it!)
- Looking at ice lollies differently and finding alternate uses for them. (Don't do this either!)
- Intense craving for tacos and margaritas.

You're welcome.

All jokes aside, this is a slow-to-medium burn, instalove **romantic comedy** with on-page explicit content. It is intended for mature audiences.

Additionally, there are scenes with:

- Light primal play

- Smidge of masochism and marking
- Medium dose of breeding kink
- Dash of edging and orgasm control
- Fun with vibrators
- A popsicle debacle
- Pierced peens and ladybits
- Sexy in public
- Butt stuff in the epilogue

Author Note:

Ben's chapters are written in British English. You will find an extra "u" and a lack of "z" in his point of view. **<u>This is intentional.</u>**

Sensitivity readers were consulted during the writing of this book to ensure both Ben and Layla's mother, Jennifer, were portrayed as accurately as possible with their disabilities. In addition, while professional piercers were contacted in the research process, this book is not a how to guide. If you're considering getting a piercing, please discuss with your piercer how to properly care for your new bling. Also, please be safe and talk to your doctor about what works best for you and/or your sexual partners regarding pregnancy and STI protection. Ben and Layla are fictional, you are not.

PLAYLIST

"Butterfly" — Crazy Town
"Cruel Summer" — Taylor Swift
"Dangerous Hands" — Austin Giorgio
"Bitter Sweet Symphony" — The Verve
"Fallin' for You" — Colby Caillat
"Fell in Love with a Girl" — The White Stripes
"Ex-Factor" — Lauren Hill
"Ruin My Life" — Zara Larsson
"Hero" — Enrique Ingesias

PROLOGUE — LAYLA

"That is *not* research. You're basically catfishing."

Becca's right. Online dating started as a great way to get into the heads of rich, hot men in the Pacific Northwest for my billionaire romance book. It quickly morphed into a fun game of cat and mouse. I use my real picture, but my intentions aren't purely educational.

"How is it catfishing? I don't doctor up my photo or bio," I insist.

"Lisa? Really?" Becca side eyes me and purses her lips. As authors, it's common to use pen names. This is no different. Why should I give any of them my real name? It's not like I'll ever meet them in-person. "Babes, you tell them you're doing research for your novel about morally gray billionaires, then flirt with them like you haven't been laid in a year."

"I do not," I grumble. "Would Julian be up for it? I need to finish this book, and finding a 'bad guy' has proven to be harder than I anticipated." She shakes her head with a chuckle. "Rude."

I've asked no less than a hundred times, getting the same answer every time. Becca's husband, Julian, is a billionaire. And he's not just any billionaire; the man could buy a small country if he wanted to. I would interview him for my book but he's entirely too nice, overflowing with fucking green flag book boyfriend energy and is completely obsessed with Becca. I need someone who has seen things —who has *done* things.

"You think you're going to find a hot millionaire—"

"Billionaire," I correct.

"*Billionaire* on a dating app? Is there a button they select when filling out their bio? Rolling around in coins like Scrooge McDuck—check!"

"No," I scoff. "That would be great if they did. The big boats usually give them away."

"You know damn well they just took a picture at a marina somewhere."

"Okay, here." I pull out my phone and open the dating app. "This guy, Blake. He's thirty-six. We've been chatting for a few days. Look at that car! Does that not scream 'money man?'"

Becca squints and zooms into the picture for a better look. "Fair enough. Doesn't look like a filter and he's actually inside the car." She hums in approval. "Looks like a smug asshole; maybe this is your guy? He reminds me of some of the fuckboys I knew in New York. You know, the ones who have a new woman on their arm every week. What questions do you ask?" She continues flipping through his photos, her expression varying from impressed to skeptical.

"I ask how they got to where they are, and a few international questions for this one since he's from England."

"Nothing personal?" She quirks an eyebrow and hands me back my phone.

"His favorite color is red." It slips out too easily.

"More like yours is." Becca snort-laughs. "Get it? Because he's a red flag." When I don't join in on her amusement, she schools her expression and adds, "Well, I doubt this guy is morally gray, but enjoy the flirty research. I'm glad you're able to make it to dinner tomorrow night, Ben will probably work better for your interview. Hubby warned me he's basically an evil villain from one of Amanda's romantic suspense books. Twenty bucks says he's under-selling it and Ben's hot as hell, red flags and all."

"Blake who?"

We both laugh but my heart leaps into my throat. I actually want to meet Blake, even if he isn't the morally gray billionaire hero I need for my book.

1

BEN

ONE WEEK EARLIER

"Mr. Turner, your two o'clock is here." My timid assistant, Bethany, adjusts her dark pink, plastic-frame glasses. Much like the rest of my staff, she's scared shitless of me.

"Send them in." I close my chat with an author who wants to interview me, then stand at my desk, buttoning my blazer.

I've been talking with an inexperienced Lisa Granger off and on since last night. A quick internet search came up empty, so she must be an up-and-coming author. I wouldn't normally entertain someone so unqualified, but there's something about her I find fascinating. To be safe, I've given her a fake name; there's a chance she's done the same.

I've been looking forward to the merger meeting with Roger Kipling all week. He marches in, boring his eyes into me as he adjusts his cufflinks. "Benedict," he groans.

"Roger. Have a seat." Holding eye contact, I take his offered hand, maintaining a firm grip until our knuckles are white. I make sure he sits first—a not-so-subtle power play, standing for a moment longer than necessary to stare down at him.

"When will this be over with?" he seethes.

I'm buying out his publishing company, effectively making him one of the richest men in the business—the least he can do is show a little gratitude. Instead, he gives me more attitude than a petulant teenager.

"I'll be heading to Seattle in a week, then New York, and back here. The arrangements have been made. You're coming with me. We need to make sure the transition is smooth." I don't add that it would be nearly impossible with him here micromanaging the day-to-day. I don't trust the prick.

"The Americans are going to eat you alive, Benedict." He shakes his head. "Why don't you just stay here and let me do what I do best? You can sit in your ivory tower and enjoy the millions pouring in."

I didn't get to where I am by letting others '*do what they do best.*' No, I got here by maintaining iron control in most aspects of my life. Under no circumstances will I allow Roger to purposefully drive the company into the ground while my back is turned.

"Absolutely not. I'll be there in-person until I can put new staff in place and conduct a few rounds of layoffs."

"You are *not* cutting my people," he growls. I can practically see the steam leaving his ears as his fists clench and jaw tics.

I relish in the sight of his anger, waiting a moment longer than necessary to answer him. "It's business, Roger.

Redundancy is inevitable. You understand." I have no issue dismantling his company if he tries to fuck me over. "We'll be letting go of author contracts as well. We'll probably start with romance, since there are so many of them."

Roger scoffs. "For someone who owns half of the publishing industry, you know nothing about books. Romance is a billion dollar industry. If you start cutting, they'll all jump ship. We already lost Merlot Bennet, we can't afford to lose any more big names."

"That may be true, but she writes contemporary. Vampire porn is hardly romance. I'm sure we could cut several fantasy or paranormal titles, and replace them with contemporary or romantic comedies." My mate, Julian, narrates fantasy audiobooks. I'll make sure his titles are safe. After that? The rest can be chucked out for all I care.

"You're a fucking idiot. Just because there's sex in a book, doesn't make it porn. And so fucking what if some of them are? Look at some of our top dark romance authors' back-lists; you'll find a mafia don who fucks a woman with a cigar, or a stalker's brother who kidnaps the heroine. Shit, that's just from one author. Don't get me started on the authors who write men with breeding or primal kinks. Those are some of our best sellers. Why would you cut them?"

I still at his words and stifle a groan. My preferences behind closed doors are of a particular variety. Keeping my expression neutral, I grip the armrest of my office chair, in an attempt to maintain my composure.

"Regardless of the sexual content of your catalogue, I will not allow you to destroy your own company from the inside by continuing to promote romance authors." Roger rolls his eyes but I press on. "Cut the authors, the editors, and the assistants, or you'll never see the inside of a board-room again. If you don't do it, I will."

Roger groans. "You're worried about me destroying the company, but you're willing to throw away millions, for what? Sex in books? You can't be serious, Ben."

"It's Mr. Turner. You answer to me, Roger. Cut them, or you can sell your shares." I smirk and lean forward in my seat. Him handing the company over to me is the most ideal outcome. If he tries to fuck me, I can sell the company for a few billion and walk away. It isn't special. I'll dismantle it piece by piece, keeping only the profitable departments, just like I've done with every other publishing house for the past decade.

"This was my wife's company!" he roars. "Over my dead body."

That can be arranged.

Last minute preparations have been made. I only have a few more days until I'm headed to Seattle and I'm dreading every minute of it. To distract myself, I scheduled dinner tonight with a blonde woman with tits big enough to double as flotation devices.

Unfortunately, it's the worst date I've ever been on. While the woman sitting across from me would be a fun shag, my thoughts keep drifting back to the unassuming, American author who contacted me last night.

When Bridget gets up to use the toilet, I open the messages on my dating app to block her from further communication; I have no interest in seeing her again after this evening is over. Scrolling through a few Seattle matches, I'm hoping to line a few women up for drinks—*maybe a shag or two*—but instead of replying to the twelve women who messaged me today, I click on the thread with Lisa. I should probably tell her my real name at some point, but I'm enjoying anonymity far too much.

> I'd be honoured to be interviewed for your book.

LISA

Thank you! I know it's not the most conventional way of finding a wealthy man on the internet to interview, but I appreciate you taking the time to talk to me.

> I'll be in Seattle in a few days, would you like to meet for a pint?

That's not necessary. I can collect all the information I need through texts and emails, if that's okay with you?

The fact that she doesn't want to meet has me wanting to even more. I enjoy a good chase.

> Messaging can be tedious. How about a video call?

How do I say this and still be respectful? Not a chance.

I can't help the laugh that escapes me. Women never speak to me this way; it's refreshing.

> Well, aren't you as tight as a duck's arse, love.

I'm sorry, is that a British term?

I looked it up. Yes, I suppose I am as tight as a duck's ass. Though the internet gave me several options to choose from.

Either you're calling me poor or stubborn. Compared to you, I'm most definitely both.

You've never heard that before?

Absolutely not. But I'll be using it often now, arsehole.

Sorry, that was meant as a joke. I think it's hilarious when someone says arse. I'm sure it didn't translate properly over text.

No offense taken. I am indeed an arsehole.

A call? Better yet, why don't we take a walk while I'm there or grab a coffee? I'll answer any questions you have for me.

I'll make you a deal: you answer a few of my questions on here and I'll agree to meet in person. It better be an actual walk. I don't run.

I'm too busy flirting with Lisa that I didn't notice Bridget taking a seat opposite me. "Shit. Where did you come from?"

"Based on that ridiculous grin on your face, I'd gather you're talking with another woman." She stands, slipping her handbag onto her shoulder. "Have a lovely evening."

The moment she's gone, I sip my rum and return my attention to my phone, finding an entire questionnaire from Lisa waiting for me.

2

LAYLA

1. How did you make your first million? What about your first billion?
2. What charities do you contribute to?
3. Follow-up to #2, are they personal to you or what your PR team has set up on your behalf?
4. What is your favorite color? (Yes, this has significance, please answer it.)
5. What is your astrological star sign? (This is for science.)
6. Where did you grow up?
7. What is the last romance novel you read?
8. Do you have any piercings? (Don't answer that.)

Chewing on my lip, I push send. I shouldn't flirt with him, yet here I am, shamelessly doing it. The other men I've contacted start a conversation with something like: "Hey, baby. What's your cup size?" Or, if they're feeling extra bold, they jump straight to the dick pics. Blake is the first who acted as if this was a business meeting, and here I am being a hypocrite asking about piercings.

Blake's status shows offline, so I take out my laptop to get some writing done. I'm already a few paragraphs into a new chapter of a side quest book I started last week—where Penelope is in prison for magical treason—and startle when my phone dings with a new message. I excitedly snatch my phone, hoping it's Blake. My face falls when I see it's Becca.

> **BECCA**
>
> I'm headed to Portland with Julian in a few days for a mini vacation. His friend, Ben, who he hasn't seen in forever, is coming to Seattle for work. So, we'll be there for a day or two.
>
> We're making a PNW week of it!
>
> I expect coffee, lunch, or dinner while we're in Seattle! In fact, I better get all three!
>
>> Yes! Name the day and time and I'll make it work.
>
> Are you up for a dinner date?
>
> Julian's setting up a dinner with Ben. Apparently, he's hot.
>
> Well, Julian says he's moderately attractive.
>
> I don't really want to have dinner with them by myself. Please say yes!

Do I want to go on a date? Is it a date? I kind of like this Blake guy. There's no way he's into me, so maybe Ben is the perfect distraction.

>> Sure. But we still need to grab coffee.

Just as I'm about to suggest one of my favorite places, a notification appears at the top of my screen from Blake. I can't click fast enough.

> BLAKE
>
> **I'll have answers for you shortly.**

Shit. I shouldn't have included my flirty icebreaker questions. He's all business; I may as well have received an email stating we'll 'discuss matters at a later date.' Disappointed, I text Becca with a few options for coffee.

I return to my writing, and my phone pings with Blake's response. I open our messages to read through his answers.

1. First million was running my own prosthetics company. Billion was after buying out a few companies.
2. I contribute to several charities. Most are recommended by colleagues or my financial advisor.
3. One in particular charity is important to me— they provide affordable accessibility options for people who need them.
4. Red, but not bright red. Almost a dark orange. Like sunset on an autumn day.
5. I had to research which sign I am. Apparently, I'm a Leo.
6. Canterbury, near London. It's where I was born and bred.
7. I don't read romance novels, but the billionaire one you're researching is intriguing.
8. Not yet, but there's one I've been wanting to get.

Oh shit! Some of those were incredibly thoughtful. I tap my nails on my desk, contemplating my response.

> A Leo? Interesting.

Why? Are we destined to be enemies?

> Sure. Let's go with that.

Ah, so lovers then. Perhaps our meeting shall be more than just an interview.

I suck in a breath. *Is he flirting? He's flirting, right?*

> I guess we'll never know. Perhaps your answers were unsatisfactory and we'll never meet.

Oh, we absolutely will. Speaking of which, should I pick you up, or would you prefer to meet me? I can send a car.

> You think I would give my address to a stranger on the internet?

Live a little, darling.

> Darling?

Would you prefer 'love?'

> Absolutely not.

Darling it is.

> Fine, I'll meet you for an interview. Nothing more.

If you say so. Now, it's only fair that you answer a few of my questions.

My stomach drops.

> Sure. Lay it on me.

The same as you asked me. Plus one. I'll ask once I see your responses.

I take a deep breath. He doesn't need to know much; I can keep it vague and respond in rapid fire.

> First million writing books—not a billionaire. Yet.

> Contribute to a few charities but should do more.

> Favorite color is yellow, but not neon yellow.

> I'm a Sagittarius, but that means nothing to you. My birthday is in December.

> Lived in New York most of my life but I've been living in Seattle for a while now.

> I enjoy writing fantasy romance but my current work in progress is my first contemporary. I just finished reading an adorable book about a guy who restores his grandmother's home and falls for her nurse. So, I'm pretty sure my next book will be about a small town.

> Were my answers satisfactory?

Yellow, but not neon?

> More of a pastel or sunshine yellow.

Sunshine yellow suits you.

You forgot one.

> I'll show you mine, when you show me yours.

Fuck. Why did I say that? I unsend the message, even though it shows he already saw it.

> Well, this is an interesting turn of events.

> I don't know what you're talking about.

A notification pops up on the screen.

You've been invited to a voice call with Blake T.

Shit. Against my better judgment, I pick up. "Hello?"

"Oh, sunshine, I do believe you told me that if I showed you mine, you'd show me yours. Why would you delete that message?" Blake's voice is sultry. He sounds tired, but his accent is doing things for me.

Is the hot billionaire flirting with me?

Should I ask him to call me a good girl? For research.

No! Fuck.

I clear my throat. "It was inappropriate. My sincerest apologies," I manage in the most professional voice I can muster. He chuckles darkly and my breath catches. "Anyway, I know it's late for you. Thank you for the preliminary interview screening. I'll have my PA reach out with additional questions, should I have any."

Ooh, that sounded good! It would help if my PA wasn't my sister—the last thing I need is her reaching out to him.

"I'll have my people contact your people. In the meantime, what do you say we continue this same time tomorrow? My follow-up questions can wait until then."

"Oh, um…"

"Fantastic. I'll talk to you tomorrow, *sunshine*." The way he says 'sunshine' with that hot as fuck accent of his—it's playful with a darkness to it. The butterflies in my stomach begin somersaulting.

"I suppose that's better than 'darling.' Have a good night, Blake."

The line cuts off and I stare at my phone for a while longer, wondering what the hell just happened.

The last few days, Blake called me in the middle of my day and we talked for hours—until what would be 3 a.m. for him. Our conversations feel like I'm talking to an old friend—if that old friend was sinfully attractive and their voice alone could make you come. While he flirts, we haven't crossed any lines. Sadly, there's been no phone sex with the hot billionaire, but the sexy banter and getting to know him is hotter than any smutty audiobook I've listened to.

Blake landed in Seattle earlier today. I hadn't expected to hear from him so soon, but we've been on the phone for four hours. It's the middle of the night, but I'm normally up late writing, so I don't mind talking to him so late. How he's still awake is beyond me.

"You'll be leaving right before football season starts. It's a big deal here. You can't go anywhere without seeing team flags and jerseys."

"Darling, American football is *not* football," he insists.

"I'm aware. You have *soccer* in England." I know my word choice will ruffle some feathers. I sink further into my pillow to get comfortable, awaiting his defense.

"I'll have to take you to a proper *football* game sometime."

"I've never been to a *soccer* game. No one gets tackled, so how much fun could it actually be to watch?"

"So, you enjoy getting tackled, sunshine? That could be arranged."

I suck in a breath. "I, um…"

"Sorry, love. I shouldn't have said that. Forgive a tired man for his blunder?"

"It was just unexpected."

Blake's full of surprises tonight. He told me about his mother, and how he has a close relationship with her. He also mentioned that his cousin is some kind of *Indiana Jones*. We talked about our favorite food and drinks; he takes his tea with a little milk but not cream, and he absolutely hates pineapple on pizza. The last one is almost a deal breaker. I love a red flag book boyfriend, but hating pineapple is taking it too far.

I change the subject away from being chased and tackled for sport. "So, what are you up to tomorrow?" There's silence on the other end. "Blake?" I listen carefully and hear the deep rise and fall of his breath, almost but not quite a snore. "Goodnight, Mr. Billionaire," I say quietly. I hang up and close my eyes, drifting off and dreaming about a flirtatious, gorgeous man I enjoy talking to a bit too much.

3

BEN

"Benedict?" The barista's voice pulls me from my daydream.

"That's me," I sneer. Why must they always use my name from my credit card in an attempt to make things more personal? I grab my latte and find a comfortable chair to settle into while I wait for my friend, Julian.

I've been fantasising about Lisa more than usual today. I can typically go several hours without her invading my thoughts. Today, she's consumed me.

Since our initial call, we've been chatting for hours on the phone. Last night, something was different. Her sweet demeanor and her full laughter have pulled me even deeper into my daydream. She's the perfect combination of strength and softness—I'm drawn to her like a moth to a flame.

My inbox is flooded with women throwing themselves at me, but Lisa's different. She hasn't flirted with me since we started talking and actually shrugs off my advances. Even when there's a slip up, she quickly corrects herself. Sure, there have been some personal questions, but she's genuine and… my polar opposite.

Fuck, I'm supposed to meet her tomorrow. I'm excited and surprisingly nervous. I don't remember the last time I was nervous meeting a woman. I quite enjoy that we talk about anything and everything.

My phone vibrates with a text. I set down my latte and find several missed messages. I'm about to click on one from my assistant when I spot one from Lisa.

LISA

Sorry I fell asleep last night!

I believe I fell asleep first.

If it makes you feel better, I dropped my phone on my face.

Twice.

You did not. But yes, it does make me feel a little better.

Meeting up with a friend for coffee in a few. Talk soon!

Same time tonight?

I woke up this morning with my phone resting on my chest and dead wireless earbuds. I've never fallen asleep on the phone with a woman before; it was one of the best nights of my life and I've never even met her in person.

The typing bubbles appear on my screen when there's a notification of an incoming text from Julian. He must be running behind to meet me. I click on it.

Wipe that ridiculous smile off your face.

I glance up, surprised to find Julian sitting across from me, stifling a laugh.

"You're such an arsehole, Jules."

"I fucking love that you say 'arse.' So, who's the girl?" Julian sits back, smugly sipping his coffee.

"There's no girl," I insist, placing my phone screen side down on my thigh. It vibrates twice. I know it's her. "Lisa." I clear my throat. He'd pull it out of me eventually. "Her name is Lisa."

Mid-sip, Julian nearly chokes on his coffee and his eyes widen. "What? So, there *is* a girl?" I nod. "Do you have a picture?"

Julian and I have known each other for years but we usually keep our conversation to business and football. He never asks about women because my answer is always the same: Never anyone of consequence. He's married now, so I'm not concerned about him trying to steal this one from me. I enjoy that no one knows about her but me—even my family, who I'm close with.

"Yeah, but I'm sure as fuck not showing you," I reply. Julian chuckles and a small smirk appears as he takes a drink. "She's gorgeous, but unlike the typical women I date. She's fucking smart and—"

"Let me guess, she's a *nice* girl? You know you can't date her."

"Why the fuck not?" Julian saying that I can't just makes me want to pursue her even more. I enjoy the challenge, especially if it's something I'm not supposed to have. The forbidden is always more enticing. Even if I ruin the girl in the end.

He winces. "You're not exactly a good guy. Let me guess. She's, what, twenty-two?"

"If I'm not a good man, then why the bloody hell are we mates? And no, she's thirty-four." I sip my latte, awaiting his response. It's still scalding hot; the milk is a little burnt. Can't anyone make a proper coffee in this country? I should've ordered tea but needed the extra caffeine today as I adjust to the time difference. Talking to Lisa until 3 a.m. didn't help.

"I wonder that myself sometimes," he teases, then shakes his empty cup. "I'm going to grab a refill. Want one?"

"This one is rubbish. Could you order me a cup of black tea with milk? They can't fuck that up, can they?" No, they absolutely can. "On second thought, just water."

"You're such an *arsehole*, Benny." He gets up for a new coffee and a water. When he returns, he asks, "What are your plans tomorrow night?"

I don't want to let on that I'm supposed to meet Lisa. "No plans, why?"

"My wife and I are meeting her friend, Layla, for dinner. I meant to ask you a week ago, and I think Becca is trying to make it a double date. Could you come? I already told her last week that you were, and I hate being a third wheel with those two."

Bollocks. I can't say no now. "Depends. What time?"

Julian checks his phone and sends me the information for a new seafood restaurant in town. "How's six?"

"Can we do earlier?" Julian frowns, so I correct myself, "I'm a little jet lagged and need to keep a consistent schedule."

He eyes me suspiciously. "How about five? We can eat with the senior citizens."

"Perfect." Now, I just need to move my date—*meeting*— with Lisa out a few hours.

―――――

After coffee with Julian, and a day full of tedious meetings with the merger and acquisitions department, I'm thankful to be settled in my temporary flat. It's the dullest place I've ever stayed, but I'll take a penthouse apartment over a hotel any day.

I've been looking forward to talking to Lisa tonight. It's only 8 p.m. here, but that's 4 a.m. my time. Still, I want to talk to my little author. I open the dating app, click on our message thread, and press call.

"Good evening," Lisa practically sings. I can't help the smirk tugging at my lips.

"Hello, sunshine," I flirt back, keeping my voice intentionally low.

There's a short pause. I swear I hear her breath hitch. She clears her throat. "How was your day?"

"I met a friend for coffee this morning and had a few rough meetings this afternoon. What about you? Find another billionaire to interview?" With all of my being, I want her to say no.

She laughs. "I also met a friend for coffee but it was otherwise an uneventful day of writing. I do know another billionaire but there's no way I would interview him."

I straighten. *I wasn't her first choice?* "Really? Why not?"

"He's too nice. I need to talk to someone who is, well, not." She doesn't think I'm nice? I'm not, but that's not exactly the impression I intended to give off with her. I take too long to respond, and she clarifies, "Not that you're not nice. That's not what I meant. The character I'm writing is a little more morally grey than my friend is."

"And you deem me to be *morally grey?*"

"Yes, no… I don't know you well enough to determine that."

Oh, sunshine. You have no idea.

"Well, what I'm taking from this is that we need to get to know one another better." It comes out as a purr. I want to entrap this innocent woman, break her down to build her up again.

"I, um… Speaking of getting to know one another. Do you mind if we cancel tomorrow? I have some last minute plans that came up. Rain check?"

Does she have a date?

"Do I mind? Of course I do. What time is your date tomorrow night?"

Lisa stumbles over her words but manages, "It's not a date. Just dinner with friends and some guy I've never met."

"Cancel on the bloke." It slips out before I can stop it. "What I meant to say is, if you can't cancel, I don't mind meeting later. I also had a last minute meeting come up and was going to ask to move our little rendezvous, anyway."

"Not a rendezvous, Blake. It's just an interview."

That's what you think, sunshine. "If you say so."

My nerves have been shot all day. I haven't been on a date in… *shit*. I don't remember the last time I went on a date. I've been consumed with writing and marketing my book for years; I didn't have a moment to breathe until Kipling Publishing took me on. Now that I have more time, I'm terrified to dip my toe into the dating pool.

Tonight, I'm wearing a crimson red silk top, black blazer, and dark skinny jeans, completing the look with red bottom black stilettos—intentionally wearing pops of red for a certain billionaire I'm seeing later tonight. I need something sexy but sophisticated, versatile enough for a dinner with Ben and an interview with Blake. I wasn't lying to Blake; I'm not sure if it's even a double date with Ben. It feels like more of a friendly dinner.

My stomach drops. If it *is* a date, I'd much rather it be with Blake. He's a bit of a flirt, and he's not interested in me like that, but there's something about him that draws me in. I don't typically interview men for my books and I'm hyperaware of why that is now. I've been so deep in research that I'm now attracted to my own billionaire.

Not yours, Layla. It's just an interview. Nothing more.

I have just enough time to grab a rideshare to the restaurant. I swipe on a coat of my favorite dark red lip stain, top it with clear lip gloss, then toss both in my purse. After one last check in the mirror, I head out the door.

The ride to the restaurant should only be twenty minutes. With traffic, it takes almost thirty. I hate being too early, but not as much as I detest being late. The rideshare drops me off and I glance down the street to the cafe where I'm supposed to meet Blake later. My shoulders slump. I should be more excited to go out to dinner with Becca, Julian, and his friend. Smothering my disappointment, I correct my posture, paint on a bright smile, and walk inside.

The host directs me to the table where they're already seated. Becca is impeccably dressed; after marrying Julian, she always is. Julian's wearing a light blue button-down shirt, sleeves rolled up. Asshole. He knows what he's doing. As an audiobook narrator, he's well aware it's Book Boyfriend Etiquette 101. What next? A doorway lean? My friend is a lucky bitch.

Ben has his back to me as I approach the table. He has the same raven black hair Blake has, making my guilt seep in. His light yellow shirt sleeves are also rolled up, his tattoos peeking out from under them. Perhaps he took notes from Julian and this won't be just a friendly dinner, after all. I envisioned him a little more conservative, even if Becca didn't give me any clues about his appearance. The only thing she mentioned is he's here for a few months.

This could be a fun summer fling?

"Sorry I'm late, everyone, traffic was awful." Ben turns to greet me and… *Why is Blake here?* I skid to a stop. "Hi."

"Well, hello, sunshine. Isn't this a pleasant surprise?" Blake's sapphire blue eyes twinkle with mischief.

I suck in a breath. I'm a fucking idiot and should've known he'd also give a fake name.

Taking the seat next to him, I whisper, "What are you doing here?" I don't care if Becca and Julian can hear me. Fuck it.

"It seems you had a date after all, *Lisa.*"

Julian eyes Ben suspiciously, then shifts his gaze to me. "I'm sorry. Becca failed to mention that you two were seeing each other."

"We aren't," I insist a little too quickly. "I have no idea what you're talking about."

"When Ben said he was meeting with an author named Lisa for an interview later, I put two and two together," Becca snickers, then gasps. "Oh, shit!" She lets out a laugh that fills the room. "Hold on, which trope is this?" Wiggling her eyebrows teasingly, I scoff in response, fidgeting with the hem of my shirt. This is so fucking embarrassing.

"Mistaken identity?" Julian offers.

"Close, but no." Becca taps her finger to her lips. "Maybe secret identity?"

"Just because you two have some weird fated mates bond, doesn't mean everything has a trope," I grumble and cross my arms over my chest, leaning back in my chair.

"Well, looks like you have your plot figured out for your billionaire romance," Ben playfully suggests, sipping his beer. My attention is drawn to his lips and I quickly look away.

"Oh, for the love. Yes, I am interviewing *Blake* for my book. How was I supposed to know that he's your friend?"

Ben reaches under the table and gently grips my thigh in solidarity. I suck in a breath. I don't remember the last time a man touched me, even if it's just a friendly, innocent gesture in response to this fucked up situation.

"We both used fake names," he says softly, but lowers his voice as he continues, "Perhaps I'm not the only morally gray one at this table." His intense, but playful gaze ensnares me and I'm helpless to look away. He doesn't remove his hand as he addresses Julian, "This is my fault, mate. I gave her a pseudonym. There's no way she could've known it was me."

"I need a drink. Does anyone else need a drink? No? Okay, well, I'm going to the bar to grab one." My voice is squeaky, my words falling out in rapid succession, but I don't give a shit at this point. I need to get far away from this gorgeous man and take a moment to think.

I get up too quickly and knock Ben's hand against the underside table. He lets out a quiet hiss. When I glance at my friends, they both give me a knowing look. They may as well say out loud, "Why is his hand on your lap, Layla?" *Assholes*. If I wasn't mortified before, I am now.

Rushing to the bar, I find a free seat at the end. Thankfully, the stools to the left and right of me are occupied, so if Ben tries to do some sort of heroic chase, there's no chance he can join me.

I signal to the bartender and order a margarita on the rocks with salt. It doesn't pair well with what I was planning on ordering for dinner, but tequila-drunk sounds like a fantastic idea right now. I rest my face in my hands and take a deep breath in and out.

Blake is Ben. Ben is Blake. Bl-en is friends with Julian, which means he's a *nice* guy. I can't interview him now. Nice guys aren't morally gray villains, even if Becca implied he's an ass. Julian wouldn't be friends with a douchebag. I'm back to the drawing board to figure out how I'm going to make this book work.

A familiar purr comes from behind me. "I didn't know, sunshine."

"Yeah, well, here we are, *Benjamin.*" I don't lift my face from my palms. I can't face him.

"It's actually Benedict. Here's what's going to happen, love. We're going to have a drink here at the bar, we'll have dinner with Julian and Becca, then we'll have that little meeting of yours at the cafe down the street. All as if nothing is amiss." Ben then says to the man next to me, "I'll give you $1,000 for your seat if you're out of it in eight seconds."

I finally glance up. "You don't ha—" Ben's handing the man a small stack of $100 bills and on the stool next to me before I can get the rest of my sentence out.

"Now, where were we, sunshine?"

5

BEN

When Julian began pursuing Merlot Bennet—who I've come to know as Becca—I thought he was out of his mind. He kept talking about an instant connection and how he knew the moment they met that she was the one for him.

It's absolutely absurd.

He's narrated far too many romance books that it's infected him with some sort of delusional idea that soulmates exist. While he might be living happily ever after with the love of his life, that's not in my future. As much as I feel an unexplainable pull toward Layla, she's certainly not my forever. She can't be.

That doesn't mean I can't have a bit of fun.

I can't deny that Layla is absolutely stunning. I knew from her pictures that she was beautiful, but I haven't been able to take my eyes off her since the moment she walked into the restaurant. Her hazel eyes I so easily get lost in, her dark auburn hair she repeatedly tucks behind her ear, the light dusting of freckles across her nose... she's breathtaking. I knew there was something special about her when we began talking, but nothing could've prepared me for this enchantress of a woman. She captivated me, to the point that I'd chase like this.

I enjoy a hunt, but I don't enjoy when my prey is someone like her. I have few friends—one, really. Julian is the only person who still sees any good in me after I've dismantled company after company, destroying everything in my wake on the path to greatness. I can't lose the only friend I have by playing with his wife's friend.

So, why am I still sitting here, with bated breath, awaiting this beautiful woman to say yes? She doesn't even know what she's agreeing to.

"You shouldn't have done that." Layla shakes her head.

"I—" I'm interrupted by the bartender dropping off her drink. "I'll have one as well, thank you." He nods and begins mixing a cocktail I normally wouldn't be caught dead drinking.

"I shouldn't have come tonight," she admits.

A swirl of emotions stabs me in the gut. I swallow my pride and dare to ask, "Why not?"

"It was supposed to be a dinner with friends, and—"

"No," I growl. "It's a date. Call it what it is, darling. I hate to admit I wasn't looking forward to tonight. But you came here for a date, same as I did."

Layla's gaze is murderous, eyes dark and burning into me. She lightly licks her dark red lips, daring me not taste her. "You didn't want to come? Why are you still here if you're so disappointed?"

Fuck. I love that she's cheeky, even though she's otherwise delightful. I tuck a few stray strands of her hair behind her ear, as she's done all night. Her breath catches at my touch. If she reacts this way to a simple gesture, I'd have far too much fun playing with her.

"You have it all wrong, sunshine. I'm the furthest from disappointed. I was looking forward to later. I didn't want to go out to dinner with my mate's friend, I wanted to see *you* tonight. I wasn't lying when I said it was a pleasant surprise."

"We were only going to grab coffee and I was going to interview you. We—"

"Call it whatever you want. Doesn't change what I want." *Shit. I shouldn't have said that. What is it about this woman that I can't keep my composure around her?*

"What do you want?" Her eyes dart between mine, searching for answers I so desperately and selfishly want to give her. She's the sunshine to my darkness. I would destroy her.

Fuck it. I don't want only want to have fun with this woman. I want all of her.

"You want to get out of here?"

Layla doubles over in laughter; definitely not the response I was looking for. When she catches her breath, she replies, "This has to be the worst date I've ever been on! No dinner, no drinks, no conversation. Just straight to it with the 'want to get out of here?' I have to say, this is a first for me—up there with unsolicited cock pics for the worst way to hit on a woman, ever."

I'm speechless, unsure how to respond, as she finishes her margarita in three long gulps. My gaze falls to her throat, watching each swallow intently. I envision my hand wrapped around it, bringing her perfect red lips to mine. Claiming her.

"Well, this has been fun. I'm going to get a rideshare and head out. Enjoy dinner with Becca and Julian." Layla swivels in her seat and hops off the stool.

Before she can get away, I wrap my arm around her waist and pull her to me until her back is flush with my chest. I'm wrapped in her citrus and lavender perfume and resist the urge to breathe her in further. Layla stifles a moan, and I know I'm risking everything but I can't help myself. She's the perfect fit in my arms and I find myself not wanting to let go.

I whisper beside her ear, "Let my driver take you home, after we have our *meeting*."

"I should go," she breathes.

I release her. "Your choice, sunshine." She turns, eyes wild with lust she's trying to hide, but she blinks it away and walks swiftly toward the exit.

I'm a man who always gets what he wants. It might not be tonight, but Layla will be mine.

6

LAYLA

Ben has some fucking nerve… but, *fuck*, it felt good having his arm around me. I'm a grown, educated woman, I shouldn't be so easily charmed by some hot billionaire.

I'm not falling. No, nope, I'm not going to do it. I refuse. I don't even know the guy; it should be easy enough to get him out of my head. Seattle is a large city, if he's only here for a few months, I'll just avoid him until he leaves.

I can do this.

I'm standing outside waiting for my rideshare when Ben's voice startles me. "Layla, I'm sorry, I shouldn't have done that."

I fumble my phone and it falls to the ground with a crack. *Damn it!* We both bend down to pick it up and his woodsy cologne envelopes me. I take a deep breath as I right my posture. Why does he have to smell so good? He hands me my phone and the screen is shattered. I inwardly chastise myself; I should've bought a better protective case.

"Come back inside. I'll leave if you want me to, but Julian and Becca leave town in the morning. I know she wants to spend time with you before they go to Portland." Ben's voice is soft; his eyes earnest. Maybe we can be friends? I can be friends with an incredibly attractive man.

Nope, I'll be a cliché female main character in a friends-to-lovers trope, pining after a man I shouldn't want. He'll leave and I'll be heartbroken.

"I had coffee with her yesterday. She'll understand." My tone is meeker than I'd like but I'm stuck in some sort of staring contest with him. I'm lost in his fucking gorgeous eyes. It's entirely unfair how attractive he is.

Ben tucks my wind-swept hair behind my ear. "Sunshine." It's quiet but laced with something almost feral. If I was in the fantasy romance books I write, I would have the characters' lips crashing into each other in an epic makeout session right about now. He'd probably be some kind of shifter or…

The villain.

Becca may have been onto something. Ben could be the inspiration for my billionaire after all. As he towers over me even in my heels, the street lights only highlight his chiseled features. He has the whole look down, with raven black hair, piercing blue eyes, and the perfectly groomed short beard. Intentional scruff is so damn hot.

It's fiction. I can make up the horrible things he does in my story.

I swallow hard. "Okay, I'll come back inside."

"Attagirl." He offers his arm. Damn it, he has gentleman

moves, too. "I can't promise I'll behave, but I promise I'll try."

Maybe he's not a nice guy?

I take his arm. "I still have to cancel my rideshare, but my phone…"

"I'll replace it," he insists. "It was my fault. I'm sure I can have it delivered before dinner is over."

"You don't ha—"

Ben silences me with his finger to my lips. I blink in surprise. His fingers travel lower, tracing my jaw and sliding into my hair. He drops our linked arms and pulls me to him by my lower back until our bodies are flush.

Is he… Is he going to kiss me?

Ben leans in until our faces are mere inches apart. I instinctively wet my lips. The movement catches his attention and his gaze is fixed on my mouth. He closes the distance and—

"Layla, there you… Oh. Sorry, I'll just…" Becca turns on her heel to leave.

Ben laughs softly and presses his forehead to mine. "We'll be right there. Something I need to do first."

Becca's long gone as I anticipate a kiss that never comes. Instead, he kisses my forehead and releases me. I try to stifle the whimper at the loss of contact, but he hears it anyway and smirks.

Taking out his phone, he types for what feels like an hour. I take a step back to head into the restaurant, but he hooks his arm around my waist and pulls me into him.

"Not so fast, sunshine. I just needed to order you a new phone. I'm not done with you yet." His eyes finally lift to meet mine as he pockets his device. "Now, where were we?"

"We were going inside."

"No, we weren't. I was going to kiss you, and you were going to let—"

I break out into a fit of giggles. I'm sure he stole that line from Julian. It's a good line, and I would've fallen for it if Becca hadn't told me about Julian using it first.

Ben frowns. "Is there something funny about wanting to kiss you?"

"I'm sorry, but you need original material."

His eyes soften and he laughs lightly. "Let me guess, Becca?" I nod, biting my lip. "Ah. Well, can't fault a man for trying."

I lift onto my toes and kiss his cheek. "Come on, let's get inside. You can continue to plagiarize over a drink and dinner."

Ben attempts to take my hand and I swat it away, but he guides me inside by the small of my back, anyway. When we make it back to the table, he pulls out my chair for me. As I sit, he leans in beside my ear and whispers, "You look incredible tonight."

My breath catches as the hair raises on the back of my neck. His hot breath coupled with that delicious accent is doing things to me I'd rather not admit. I squeeze my thighs together, since my damn body insists on betraying me tonight.

He takes his seat next to me and types something on his phone, showing it to me. "See, your phone is already enroute."

Except it's not tracking; he shows me his notes app.

You know red is my favourite colour, but that sexy top of yours would look better on my floor in the morning.

7

BEN

A blush creeps up Layla's neck, painting her cheeks a beautiful shade of crimson. I shouldn't be flirting with this innocent woman, but when she looks at me with those fucking enchanting hazel eyes... I can't help myself. I'm dead certain she wore red for me, just as I wore yellow for her.

"I, uh, thank you," she manages.

"What happened to your phone?" Becca asks Layla with a raised eyebrow.

Layla hands my phone back to me. "It, um, shattered. I was—"

"It was my fault. I startled her. A new one will be couriered over to us within the hour." I am enjoying this chase more than I should. Placing the napkin on my thigh, I signal to the waiter to order a round of drinks.

Julian huffs a laugh. "You're here less than a week and already breaking hearts and phones."

"I haven't broken any hearts." I glance at Layla, well aware I will absolutely break hers. "Just a phone."

"I'm going to use the restroom," Becca announces, then asks Julian, "Would you mind getting me a refill on my Manhattan?"

Julian takes her hand, kisses her knuckles, and nods. Part of me wants to be disgusted by my love-sick friend, but I can't help a pang of jealousy seeing him so happy.

"I'll join you." Layla cannot get away from me fast enough. She scurries off to the loo, leaving Julian and I alone.

Immediately, his smile fades. "No," he growls. His previously friendly demeanor is replaced with a scowl; his tone laced with venom.

"No, what?"

"Not Layla."

"I don't know what you're talking—"

"I said no, Ben. You're not going to hurt one of the sweetest women I've ever met. You want to fuck around with someone? You want a toy to play with? Find someone else, *anyone* else. You destroy authors' careers, she's an author, how do you really think that's going to work out?"

The waiter interrupts before I can defend myself. "May I bring you another, Manhattan, sir?"

"Yes," Julian replies, not breaking eye contact with me. "Two please. And a margarita with salt for her *friend*." The emphasis on his last word isn't lost on me and I sit back in my chair, contemplating my next move. He should know better than to present me with a challenge.

"I'll have a dark rum, neat."

"Are you a pirate, Benny? Fitting."

The waiter mumbles something to himself and walks away. Julian's eyes still haven't left mine. He knows I always get what I want, so I'm unsure why he's goading me. Jules can try and chase her away but there's no corner of the earth that she could run to that I wouldn't find her.

What am I saying? She's a good woman, why am I considering getting involved with her? I may be a villain to some, but I'm not her villain. I won't allow it.

"You're right. I won't pursue her." It doesn't mean I can't help with her book or spend time with her. Also, I'm lying. I will absolutely pursue her if the opportunity arises.

Julian visibly relaxes. "Thank you. It would devastate Becca if you hurt Layla. I know you enjoy the"—he looks around and lowers his voice—"whole prey and hunter bit, but I'm asking you as your friend. Don't do it with this one. Okay?"

My jaw tics. That's exactly what I want with Layla. I hardly know her, but something about her has me itching to—

"So, what did we miss?" Becca cheerfully asks as if I wasn't just fantasising about her friend.

The rest of dinner is uneventful. No mention of work, which I'm grateful for. I'm not particularly keen to share that I dismantle publishing companies and subsequently destroy careers in the presence of two authors and a narrator.

Layla's phone arrives right on time—which unfortunately means she can order a rideshare home instead of letting me drive her. Thankfully, she's agreed to meet me for coffee as we originally planned. She offered to pay, but if I do, technically, this could be a coffee date.

Not a date. But, fuck, what I wouldn't give for a shot at having this woman as mine for the night… *or so many more.*

The coffee shop is busy but we are able to find an empty table. After ordering, we take a seat. I keep my distance and ignore my unexplainable need to be near her.

"Okay, sunshine, lay it on me. What questions have you prepared?" Awaiting her response, I sip my latte, which is decidedly better than the one I had with Julian. She sets down her white mocha; how she can drink something so sickeningly sweet is beyond me. Her plump, red lips open and close a few times as she figures out what exactly to ask me. "Or should I ask you a few, first?"

"Oh, no, I have them right here in my… Shit. Where's my purse? I must've left it at the restaurant."

Layla didn't leave it at the restaurant. She forgot it on her chair and I covertly tossed it in the bin outside the restaurant when she wasn't looking. I'm never impulsive. With her, though, all bets are off.

"We can head back to the restaurant and see if they have it?" I offer.

"Do you mind?" she asks hopefully.

Fuck. I'm such an arsehole. I threw her fucking purse away to force her to spend more time with me. Who the fuck does that?

We leave the cafe and walk two doors down to the restaurant. My palm itches to hold hers, but I can't bring myself to do it. There's an unfamiliar feeling in my gut—a tinge of guilt?

Approaching the host stand, the woman greets me, "Back so soon, Mr. Turner?"

Layla's head whips in my direction, her eyes narrowing. "Turner? You're not… Benedict Turner? As in Turner Publishing?"

"The very same." Before she can reply, I ask the hostess, "My date seems to have misplaced her purse, could you take a look around for it?"

"It's not a da— Nevermind. Maybe I left it in the restroom? I'll check there."

Layla walks to the back of the restaurant, and while the hostess is preoccupied, I step outside to see if her purse is still in the bin. Sure enough, it's sitting on top, unscathed. I quickly grab it and walk back inside. The hostess is nowhere to be found, so I find the barstool seat she was in earlier.

If I let her find me here, I'll be the hero who found her handbag. Perhaps my plan wasn't in vain? Moments later, Layla finds me in the bar. I lift up the purse with a small wave of victory and she lights up.

That same feeling of guilt fills me. I righted a wrong, so why do I still feel this way?

"Thank you, *Benedict*." Layla takes her bag, and I sigh as she lifts onto her toes to kiss my cheek. "But perhaps I should call you Mr. Turner, seeing as you're now running the publishing company I'm signed under."

I think back to my conversations earlier today with the acquisitions department. I had them cut most romantic fantasy and thriller editors and titles. Thousands of authors lost their contracts, but I tried to keep most of the fantasy titles in case Julian wanted to narrate them. Most contemporary romance was cut.

"What's your last name, sunshine?"

"Thorne. Why?"

Fuck.

8

LAYLA

The blood drains from Ben's face the moment I tell him my last name, and he nervously asks, "Layla Thorne? You write fantasy and romance books?"

"Yep, that's me."

Ben looks around as if we're about to be caught doing something illegal. "We need to go." He guides me by my elbow out of the restaurant, thanking the hostess over his shoulder.

"What's going on?" I keep my eyes on him but he refuses to look at me. "Ben, what's wrong?"

"My driver will take you wherever you like. I need to get back to the office." He rakes his hand through his hair. For a man who was stoic moments earlier, he's now anxious.

I place my hand on his forearm. He finally looks at me. "Whatever it is, I'm sure it'll be okay."

"You're right. It will be. Something came up. Can I call

you tonight?" There's so much pain and anguish in his eyes. Whatever is bothering him, it must be heavy.

"Of course," I reply with a small smile. I should say no, since it could be deemed a conflict of interest. He just seems so sad and lost. "Don't worry about a ride for me, I'll just order a—"

"No, I insist, love. It's the least I can do. I'm sorry, we'll have to continue this date of ours another time."

"We're not on a…" His eyes darken and I can't continue. I'm beginning to question how much of a good guy he is when he looks at me like this. I clear my throat. "I'll accept the ride home. Thank you."

A honk breaks the spell he has me under, but neither of us look away. Ben tucks his phone in his pocket and mutters, "Fuck it."

In an instant, he takes my face in his hands and nearly kisses me, stopping with his lips less than an inch from mine. Another honk startles both of us. I can't help but laugh at the horrendous timing his driver has.

Probably the best timing, since I shouldn't be kissing this beautiful man.

I cover his hands with mine and pull them away, whispering, "I should go."

Ben groans but it comes out more like a growl of a fae in the books I write. My heart jumps into my throat, and I have the instinctive need to run, but I don't feel unsafe. There's something about him I can't explain; I remain rooted in place.

"You said you should go, but your eyes betray you, darling."

More like my whole damn body. "So, if I don't go?"

"Run away, sunshine. Before I do something both of us will regret."

I chew on my lip, glancing behind me to the car and then back to Ben. Something spooked him when I told him my name. Curiosity gets the best of me. "Can I come?"

"Oh, you're absolutely going to c—" His jaw tics and a growl erupts from his chest. My eyes widen. "I'll call you."

Despite the weird static electricity between us, I step away from him and walk to the car. As I open the door, I take one last look at the man who makes my breath hitch and time stop. Maybe Becca and Julian aren't the only ones living a real life romance novel?

I close the car door behind me and give the driver my address. The drive home is quiet, and I don't attempt to fill the silence with small talk. When we arrive at my apartment, I go upstairs, change into a comfortable pair of black and white buffalo plaid pajama pants, and climb into bed.

There are no calls, no messages in the dating app. I doze off, disappointed that I let myself fall into the trap of a flirty billionaire.

I wake up to the smell of coffee. It takes a moment for my brain to catch up with my body.

Who the fuck is in my apartment?

I grab my baseball bat and dart to the kitchen. In a perfect world, I'll walk into my kitchen and find a hot man making me a cappuccino, but one can't be too careful. Unfortunately for me, it's only my friends, Becca and Amanda. I lower the bat in relief.

"What are you two doing here? Amanda, I thought I wasn't going to see you until Harriet's wedding."

"Hey, bitch," Amanda calls over her shoulder. "Julian flew me in last night. Something about keeping you away from some hot as fuck British billionaire. What is it with you two? And where can I get one of my own?"

Becca smacks Amanda's arm. "It's not to keep her away from Ben, it's to keep her busy so she isn't tempted by a charming man who is only here for a few months and is *way* too into her."

"Same fucking thing, Becs. Anyway, put some real clothes on. We're going out today."

I check my phone for a missed call or text. There's one from Becca saying she'll be by this morning before she leaves for Portland with Julian. Nothing from Ben. I squeeze my eyes shut. Was last night a dream? What did he mean by doing something both of us would regret? He almost kissed me!

"Sure." I wish away the disappointment painted all over my face, and plaster on the most genuine smile I can manage, then head to my room. Thankfully, neither of them seem to suspect anything.

When I return to the kitchen in dark skinny jeans and a dark red tee, Amanda and Becca are sitting at my kitchen table. Amanda is checking her phone with a scowl. Something's wrong. It takes a lot to upset her.

"Did you get an email from our new publishing giant?"

Amanda's a top three romance novelist, what on earth could she be upset about? I check my phone—which will now be a constant reminder of what happened with Ben last night. There are no new emails.

She continues, "They're making major cuts. They fired everyone on my team and said they won't be publishing any new titles. *Fuck!*" She tosses her phone onto the counter without care. Unlike my old phone, hers doesn't shatter. I take note to ask her later what case she has when her world hasn't just been flipped upside down. "They cut a ton of romance, fantasy, and young adult. Thousands. Becs, maybe going the indie route was the right move. You're saved from this shitshow."

"YA and fantasy? *Shit!* I need to check with Harriet and see if her books are safe." Becca texts our friend, Harriet— she's getting married next month and this is not the kind of news she should be getting before her wedding.

How could this happen?

Ben.

His company took over. It's the only explanation. Do I call him? No. It would be unprofessional to inquire about another author. I find the contact information for my agent and send her an email. The girls are talking in the background, but I don't hear any of it. All I see is red. Fitting that it's his favorite color, seeing as he just cut contracts for romance authors world-wide.

Still typing, I rush off into my bedroom and strip off my shirt. I don't want any sort of positive association to be made with that man. I put on a pastel yellow shirt and press send on the email. I'm about to leave my room when there's an incoming text from an international number.

+44 7970 123456

My sincerest apologies about last night.

It has to be him. Sincerest apologies? What the actual fuck?

Benedict? More like Ben's a dick.

I begin typing: *Did you have anything to do with the cuts made to authors and their teams?* Then, I delete it all. I opt for a lie and save his number into my phone.

It's fine. I went to bed early.

BEN'S A DICK

I'll be in touch, sunshine.

Oh, so we're back to 'sunshine' now? Fuck this guy. I don't respond and shove my phone in my back pocket.

I return to the girls, rage filling me. "All right, let's go."

Maybe he's the morally gray billionaire I've been searching for, after all.

9

BEN

"What do you mean it can't be undone? Figure it out." I slam the phone onto the receiver and blow out a long breath. I have to save her books, no matter the cost.

I slept in my office so I could get an early start this morning. Last night was utterly pointless; everyone was either asleep or ignoring my calls. After a solid three hours of shut eye, I woke up to begin a round of calls back home. No one in the UK, France, or Germany were able to help. I dozed off for a few more hours and started with the East Coast.

An idea comes to me: I can change the language in the contracts. It would require saving the jobs of the staff we let go, potentially losing millions. I pocket the thought as a last resort. There has to be another way.

Thankfully, an email from the man in finance I hung up on comes through and he's able to assist me in restoring Layla's contract. Her editor and cover designer are already gone, but keeping her on as an author is my top priority.

I pull up my contacts. As much as I wanted to call her last night, I couldn't bring myself to do it until it was all solved.

My sincerest apologies about last night.

SUNSHINE

It's fine. I went to bed early.

I'll be in touch, sunshine.

Something's amiss. I stare at my phone for a moment before shaking away the thought; I'm reading too much into it.

What has this woman done to me?

I pocket my phone. Saving her books doesn't feel like enough. Was Roger right? Did I take things too far by cutting romance? Should I have cut other genres instead? I'm questioning everything because of a woman I've been talking to for a week and only met last night.

No, my decision was correct. I shouldn't be second guessing myself.

I work for a few more hours, even though my mind continues drifting to Layla. Having her in my arms, our almost-kisses, the way she made me feel more in one week than I've ever felt in a lifetime. There's something about her; she's unlike any other woman I've known.

Opening the messages in the dating app from earlier this week, there are eighty-two new ones from matches. I scroll past them and go straight to hers, finding nothing more than occasional, innocent flirting between the two of us. She was cautious; so was I. Reading them over again, it's as if we're no more than business acquaintances or friends. But, my chest warms, recalling our phone conversations where neither of us talked about writing or publishing. It felt... *real.*

Not talking to her feels wrong, but what can I tell her? "I'm the twat who almost destroyed your career." I don't think that one will go over well with her.

I need to see her again.

As I'm about to dial her number, there's an incoming call from Julian. "Jules."

"What the hell? You cut Amanda's contract?"

Bloody hell. Who the fuck is Amanda?

"You know I can't discuss contracts with you. Your current audiobooks are safe. There's nothing else I can disclose."

He groans. "Don't be a dick. Becca and Layla's friend, Amanda Storm. She's a top three bestselling romance author, and you pulled her contract? What the fuck?"

"As I said, I—"

"You can't discuss it. Fine. But this is bullshit and you know it. What do you have against romance? I saw how you were looking at Layla last night."

"That's not—"

He interrupts again. For a moment, he continues to rip into me about how I'm an arsehole. I'm hardly listening, but he catches my attention and surprises me when he asks, "You've never been in love, have you?"

No.

"Of course, I have," I lie.

"Who?" he barks. "Name one woman you've been in love with in the past decade."

"What does it matter?" I roar back. My volume now matches his, so I bring it down. "It doesn't. My love life has nothing to do with my job or layoffs."

"Bull fucking shit. Are Layla's books safe from the cuts? I bet they fucking are. I knew you were ruthless, but I never would've imagined this. You cut thousands." He lets out a disappointed sigh. "Just leave Layla alone, like you promised. She doesn't need an asshole like you in her life."

Julian hangs up, leaving me alone with my thoughts in my quiet office. In one day, I not only ruined careers, I managed to ruin my friendship with Julian and… I stole a goddamned handbag. Is this what I want to be remembered for? Maybe Julian was right and I am a fucking pirate.

That's ridiculous. I've been doing this for years. Taken over dozens of companies. This should be no different.

Layla.

She makes this different. I need to fix this. I need to see her. There's just one problem: I know damn well I won't be able to keep my hands to myself if I do.

But there's one way I can guarantee I won't sleep with Layla…

10

LAYLA

Becca left with Julian to Portland this morning, so Amanda and I decided to enjoy pedicures and massages, just the two of us. Amanda and I spent quite a bit of time together two years ago, when we stayed at Julian's vineyard home in California. In the past couple of years, we've had maybe three opportunities to see each other, so I'm grateful for the time to catch up.

Amanda's idea of a good time is tacos and margaritas. Okay, so *my* idea of a good time is tacos and margaritas. After some self-care at the spa, we're devouring the best guacamole in the city, paired with heavy-pour margaritas.

"Hand me your phone," she demands between bites. I pass it to her. "Holy shit! This model isn't even out yet. How did you get one?" I don't get a word out as she asks, "How do you even unlock it?"

Amanda gives me back my phone. I unlock it and hand it back to her again. "What are you up to?"

"Nothing," she replies with a shrug. She types something for entirely too long. My phone vibrates in her hand and her sly grin spreads across her face. My phone vibrates a second time and I snatch my phone back.

> If you are still up for an interview, would you meet me for a drink?

BEN'S A DICK
> Of course. What time?

> Now?

> My darling Layla, I didn't take you as a day drinker.

"Damn it! What did you do? Becca said you're supposed to be helping but how is *this* helping?"

"What? I wanted to meet this guy who pissed you off so much that you didn't even enjoy an hour-long massage from a hot Swedish man. Love that he's in your phone as Ben's A Dick, by the way."

I startle as my phone vibrates with an incoming call from Ben. "Do I answer it?"

"Fuck yes, you do! Use a sexy phone voice. Make it all breathy. *'Oh, Ben, I've missed you.'*"

Answering the phone, I can't help laughing at Amanda's theatrics. "Hello?"

"Hello, sunshine." Ben's voice is smoother than silk. I'm half tempted to record it, just to listen to it again later.

No. I'm mad at him.

"Don't mind the texts, my friend sent them."

"Oh," he sighs, his tone oozing with disappointment. "Well, I was calling to let you know that I have an appointment downtown in two hours but could meet you before or after. But since you—"

"Yes," the words tumble from my lips before I can stop them. "I mean, yes, I can meet you." If he's the morally gray billionaire I think he is, I really should interview him.

He agrees to meet us in fifteen minutes, giving Amanda ample time to help me revise my interview questions. Having her here will be a great buffer and might keep the discussions on track—I'm not sure what would happen otherwise.

I'm sipping my third margarita when I feel him behind me before I hear him. It's as if the air around me changes. "Hello, sunshine," he purrs.

I suck in a breath and Amanda does her best to not spit out her drink when she spots him behind me. "Holy shit. You didn't tell me he was hot!"

Really, Amanda?

Ben sits next to me. "You didn't tell her how incredibly handsome I am? Such a shame, considering I have no issue telling anyone that you're the most beautiful woman I've ever met."

I snort-laugh; the tequila is definitely doing its job. "Yeah, okay."

"So, publishing daddy, thanks for releasing me from my contract. Love that so fucking much." Amanda seems to also be a little more buzzed than she let on.

I look anywhere but at him, even though his eyes have been on me since he sat down. "It's Amanda Storm, isn't it?"

"That's me!" Amanda raises her margarita with a bit of a sneer.

"Check your email, Ms. Storm." He still doesn't look away from me as he addresses her.

I finally meet his gaze. "What did you—"

"What needed to be done, darling."

Amanda's already scrolling her emails on her phone but her eyes lift to Ben at 'darling.' "I'm sorry, what's happening? Why are you calling her... oh. *Oh!* Okay, I should head out and leave you two to eyefuck. Or fuck-fuck. You know, the whole, spread her out right here on the table, and feast on her thing. Could be hot. Could get you arrested."

I was mid-drink as she spoke and choked on my drink. As I'm about to defend myself, he beats me to it. "That won't be necessary, Ms. Storm. Please stay, my feasting will have to wait. I'm headed to an appointment shortly. I'd like to think I'll be able to join you right after, but this one can be unpredictable. We might need to push out your questioning to this evening, sunshine."

"Okay, but now you have to tell us what the hell this appointment is. A tattoo? A mole removed? One of those water spas? A drug deal?" Amanda rests her chin on her fists, elbows on the table, in anticipation.

"A piercing," he replies matter-of-factly.

"What kind of pier—" I swallow my own words. "Never-mind, it's none of my business."

Ben leans in and whispers, "I'll show you mine, if you show me yours later." A shiver cascades down my spine at his words. He kisses my temple as he stands. "Enjoy the rest of your meal." Without another word, he walks away. Stopping at the host stand for just a moment, he hands her something, then leaves the restaurant. I'm left questioning what would've prompted him to get a piercing.

Amanda's voice pulls me from my thoughts. "He's totally getting his dick pierced. What do you think? A Jacob's ladder? Or maybe a Prince Albert?"

"I… I don't know."

Is he getting his dick pierced? No, that's incredibly impulsive. Probably an earring like a pirate. I laugh to myself at the thought.

We finish our meal and anticipate a check that never arrives. When we question the server, she insists that an attractive British man paid for everything and left something for me. She hands me an envelope.

SUNSHINE,

I KNOW YOU'RE WONDERING,
SO HERE'S A HINT:

ONLY WAY I COULD GUARANTEE
I WOULDN'T TRY TO FUCK YOU
ON A SECOND DATE.

SEE YOU TONIGHT?

—BEN

Shit! He's totally getting his cock pierced.

The back has information for a restaurant near the water and a designer boutique with an appointment time.

"Let's go shopping on his dime," Amanda sings. "Then, you're so meeting that hot as fuck billionaire for dinner. Sorry, Layla-love, it's *totally* his dick, so no hanky-panky for you."

Fuck. That hurt worse than I thought it would. I've been wanting to get a Prince Albert done for a while now; the timing couldn't be better. The piercing guarantees I can't touch Layla for at least a month; it's worth it.

The weather has made things extremely difficult for me. It's warmer and more humid than I'm used to, so my leg is in a bit of pain—in addition to other things. Thankfully, my driver came prepared and brought me over-the-counter pain medication, which should hold me over until I get home.

On the ride to my flat, an email from the boutique I sent Layla to pings my phone. She picked out a dress but didn't leave with it.

Well, this won't do.

I send a reply, asking them to contact my assistant, Ryan, for Layla's address to deliver it directly to her within the hour. I shouldn't use the directory to my advantage, but when have I ever followed the rules?

I should send her flowers or some other romantic gesture. I don't want to scare off my doe-eyed darling, and look into something less sentimental, but come up empty.

As I open my messages to send one to Layla, I find two missed texts from her.

> **SUNSHINE**
>
> Thank you for the offer but I respectfully decline. I'll find something in my closet that will work.
>
> See you tonight for the interview.

> Call it whatever you like, darling.

You're mine for the evening.

> Your dress will be delivered shortly and a car will be there in two hours to pick you up.

She's typing but the dancing bubble disappears moments later. Did I push too hard? Is she going to back out?

They reappear with a new message; I release a breath I was holding for far too long.

> You'll have to return the dress.

I call her; I'm not having this conversation over text

"Hey, Ben." Layla's usual upbeat greeting is vacant.

"I'm not returning the dress. This isn't up for negotiation," I growl. She sniffs once. *Shit.* "What's wrong, love?"

"Sorry, allergies. I, uh, I can't wear it. I'll find something here to wear."

"You don't have allergies; you told me yourself a few days ago. What's wrong, sunshine?" Whatever it is, I want to fix it, *need* to fix it.

"It's nothing. I'm fine. I'll see you later."

I hang up and have the driver reroute to her flat. Twelve minutes later, I arrive. A woman with her small child has her hands full with groceries and is about to enter the building. I offer to get the door for her, my chivalry gaining me access. There's no security here, something I'll remedy later. I have an inexplicable need to keep Layla safe—even if it's from me.

I take the lift to the fifth floor, leaving the woman and her child to continue to theirs.

What am I doing? I shouldn't be here. I turn back and press the button to return down stairs. The doors open and…

"Sunshine." Her eyes are swollen, cheeks stained with dried tears, but still remarkably breath-taking.

Layla steps out of the elevator and my heart stops. I instantly wrap my arms around her. I want to protect her from the world, destroy whoever did this, and let her piss on their ashes. Whoever caused this will pay dearly.

"Ben? What are you doing here?"

I don't immediately reply, instead hold her tighter. She sighs into me, returning my embrace. "What's wrong, darling?"

"You are," she whispers.

I pull back and tilt her chin so she'll look at me. Does she know about all of the horrible things I've done in my life? Did Julian tell her?

I ask softly, "How can I fix this?"

"I can't wear the dress. It… it didn't fit."

"Oh, sunshine." I kiss her forehead. "I assumed you didn't want it because I was paying for it." I pull back an inch to look into her bloodshot eyes. "I'll cancel it. You can wear whatever you'd like, even pyjamas. You're perfect, just as you are."

She laughs softly. "Hardly; you don't have to be nice. I know I'm not perfect and I'm okay with it."

"You're more than perfect, love."

Layla has the most delicious hourglass figure, sparkling hazel eyes that see into my soul, and a smile that could chase away the darkest clouds. How could she not think she's absolutely stunning? Having her in my arms, I have to resist running my hands over her curves. Or, worse.

My now hard cock is pressed against my trousers, making me wince. I need to think about the least sexy thing I can…

Bundt cake… No, cake just makes me think of her perfectly round arse. Trains… Nope, now I want to rail her…

My leg throbs almost as much as my cock, the pain nearly unbearable. "Do you mind if I sit for a moment?"

"Are you all right? Your face just turned white." She wipes her tears and my heart falls into my stomach. "Come on."

I release her and she gestures to her door. I don't normally limp, but I also normally have my medication on me.

Layla's place is quaint but full of colour. It doesn't surprise me; it matches her personality. Whilst otherwise immaculate, there are stacks of books and journals everywhere. I take a seat on her sofa and she sits beside me.

"Can I get you anything? You seem like you're in pain. Is it... *Oh*." She clears her throat, then mutters, "Amanda was right."

"What was Amanda right about?"

"Do you need an ice pack for your, um...?" Her eyes fall to my crotch.

I let out a hearty laugh, but it just makes the pain worse, though it's worth it to see the light blush dust her cheeks. "A bag of frozen peas should do the trick."

"Of course. One moment." She stands and hurries to her kitchen, her hips swaying with each step. Fuck, is she doing that on purpose?

Layla returns with a bag of frozen vegetables and hands them to me. I place them just below my knee, feeling the pain subside almost immediately. "Thank you."

"Well, if your dick is pierced, this would never work out. It would break me."

I can't help but laugh again; she's fucking adorable. "No, sunshine, my cock doesn't reach my knees."

"What, uh..." She chews on her lip. "What's going on with your leg? Sports injury? I'm sorry, I shouldn't pry."

"Motorbike accident." As much as I want to show her, I don't want her pity. "I'll be all right. Just need to grab my medication before tonight."

"Here I was, complaining about a dress not fitting my hips,

and you look like you're a step away from needing morphine. Damn, I'm such an asshole."

I turn to face her and take her hand in mine. "You are the furthest thing from an arsehole. My accident was ages ago. I shouldn't have come, but more importantly, I shouldn't have bought a dress for you."

"No, it was sweet. A little 'Pretty Woman,' but sweet. What do you say we have dinner here instead of going out? I'm a pretty good cook, you know. I'll order you something comfy for you to wear and maybe you can call the pharmacy to see if they'll send your medication here?"

Dinner? Here? With the most beautiful woman I've ever known? This can't be real. I must be hallucinating from the pain.

In case this is indeed happening and I'm not imagining it, I insist, "I will absolutely not let you pay for a single thing, sunshine. Tell me what you need and I'll take care of it."

"I'll make a list." With a wink and a bright smile, she squeezes my hand once and releases it as she gets up to saunter into the kitchen.

12

LAYLA

I rush off to the kitchen to figure out what the fuck I'm going to make this man. I'm not a good cook, by any stretch of the imagination. I'm a 'what can I have delivered for dinner in less than forty-five minutes' kind of girl. My pantry is filled with writing snacks—gummy bears, three half eaten boxes of cereal, and grapes.

Okay, so they are fermented grapes...

In a bottle...

2010 Syrah.

What the hell am I going to cook? I had tacos for lunch, so while it's easy, it's not appealing.

My hand braced on each door of the cabinet, I holler over my shoulder, "What are you in the mood for?"

"You don't need to cook, love. I can order something. I'll have one of my assistants drop off my medication, a change of clothes, and dinner."

"She's going to think you're staying the night. Don't you think that's a little fucked up to ask of a new assistant?"

"*He* isn't going to think anything. Ryan has been with me for years. I'm not exactly known for sleepovers."

I spin on my heel and can't help but feel both excitement but disappointment at his statement. On one hand, he fits the morally gray billionaire persona I was hoping he would be. On the other, a pang of jealousy settles in my gut.

Deciding to make light of it, I ask, "Don't stay the night? A bit of a manwhore, Ben?" *Not the most appropriate thing to ask someone you have a working relationship with, but too late now.*

"Hardly," he insists with a light chuckle. "I'm in the public eye back home. I was hoping to have some staged dates here, to ensure the media stayed off my back, but that's the extent of it."

"When was the last time you got laid? *Shit*. I'm so sorry, I shouldn't have asked that. Is this workplace harassment since you're the new boss daddy for my publishing house?" Ben's eyes darken. I don't think I could dig the hole any deeper, yet here I am, with a shovel.

"I told you that your top would look better on my floor in the morning, and you're worried about asking me when I shagged someone last?"

He has a point, but I backpedal. "You were joking."

"Was I, sunshine?" Ben cocks an eyebrow, lightly biting his lip. With his blue eyes piercing me with his gaze, I can't look away. We remain in a staring contest for what feels like a month. "Well?"

I shake away whatever the fuck that was and clear my throat. "You were."

"I don't joke, love." He moves to get up, the pain evident on his face. Whatever happened to him in that accident really fucked up his leg if he's feeling it years later.

"Don't get up!" I rush over to him. "What do you need?"

He sits back down and groans. Not from pain. Or maybe it's pain? I can't tell, it just sounds sexy and growly. "I'm fine, I need to get up and move so I don't end up stiff."

"Sit your ass down, right now, mister. Take off your pants." That didn't come out quite as I intended, but after years working as a massage therapist to supplement my writing career, I want to help.

"I'm sorry, come again?" he laughs.

"You heard me. I'm a certified massage therapist. Or, at least, I was. My license expired. Anyway, pants off. I'll help that leg of yours."

"You just want to get me naked, darling." While it comes out as a joke, he actually looks a little… afraid?

"You'll have your boxers on. Are you a boxers guy? Or briefs? I'd gather you're a boxer briefs man. Maybe navy blue?"

"What… How…?"

"Years of seeing people nearly naked." I cock an eyebrow and cross my arms over my chest, but it forces his gaze lower and his eyes darken. They are one of my greatest assets, so I don't mind him staring. Flirting with this gorgeous man is far too much fun, I may as well enjoy it while I can.

He's in pain. What the fuck am I doing?

Ben lifts his eyes back to mine and surprises me when he jests, "And you were worried about workplace harassment with your previous comments."

He *is* joking, right? He said he never jokes…

"Hey now, no need to bring HR into this," I say nervously.

"Wouldn't dream of it, love."

I gesture to his feet. "Start with shoes and socks, and we'll go from there."

"I don't think so, sunshine. Nice try."

"What are you afraid of?"

"Pity." He clears his throat. "I mean, nothing. You're reading into it."

Pity? Maybe he has weird feet from the accident. "I'll admit, it's probably unusual having a woman you hardly know touch you. I just want to help you feel good… better. I mean, *better*. Not in pain. Totally professional, though, nothing sexual about it," I reassure him, despite my gaff.

"Oh, darling." He takes my hand and brings my knuckles to his lips. "There is nothing professional about what I want to do to you."

"Gah, you're such a flirt! Does that line work on all the girls? You have the whole broody, mysterious billionaire thing going for you. I bet it does, and you're rolling in pussy back home."

He leans back his head and groans. "Why must you insist upon bringing up other women? Do you really take me for some kind of philandering playboy?" He lifts his head from the back of the couch, the blue from his irises is nearly gone. "I have my eyes on one woman. Only. One."

I unintentionally lick my lips, drawing his attention to them, and swallow hard. I have the same need to run that I did last night, but not from fear. With the way he's looking at me, I feel sexier than I have in years.

Ben sighs, breaking the spell he had me under. He averts his eyes and says softly, "You'll find out eventually, but I swear if you try to apologize, or feel sorry for me in any way…"

"I can't promise that, but I'll try," I offer.

He lifts his pant leg to his knee and reveals what can only be described as a bionic leg.

Prosthetics company is how he made his first million.

"Ben," I breathe.

"You said you'd try, darling," he warns.

"Sorry. I mean, I'm not sorry for that. It just clicked that you owned a prosthetics company." I gasp. "The charity. That's why you're in pain? You lost half your leg in that accident?"

He nods and lowers his pant leg. "Let's get dinner ordered, shall we?"

"No." I shake my head. "Get your medication first. Dinner can wait. But now that I know, will you let me help?"

He chuckles and mutters something under his breath that sounds remarkably close to, "You don't deserve her."

One week. Less than a fucking week, actually. That's all it took for Layla to come into my life and flip it upside down. We've spent hours on the phone together this week, but nothing could have prepared me for this siren of a woman to make me question everything. She's too good, too fucking perfect. I want to keep her, but I'll just hurt her. I know I will.

I need to downsize Roger's company, which as of next week, is officially my company. The more time I spend getting to know Layla, the more I consider slowing down my acquisitions.

Do I need to monopolize the market? I've been doing this for so long. At this point, how do I stop being the villain of the publishing industry?

"Ben." Layla's voice pulls me from my downward spiral.

"Yes? Sorry."

"Order your pain meds. You look like you're about to be sick."

"Right. They're more anti-inflammatory than pain management." I shake my head and say mostly to myself, "Why am I telling you this?"

She smirks, biting her lip. *Damn it.* I know Julian wanted me to stay away from her, but there's no way in hell I'm going to. There's absolutely nothing on this earth that could convince me that being anywhere but here, with her, in this moment, isn't...

Oh. Shit.

I'm falling for her. At least, I think I am. I know nothing about love. We hardly know each other, but I know more about her from one week of late night conversations than I do about any other person in my life.

"Can I help while you wait for Ryan?"

If she touches me, it's a guarantee I'll be hard. It's the fucking conundrum of the century. After getting the piercing earlier, I don't think it's wise, but my leg is killing me. I reluctantly nod. "I'm not taking my trousers off, sunshine."

"Do you really think I can do *anything* with slacks on? I'll go grab my coconut massage oil and a few of my favourite essential oils. You can pick which one you like best. When I come back, I expect to find that your pants aren't on and your meds are out for delivery, Mr. Billionaire." She stands and saunters off to what I assume is her bedroom or bathroom.

I can do this. It's just a leg massage from the most incredible woman I've ever met. Nothing more.

After taking off my shoes and socks. I unzip the leg of my trousers from the bottom to my knee, unbuckle my belt, remove and fold them neatly, then set them to the side. I make a mental note to order additional accessible trousers. With how things are going with Layla, there's a good chance I won't be going home for a long time.

I'm left vulnerable. I know with absolute certainty that most women I've been with didn't care about my leg because of my money. I care what Layla thinks. While she's gone, I message Ryan to grab my medication, a duffle of clothes, and dinner.

When Layla returns, she's wearing a red top and a pair of black and white plaid pyjama bottoms. It's mid-July. In what world would they be an appropriate option? Though, the mere sight of her has me hard. My hand flies to my cock to cover up. The last thing I want to do is scare her off.

"Okay, I've got orange, a clove and cinnamon hodgepodge blend, lavender, and wintergreen. But that one will clear your sinuses for a month. Pick your poison?"

"Whatever you recommend, Ms. Massage Therapist."

She chuckles and pours a few ounces of massage oil into a small container. "Well, I use a combination of orange and lavender for myself as a perfume, so let's go with that. I'll just increase the lavender so you don't smell like me."

I raise an eyebrow. "You don't want to mark your territory, love?" I certainly don't mind smelling like this little vixen.

"I don't know what you mean." Layla pulls her lips into her mouth to hide her smile. She adds several drops of each fragrance into the massage oil and mixes with a small wooden stick. "All right, sassypants. Want to keep that on or off?" She gestures to my prosthetic leg. "I'm not sure if it's one of the robot ones or not and don't want to short circuit it." She takes a seat in front of me on the coffee table, my leg between hers.

"Can I leave it on? I don't want you to see—"

"Say no more" Layla takes a small amount of her concoction and pours it into her hands, rubbing them together several times. She hesitates, her hands hovering above my thigh. "Are you sure this is okay? I don't want to make you uncomfortable."

"I'm more worried about you making me *too* comfortable, sunshine."

"Looks like someone didn't end up getting a piercing below the belt today, after all," she teases.

A small smirk creeps on my lips, even as I attempt to keep my expression neutral. "I'll show you mine, if you show me yours. I believe that's what you told me?"

"Well, there's no way I'll be turning you on today, so I may as well get started."

I grip one of her wrists in warning; her other falls to my thigh. "Layla." It's the only word I can get out. As much as I'm craving her hands on me, I shouldn't risk it. I don't think I've wanted anything or anyone more than her. Not only do I have the issue of a stupid fucking piercing, but I can't do this. Not with her.

Unless… Can I change? Is there a chance I could be good enough to deserve her?

"Sorry, I shouldn't joke. I promise I'm not trying to—"

"You don't get it, do you?" I kiss the inside of her wrist. "I'm not a good man; I'm not a nice guy. I'm a fucking menace, sunshine. Yet, I want nothing more than to be…" I sigh. "*Yours*. But, darling, I would ruin you."

Layla looks away in thought for a moment, then a small smirk tugs at her lips. "Even villains deserve a chance at a happily ever after, Ben." Her gaze shifts to mine and, in one swift motion, her oil-slicked hands slide across my beard and into my hair, her soft and sweet lips on mine. Through the pain, through the indecision of whether I should kiss her back, I do the only thing I want—I claim her as mine. I lift her up onto my lap, straddling me inches from where I want her.

"I don't want to hurt you," she whispers against my lips. She's fucking heaven. I want to taste every last inch of her.

"You could never hurt me," I reply, tangling my hands in her hair and bringing her closer. I want to own every piece of this incredible woman.

Layla lets out a soft laugh. "We're making a mess."

"You want to see a mess?" I stand, keeping her legs wrapped around my waist.

She tries to wriggle out of my hold. "Put me down! Your leg and your… *other leg*… and I weigh like double what you do."

"Sunshine, I'm going to need you to stop with that bullshit. You're fucking perfect. Now, where's your bedroom? I want you to make a proper mess all over my face."

"Second door on the left." She holds on tighter, still worried I might drop her. There is no way in hell I would. After tonight, I'd happily live the rest of my days with her soft, beautiful body wrapped around mine. I open the second door on the left but it's a bathroom. "Sorry, my left," she chuckles. "Just set me down, and I'll—"

"Over my dead body." I find her bedroom and walk in, tossing her onto the bed. I lean over her, bracing myself with one hand on either side of her. "I've been dying for you to show me yours, love." I kiss her stomach and hook two fingers into her waistband. I barely tug them down an inch when the doorbell rings. "Bloody hell, fucking arsehole had to be early." Layla lets out a full laugh and I nip at her inner hip in response. She yelps playfully. "I want you naked, right now, but you do not move from that spot. Do you hear me?"

I head to the door, realising I'm wearing only my boxer briefs, but still have my collared shirt and undershirt on. I toss off my button up shirt, feeling restricted, but put on my trousers. Ryan has seen me nearly naked a few times, but we don't need to add one more into the mix. It takes longer than I'd like, but I'm determined.

The most beautiful woman in the whole fucking world is laid out in bed and I'm struggling with my trousers. There's a knock and another ring of the doorbell as I'm still getting dressed. It dawns on me that he got inside with little to no effort. Tomorrow, I'll look into buying the building and revamping the security.

I fling open the door. "Ry— Oh. Hello, Ms. Storm."

14

LAYLA

As I'm lying in bed, I hear Amanda from my entry way, "Well, aren't you a thirsty bitch. Your fly's down, by the way… Just kidding. Where's Layla?" She has the worst possible timing.

"In here. Just, um, grabbing something," I yell.

If he really got his dick pierced, he won't be able to have sex for at least a month. When I got my clit pierced, it took six weeks to heal. My nipples took almost a year. What did he think was going to happen? There's no way we could have sex tonight, if he got anything done.

"Layla-love," Amanda calls, "home early. Didn't know you had company." Her voice gets closer and I panic. "If you need some alone time…" She opens my door the rest of the way and walks in, barely containing a cackle of amusement. "Oh. Well. Have fun with the billionaire." She lowers her voice to add, "If he's newly pierced, you're fucked in the most un-literal sense, babes."

"I know," I whisper-shout. "He was all 'make a proper mess all over my face' but it's not like we could have sex. What if he got a Jacob's Ladder? That shit takes months to heal!"

"I didn't get a ladder, sunshine." Ben's voice pulls our attention to the door, where he's leaning against the frame like a damn book boyfriend. I'm certain Julian gave him notes. My hand flies to my face in embarrassment. "Ms. Storm. Pick a hotel, any hotel, and I'll cover your expenses for the night. Want a penthouse apartment downtown Seattle? I'll give you my key."

"Sold." Amanda offers her hand, palm-up, awaiting his fob. Without hesitation, he gives it to her. "Oh, shit. This might be more fun than the writing retreat at Julian's."

"Order whatever you want, my food delivery app information is on the counter by the refrigerator, but any damages to the flat will be billed to you directly." This business side of Ben surprises me. He doesn't talk to me this way, it's as if he's talking to...

Oh. My. God. I kissed my boss! He's not technically my boss. He's the equivalent of a boss's boss's boss's boss's boss. And he wanted to, what, go down on me? I'm in way over my head here.

Amanda steps past Ben, waving the key in the air and shouting as she walks toward the door, "See you in the morning, Layla-love. May you have many orgasms!"

I shut my eyes and fall back onto my bed. "Fuck."

"I thought I told you to be naked, sunshine."

"You know, for a man who claims to be in a lot of pain,

you seem to be doing just fine." I cover my eyes with my palms.

"What's a little pain if I can still ensure your pleasure?"

I pull up onto my elbows. "What did you just say?"

"You heard me." Ben pushes off the doorframe and stalks toward me. When he reaches the bed, he removes his shirt, and tosses it to the ground, revealing his full sleeves of tattoos and a few on his chest. My eyes narrow in one a black 'x' over his heart. My fascination with his art quickly comes to an end when he climbs onto the bed and hooks a finger in each side of my waistband but doesn't pull down. "You're a very dangerous creature, sunshine. I'm a man who always gets what he wants. Yet, you have me on my knees for you."

"Whatever happened to 'I'll show you mine if you show me yours?'" I swallow hard. "If you did what I think you did, this will be a much shorter night than I thought."

"Do you want to know why I did it?"

"So, you did do it?"

"Do you want to know *why* I pierced my cock, love? Answer the question." His voice holds no malice; it's full of lust.

"Yes," I breathe.

Ben's eyes darken. "I needed to guarantee I wouldn't sleep with you. I want you for more than a quick shag. The only way that is going to happen is if I'm not buried deep inside you for the foreseeable future."

"You know how ludicrous that sounds, right? You got a piercing a day after meeting me, so you wouldn't have sex with me? I mean *'tell me you don't want to fuck me, without telling me you don't want to fuck me, I'll go first…'"*

His fingers toy with my waistband before ripping my pants and underwear off and tossing them to the ground. "In case I haven't made myself clear, I would spend eternity exploring every inch of you." His gaze falls to my pussy, and I'm incredibly thankful I got a wax recently. I can't help whimpering as he peppers kisses down the inside of my thigh. "You might not be able to touch me, but I sure as fuck will be touching you." He licks up my slit, making me shudder. "What do we have here, sunshine?" My head falls back and I cover my eyes with my fists. "I don't think so. Eyes on me."

"Ben, you know I write romance. As hot as that is, there is no way in hell I can come, if I watch you go down on me."

He climbs further onto the bed until he's settled between my legs, his face an inch away from mine. "If you won't watch me pull one after another from you, then I'll swallow your screams with my fingers deep inside you, as you fall apart."

Ben glides two fingers inside me in one swift motion, curling them up and teasing my piercing with his palm. My breathing picks up but, as promised, he kisses me hard, silencing my moans. He takes his time pushing in and out of me, keeping the same pace and pressure. I grip his shirt and pull him closer to me.

"So greedy," he chuckles against my lips. "I'm going to have far too much fun with you." He skates his free hand up my body, landing on my now heavy breasts. "Well, aren't you full of surprises? Take it off."

"Take what off?"

"You're shirt, love. I want to see you." I reluctantly remove my shirt, tossing it haphazardly to the side. "Fuck, you're stunning." Ben trails kisses along my jaw to my neck, grazing his teeth along my collarbone, eliciting a moan from me. He continues lower, until he reaches my peaked, pierced nipples, swirling his tongue around one and blowing cold air across it.

"Ben," I moan.

"Yes, darling?"

"Don't stop," I say breathlessly.

Ben grips my hand, interlaces our fingers, and holds it a few inches above my head. He continues licking and sucking, teasing me. The sensation is almost enough to make me come. He picks up the pace as he fingers me, driving them deeper into me. My pussy begins to clench around him, I'm so damn close. All I need is—

My buzzer chimes for someone to be let into the building.

"No. Absolutely not, love. You're going to come for me. Right now. I don't care if it's Ryan, or Amanda, or your eighty-seven year old grandmother." Ben lets go of my hand and kisses down my body until his face is between my legs. "Right now, you're mine, sunshine." He sucks hard on my clit and I cry out, arching my back and gripping the sheets. Circling his tongue around my piercing, he continues the deliciously punishing thrusts of his fingers.

"I… I'm right… Just… *Ben.*" I shatter, my body vibrating, vision blurred, as I come harder than I ever have. He slows his pace, helping me come down from my orgasm. When he said he could ruin me, I didn't think he meant like this.

How the hell am I supposed to ever let a man touch me again, when I have the memory of what he just did to me?

"Stay here. I'll get the door," he whispers. I reply in a hum or some guttural language I'm sure no linguist could translate. He chuckles as he kisses my stomach, then slowly removes his fingers, bringing them to his mouth and sucking them clean.

Ben puts his shirt back on and leaves my room. I hear him over the intercom talking to a man who must be Ryan. He buzzes him up and moments later appears in my bedroom with a glass of water.

"Fuck, come here." I sit up. He grips the nape of my neck and kisses me hard. A whimper escapes me. "You're extraordinary." When he breaks away, he adds, "Here. You're going to need more than just one glass before I'm through with you." I take a few long gulps but I look down and realize I'm still completely naked and he's fully clothed. My embarrassment must be apparent because he growls, "Don't you dare, sunshine. You're fucking beautiful. Drink up, put on clothes if you must, and I'll take care of the rest." He leaves again when there's a knock at the door.

15

BEN

I leave my gorgeous, naked temptress breathless on the bed while I answer the door. The pain in my leg subsided after icing it, but it's been replaced by a sharp ache in my cock. This fucking piercing was likely the biggest mistake of my life. For the next month or so, I won't be able to sink myself into her.

That was the point, arsehole!

When I open the door, Ryan is grinning from ear to ear. "Hey, *Captain.*"

"Bloody hell, it's not that bad." I can't help but laugh. One night a few years ago, I had too much to drink and Ryan had to make sure I made it home in one piece. Never again will I drink cheap rum. Now, whenever he comes to the rescue, the nickname comes out to play.

"What debauchery are you getting into tonight that you need clothes for tomorrow and dinner at Layla Thorne's flat?" he teases, attempting to peer inside the apartment. I pull the door mostly closed with a stern look. "Have you read her thriller? It's fucking brilliant. Almost better than her fantasy books."

"I haven't, but please make sure her entire backlist is delivered to my office tomorrow morning, and the audiobooks are downloaded on all of my devices." I'm sure he's right and they're all incredible, but guilt seeps in that she could've lost everything because of me. "Now, if you'll allow me to get back to my evening." Ryan hands me my duffle and dinner, which includes a bottle of wine. "Really, Ry?"

"I wouldn't be a good first mate if I didn't ensure you were properly prepared. There are condoms in the bag as well," he adds with a smirk.

"I don't need… Nevermind." I shake my head. "Thank you, Ryan."

He winks with the back of his hand to his forehead in sailor's salute and a light chuckle, turns on his heel, then heads toward the lift. I close the door behind me and wander into Layla's kitchen to drop off the food. I place my duffle on one of the counter stools, looking up to find Layla on the balls of her feet. She's reaching to grab something from the top shelf of her cabinets, wearing only my collared shirt and a lacy red thong.

I walk up behind her and kiss her neck, wrapping my arm around her middle. With her back flush with my chest, all I want to do is bend her over the counter and claim her. I *can't*. "Would you like help, love?"

Her voice squeaking, she replies, "Oh, yes, um, Amanda put my wine glasses on the top shelf, just out of reach. Do you mind?"

"Not at all." I nip her earlobe and bring down two stemless wine glasses, setting them on the counter. I take half a step back and she turns to face me. As I lift her up onto the counter by her waist, she gasps, and I stand between her legs. "You look good in my clothes, sunshine."

"Yeah, well, I figured I might as well take advantage of wearing a shirt that costs five times my rent. Not sure when I'll have another opportunity."

I frown. "What's that supposed to mean?"

"You're here for a few months, then you'll be back 'across the pond,' or whatever you British people say. Why shouldn't I enjoy myself while I can?"

"Who says I have to leave?"

"At dinner, you said yourself you have maybe a few months."

"What if I gave it all up? Throw my billions into the Boston harbor, like an American tosser?"

Would she have me, then?

Layla fists my shirt and pulls me closer, our noses nearly touching. Her worried eyes dart between mine. "Don't joke. Not about this. I'm not"—her breath shakes—"I'm not like Becca or Amanda. They're stronger than me. I like you, Ben, but I can't get my hopes up that you might stay like Julian did."

I slide my hand across her jaw and into her hair. Layla's right, I'm not Julian, and she deserves better than me. If she wants me, I'll be whatever she wants me to be. Closing the distance, I bring her lips to mine. She's cautious at first, but melts into me a moment later. Fuck, I love kissing her. Her hands glide over my shoulders, her nails digging into my back. I relish the sting. She allows me to take from her as her tongue dances with mine and she moans into my mouth.

A growl erupts from my chest and Layla pulls back suddenly. "Oh shit, are you okay? Are you in pain? Did I hurt you? Did you take your medication?" Her questions come out in rapid succession.

"Yes, I'm fine," I chuckle. "I haven't taken anything yet but I probably should; sooner rather than later."

"Are you sure? Because you just… *growled*. Did I make a man growl? I didn't think that was a real thing! I write about it in books, but… you *growled*." She laughs and I feel it everywhere. It's infectious and I can't help but join her. Layla's smile widens, looking at me with dazzling eyes. "You have a beautiful smile; you should do it more often."

"I don't smile, darling, I'm British."

"You totally smiled, *darling*." Hers is now beaming; I kiss it away. "Come on. I'm hungry and you need to not be in pain. No friend of mine should be hurting in my home."

"Friend? Oh, sunshine, I am not and will never be your friend." I place a chaste kiss on her forehead and step back, bracing myself on the counter. I can't bring myself to move away from her, not yet. "I had Ryan pick up gyros but I got you falafel. Hope that's all right?"

"You remembered," she says softly.

"How could I not? You said these are the best in town." I shrug as if it's no big deal, but I remember every detail of every conversation I've had with Layla. "I know I gave you the option of not wearing clothes, but did you really have to wear these?" I trace the outline of her knickers until my fingers are between her legs.

Layla sucks in a breath. "We should eat, and you should take your medication."

"I know." I place both hands firmly on her thighs. "I have all night to play with you."

"All night? That's a little presumptuous. I didn't invite you to spend the night, I invited you to stay for dinner." She tries her best not to smile but fails miserably.

I lean in and trail kisses from her cheek to her neck. "You mean to tell me, you don't want to wake up with my face between your legs, nipping at your clit as my tongue teases that sexy as fuck barbell piercing you have?"

Layla chews on her lip, shaking her head. "What am I going to do with you? Coming in here like some sort of sex god who selflessly pulls orgasms from women."

"Woman. Not plural, love." I step back, needing to put distance between us. Not only is my cock throbbing uncomfortably, I'm determined to make this relationship of ours more than sex. I open my duffle on the stool, searching for my medication. While I search, I find the box of condoms at the bottom—at least Ryan had the decency to hide them under my clothes.

"Do you need a glass of water?" she asks, hopping off the counter.

I glance up from my bag. "Did I say you could move, love?"

"You didn't say I couldn't."

"With that smart mouth of yours, do I need to strap you to your bed?"

Fuck, please say yes.

"You'd have to catch me first."

I groan. A man can only take so much of this torture. I take two pills from the bottle, pop them in my mouth, and swallow. She slides a glass of water across the counter to me and I finish it in four long gulps.

When I'm finished, I meet her gaze. "You better run, sunshine. If I catch you, I'm staying over and you're mine for the rest of the night." *Or indefinitely.*

Layla's eyes widen with a swirl of fear and lust. She bites her lip, rocking back on her heels once before darting down the hall. I watch her go, and don't chase; she isn't ready for what I want to explore with her.

As tempting as it is to go after her, I take a seat on one of her stools and open the takeaway bag. I unwrap my gyro and take a few bites, wondering how long she'll last without someone hunting her. She was right, it's some of the best I've ever had.

The anticipation must've been too much for her; she pads back into the kitchen and sits on the stool next to me. She's wearing the hideous plaid pyjama bottoms from earlier, but still wearing my shirt.

"Here I thought you were going to catch me, tie me up, and have your way with me, *darling*," she teases.

"Oh, I intend to. Part of the fun is seeing you squirm." I hand her the falafel. "Here. You'll need sustenance for what I have planned for you."

Layla pouts for a moment, and I do my best to hide my smile. I want her aching for me before I spend the rest of the night worshiping her.

"Thank you. Tacos twice in one day, I'm spoiled." She drizzles tzatziki sauce on her falafel and takes a bite.

"It's not a taco, darling."

"The fuck it's not. Look! There's a shell… *ish*, lettuce, tomato, a meat alternative… It's a Greek taco." She takes another bite and a small drip of sauce remains on the corner of her lip.

I can't help myself. "You have something right…" I lean in and kiss the side of her mouth. "Got it."

"You're such a dork," she laughs.

"A dork?"

"Yeah, a dork." Her smile meets her eyes with a little crinkle of her nose.

"If you say so, love."

We sit in comfortable silence while we finish our dinner. When she's done, I suggest, "You might want to slip into something a little more comfortable."

16

LAYLA

"This is *not* what I had in mind when you said you'd have your way with me, Ben! I'm not a runner. I don't jog. Actually, I don't even powerwalk. The best I can do is a thirty-minute spin class."

Ben jogs backward, grinning ear to ear. "I only have one leg and a freshly pierced cock, sunshine. If I can do it, you can. I told you earlier this week that I go for a run *every* night. You think I'd take two evenings off?"

"Why didn't you run last night?" I ask, winded. His face falls and he stops suddenly. I crash into him, nearly knocking him over. "*Fuck.*"

"Sorry, love." He briefly wraps an arm to my lower back to steady me. When he takes a step back and releases me, I immediately miss his touch.

"Why did we stop?"

Ben pauses and rubs the back of his neck. "I told you I'm not a good man. I… I didn't go for a run because I didn't go home last night. I had to fix something." He closes the distance, tucking my wind-swept hair behind my ear. "But it's settled."

I suck in a breath, pursing my lips as I glance up at him. "I had a feeling I was on the chopping block. Why did you save my contract?"

"Sunshine," he whispers the word like it pains him.

"Don't you 'sunshine' me. What about all of the other authors and staff?" I chew on my lip. "Is it true that thousands lost theirs?" I'm actually not sure I want to know the answer.

"Cuts had to be made. This is what I do. I buy out smaller publishers…" He looks away. I can't tell if it's embarrassment or regret.

"And cancel author contracts," I finish for him. "I know it's only business to you, but what if you expanded the smaller companies instead of destroying them?" He could do so much with the money he has, if only he saw publishing as an investment and not just a way to line his pocketbook.

"It's not that simple, love."

"Isn't it though?" I ask hopefully.

Ben takes a small step back from me. Maybe I lost him? "I warned you I'm not—"

"A good guy." I replace the step he took with my own. "Yeah, I know what you said. I don't buy it. You saved my contract *and* Amanda's. I understand hers: she's a top three author. I think she's rooting for us being in some weird star-crossed-lovers trope in her head, so don't be surprised if her next book is also a billionaire romance. I still don't understand, why would you save mine?"

"I don't know," he admits earnestly, shaking his head. "When I realized your name was on the list, I couldn't"— his jaw tics—"I couldn't let you lose your contract, love." His eyes close, slowly shaking his head, then asks himself, "What have I done?"

"What do you mean 'what have you done?' What did you do? Can you fix it?"

Ben shakes his head and I know the answer as his shoulders fall. He can do the right thing, but he's conflicted. I want to help him through this but, unfortunately, he needs to figure it out on his own. If he wants to make real changes in his life, he has to want it for himself and put the work in. I've never had the moral dilemma he has, but I worked hard to get where I am and know that, if he wants this bad enough, he'll make the right decision.

"You are *not* a bad man. Have you made questionable choices in life? Absolutely. Making me run is probably at the top of that list. But, you wouldn't have saved my career if you weren't a good man. And, while I'm on my soapbox, who the hell gets their cock pierced a day after meeting a women so they won't fuck them?" He looks away and laughs, almost embarrassed. Then, he stills and his eyes widen with a hint of fear. Why is he so afraid to have feelings? I press further, "Why would you do something so drastic? Saving my career—and the whole pierced cock thing—for someone you don't care about?"

Ben's eyes snap to mine. My breath catches, only a blue rim frames his pupils. "Careful, Layla." He almost never uses my name. It's always darling, love, or—my personal favorite—sunshine. I don't know what to make of it.

"Answer me." The sun hasn't completely set and a beautiful combination of yellow, red, and orange paint the sky. It would be romantic if I wasn't a sweaty mess. I look around to ensure no one is nearby, in case he is worried about eavesdropping. Our run took us along the path of a familiar park, and while there isn't a soul within a quarter-mile, I don't feel unsafe with him. "Ben," I whisper. "It's just you and me. You're allowed to be the hero, not the villain."

"Julian warned—"

"Fuck Julian. He's a nice man. Too nice, if you ask me. He let me shack up with Amanda at his place in Temecula for entirely too long. But you shouldn't listen to him. You're also a good person. You think I didn't run to a search engine to do a background check when I found out who you are?" I didn't, but he doesn't need to know that. "*You* make your choices, Ben. Not him. You get to choose whatever you—"

Ben takes my face in his hands suddenly, sliding his fingers into my hair. He keeps his thumbs firmly placed on each of my cheeks and I'm officially living every romance reader's fantasy. His eyes dart between mine before he kisses me. I can't help the whimper that escapes me. His tongue teases my lips, demanding entry I'm more than willing to give him. If he keeps kissing me as if it's his last, I might—

Shit. I'm going to fall hard for Ben, aren't I?

He pulls back an inch, pressing his forehead to mine. Per usual, I'm left breathless. "What if I choose you?" he asks, almost pained.

"You don't know me," I counter.

He laughs to himself and straightens, his eyes never leaving mine. "And you don't know me. You really believe a man known to be the most ruthless in the industry can change? I enjoy the sentiment, but…"

"Do it. Change. Right now. You have me out here, in the middle of a fucking park, at sunset, running." My arms fly wide to drive home the ridiculousness of his question. "People change, Ben. You don't have to take my word for it. People. Fucking. Chan—"

Ben pulls me to him until our bodies are flush, stealing my breath and cutting off any sort of speech I had prepared for him. "You plan on being the light to my dark, sunshine?" I avoid his gaze and look off to the sunset in the distance, the blend of red and yellow making me chuckle to myself. He's not gray, not even close. "Is there something funny about that?"

"Orange. You're a morally orange billionaire," I reply with a laugh I can't contain.

"I'm not following."

"Look." I point at the horizon. "Red and yellow make orange. There's more sunshine in you than you think, Ben."

"I suppose it beats gray." A small smirk tugs at his lips. "But I think I'd rather be inside you than the other way around," he adds with a wink.

I snicker, rolling my eyes. "Really? I'm trying to create this sweet metaphor around the sunset and you make a sex joke?" He pinches my side. I sigh, "Okay, fine, it was kind of funny. Well, I'm disgusting and drenched in sweat. Why don't I race you home? Or we can raise the stakes. If I win, you get to stay the night. If I lose, you have to leave, never to be heard from again. Ready… set… go." I can keep a slower pace on the way home—he wants to stay over and won't let me lose.

I take off in a sprint. There are no footsteps behind me for several seconds. I slow to a stop and look back, finding Ben exactly where I left him, hands stuffed in his pockets. I walk back, chin held high, swaying my hips. "Did you not understand the game?" I ask as I reach him.

"Oh, I heard you just fine, love. Why would I risk even the slightest chance of never seeing you again?" His gaze burns me and I take a labored breath.

"I was trying to be cute and flirty and—"

"You know, I have at least three kilometers left to run. Why don't you join me? Though, I would prefer to expel the calories fucking you until you can't move for a week." I'm about to respond when he continues, "I know. I can't fuck you for *several* weeks, maybe even a full month or two. But, darling, I don't need my cock inside you to make you come."

I suck in a breath. "I am not running, no matter how many orgasms you might promise me. Counter offer: I walk briskly home, take a long hot shower, and when you're done with your torture-run, you may stay the night with me, clothes on, no orgasms for either of us."

"I've tasted you, love. You expect me to not go back for seconds? How is that fair to either of us?"

"Take it or leave it," I offer with a shrug.

Ben groans. "I accept your terms. Better run along, sunshine. I warned you what will happen if I catch you." He winks and begins running in the opposite direction. While his dark gray joggers hide the bottom half of his right leg, I can still see the outline of his prosthetic if I look carefully enough. I'm fascinated by his perfect form. Once he rounds the corner, I turn and head back to my apartment.

On the walk back, I'm lost in my own thoughts, wondering how different things could be, if only he had made different choices. I take my time, meandering through the park, and really should take more evening walks; they're very relaxing. I appreciate the faint sounds of the traffic, the annoying mallards who are mating off-season, the loud footsteps approaching from behind me…

Not today, weirdo.

Someone has the nerve to place their hand on my shoulder. I swing around and karate chop the creep in the stomach, forcing them to double over.

"Fuck! Ben, I'm so sorry!" I place my hand on his back and, through the obvious pain I caused him, he's still laughing.

"That's no right hook, but you can certainly take care of yourself, sunshine," he chuckles, gasping for breath.

I wince. "Did I hurt you?"

When he finally rights his posture, he chokes out, "I'll be fine. I wanted to walk you home, if that's all right."

"Such a gentleman," I chuckle, and continue in the worst possible British accent I can muster on short notice, "Yes, you may escort me home, fine sir."

He shudders. "If you never do that again, it'll be too soon."

"Right? It was so bad! Are you sure you're okay?"

"More than okay," he replies with a small smirk.

Ben takes my hand, interlacing our fingers. I expected fireworks, or some sort of magic when he took my hand. Instead, I found something better—comfort. I feel safe with him. While I know that's a commonality with serial killers, I choose to believe that my morally orange man taking my hand is just a sweet gesture; not him trying to lure me into some sex dungeon or kill me.

I should really lay off the thrillers and dark stalker romances for a while.

"You don't have to stay the whole ni—"

"Morning?" he offers with a small smile, meeting my concerned gaze. "I'd love to have breakfast with you."

"You know that's not what I was going to say." I swat at his arm with my free hand.

"I do. I've already set my alarm for an ungodly hour. I'm absolutely staying the night, but I'll have to leave early in the morning for a call."

"How early?"

He winces. "I need to call back home. It's going to cause issues with my adjusting to the time difference here, but it's an important call."

"I'm not a morning person, so don't mind me if I'm sleeping in while you're off collecting companies like…

What's something super British you collect back home? I feel like baseball cards are an American thing."

"It's my mum." He squeezes my hand tightly, giving me pause. "No companies to be collected tomorrow, love."

We approach my building and I swipe my fob to gain entry. It's kind of sweet that he's calling his mother and not destroying a company tomorrow. I need to reevaluate my standards for men.

"You can call her while you're here," I offer. "I promise I won't eavesdrop."

He stops before the elevator. "You don't mind?"

"Why would I mind?"

"I don't know," he replies, seemingly surprised by his own answer. His soft smile reaches his eyes, creating small wrinkles in the corners as he shakes his head.

"Come on, I'm gross and need a shower." I tug on Ben's hand toward the elevator but he pulls me to him. "I literally just said I'm disgusting."

"You think I care?" He leans in and kisses me softly. I can't help the moan that escapes me as I melt into him. "I promised I wouldn't play with you tonight. However, you do realize it's tomorrow in England."

Ryan was thinking ahead when he packed my bag, even though I insisted I wasn't staying the night. He made sure to include my usual wraps for my leg and my charger for my prosthetic. I make a mental note that I need to give my 'first mate' a raise or, at very least, a promotion.

I haven't spent the night with a woman in years. What if she wakes up and forgets about my injury? Does she have a bath or just a shower? I'm sure her shower doesn't have bars installed or a rain shower head with an attachment, like I'm accustomed to.

As we enter her flat, I ask, "Mind if I use your bathroom?" While I don't desperately need to use the toilet, I need to take note of my possible bathing options.

"Of course not; knock yourself out. I'm going to drink eight gallons of water and wait for my muscles to forgive me for torturing them. Let me know if you need anything." She takes a seat on her couch, leans her head back on the cushion, closes her eyes, and crosses her feet on the coffee table.

"Are you okay, love?"

She waves me off. "Go do whatever it is that you need to do, I'll be here marinating in my own sweat until I can get my ass off this couch."

"You have two minutes." I keep my tone intentionally commanding. As predicted, she lifts her head and looks at me.

"Two? That's all I get?"

"Are you going to be my good girl and not move from that spot?"

Layla smirks. "Good girl? I think you have me confused with someone else."

"So, that's a no, then?" I stifle a groan.

"Go tinkle, or whatever you people call it in England. I'll just sit here and contemplate my life choices."

"Oh, sunshine," I laugh to myself. "Prepare for a nightly run with me, indefinitely. I promise I'll make the reward worth your while."

"We'll see about that."

"I apologise for the personal question." My cheeks heat and I clear my throat. "Do you by chance have menstrual pads? I'm supposed to use them with my piercing. I forgot to ask Ryan to pick them up."

"Under the cabinet." She waives me off again and closes her eyes, returning to her nearly meditative state on the couch.

I make my way down her hall to her bathroom, praying I find something other than a standalone shower. Opening the door with hesitation, I turn on the light. I scan the room, then do a double-take of the shower. There's a walk-in shower and bath combination with a watertight door. I remain rooted in place, in awe.

Layla isn't in a wheelchair and she doesn't appear to have mobility issues. Why would she have an accessible showering option? I walk in and take a closer look. There are jets, handrails, slip resistant floors, and a rain shower head with an extension. I shake my head in disbelief.

Walk back to the door, I close it, then carefully pull down my shorts and boxer briefs. The head of my cock is still wrapped; I take my time removing it. Surprisingly, there's nearly no blood on the bandage, even after my run.

After relieving myself, I tuck the bandage in my pocket to discard later, and locate a pad under her sink. I put it in my underwear. It's not comfortable and I'm grateful this isn't a monthly occurrence and will be short lived. I don't know how women do it.

I walk out to find Layla. She isn't where I left her, which I should've expected. Instead, she's in the kitchen, bent over and rummaging through her fridge. The urge to take a playful bite of her beautiful round arse is squashed when my cock presses against my shorts, making me wince. She rights her posture and turns to face me.

"Everything okay?" Layla closes the fridge and rushes over to me.

"I'm regretting my decisions today."

Layla's face falls. "Oh, okay. Um, if you need to go, I totally understand. You know, with the whole 'we only officially met yesterday' and all." She gasps. "Oh. Fuck. Is this because of me being signed under Turner? Say no more. I get it. I—"

I pull her into me, ignoring the pain I'm causing myself, and capture her words in a searing kiss. This gorgeous woman has no fucking clue. I have never wanted to acquire a company, a brand, or a woman as much as I want Layla. It defies logic, my nature, and common fucking sense. When she kisses me back, she surrenders, giving me all of her. I shouldn't want her, shouldn't crave her, and most definitely shouldn't be pursuing her. In one week, she took everything I knew about women and threw it in the bin.

"No, love," I whisper against her lips and pull back an inch to make sure she really hears me. "I wanted a piercing for years. I thought, by getting it done, that I could stay away from you—protect you from me. Instead, I'm counting the days until I can…" *Do not say make love, you fucking tosser.* "…properly worship you."

I will absolutely make love to her.

"It's because I have a really cool tub, isn't it?" She bites her lip, pleased with herself, and continues, "My mother is in a wheelchair and drops by unannounced often, so I had it installed a few years ago. Not going to lie, it's like my own personal hot tub most days. Glass of wine, a good book, waterproof vibrator while the jets swirl water around me. Plus, my lazy ass doesn't have to climb out, because of the door. It's heaven."

I don't think I've smiled this much in years. She's a breath of fresh air I didn't know I needed. "Did you just say—"

"Vibrator? You've seen my pussy. You think I would shy away from vibrator talk?" she asks, as if it's a normal conversation to have with someone.

"Come shower with me." It isn't a question. I don't want to spend a minute away from her.

Fuck. I'm turning into Julian.

"I don't think there's room," she chuckles. "Go enjoy a hot bath or… Oh! You can't take a bath yet with your new peen piercing. Okay, well, enjoy a hot shower without me."

Did she just say 'peen piercing?' Fuck, I need her naked. Now.

"Darling, there's no way to say this respectfully: Get in the fucking shower." I gesture with a nod down the hall.

Layla giggles. "Sorry, *sir.*" My cock twitches and I bite my cheek to keep another fucking groan from escaping me. She bites her lip, not catching my discomfort. "Especially since I sweated out eighteen pounds on the little night run you imposed on me. Hard pass next time, by the way. Not a runner. Oh and I'll take my own shower, thank you." Layla takes a step back and attempts to cross her arms over her chest.

"Get back here." I pull her to me once more. "I want you a drenched, sweaty mess. Expect another eighteen pounds of sweat shed by the time I'm through with you tonight."

"Says the guy who insists he wouldn't touch me." She narrows her eyes.

Fuck, she got me.

I sigh dramatically. "I need help, you know, getting in and out of the shower," I lie. "Missing limb and all. Wouldn't want you to get all *wet* from me; it would really be much easier if you're naked while assisting me."

"You're such a flirt. Fine, you win. I'll shower with you, but only because I want to see *you* naked and that new piercing of yours."

I steal her breath as my own as I grip her throat and kiss her deeply, needing her impossibly closer. Layla moans into my mouth and I slide my hands down until they're on her arse. They wander lower, about to lift her up and around me...

This is a horrible idea.

As much as I want to carry her into the shower and pull orgasm after orgasm from her, I can't risk an accidental injury to my dick. Fuck, this piercing was the biggest mistake of my life.

Layla's tongue sweeps across mine, and I can't help the growl that escapes me. "Don't you dare pick me up," she mutters into my mouth. "I know you're no longer wrapped."

"Fine," I reply, ensuring my lips never leave hers. "You're still coming."

She chuckles and pulls away. "If you keep talking like that, I probably will."

I kiss her once more and take her hand, guiding her down the hall toward the shower I so desperately need her in. She laughs the entire way and warmth fills me in a way I can't explain or comprehend.

I still. "Would you mind grabbing my duffle. I, uh, have a few things I might need."

Layla rushes back to the kitchen to retrieve my bag, returning a minute later with it. My fear must be painted on my face because she states without a hint of sarcasm, or pity, "If you need help, let me know." Her beaming smile is all the reassurance I need that, while getting a piercing was a mistake, wanting Layla is the furthest from it.

I don't know anything about her mother or what injuries she may have endured, but Layla's willingness to assist me makes my heart ache. Most joke that I don't have an actual heart—could Layla have ignited something I had hidden away for so long? It's as if I was a broken watch that began ticking again when I met her.

My pride chimes in. "I'm used to managing by myself."

"Ben," she sighs softly. "It's okay. I did an internship at the VA to get my massage certifications. Mostly back and knee injuries but I've seen it all. I wouldn't have offered it if I didn't think I could actually help."

"I have to"—I swallow hard—"remove my leg and charge it for the night. Then unwrap it and… I'm sorry. I'm just not used to this."

"Used to what?"

My heart stops. "Someone caring," I admit softly.

Her bright smile appears. "Well, I do. Will you let me help?"

With Layla looking at me like this, I can't help but give in. I nod and she helps me into her shower-bath combination. I take off my joggers and sit on the bench for her to assist me with removing my leg. "The cord is in my—"

"I got it, Ben. Trust me. It's okay." Layla works like an expert, finding the cord in my duffle and plugging it in. Thankfully, she didn't spot the condoms. "That should do for now. My mother has diabetes. She lost part of her leg because of it. Her peg leg, as she calls it, isn't nearly as advanced as yours, but I've done my research on prosthetics." She pauses and takes a deep breath. "It's not easy. I understand the need to be independent, but I know it's a hell of a lot easier when you accept someone's help."

"Sunshine," I whisper, "I'm sorry."

"Don't. Please. Just as you asked for no pity, do not pity me or my mother. She lives a full life, even with her disability."

I nod and she helps me unwrap my bandage. "Darling, I can—" Her eyes snap to mine in warning. I clamp my mouth shut. "Thank you."

"Don't thank me yet, you have four hundred layers going on here and I know damn well you didn't remove them last night. Just let me help, okay?"

"I don't think I could ever say no to you, love."

She replies with a smile, and all the concern lifts from me, disappearing into oblivion.

Layla is beyond perfect; there are no words for what this means to me. I certainly don't fucking deserve her. It doesn't change this inexplicable yearning I have, despite her standing right in front of me.

As soon as she removes my bandages, she takes a step back with her hands on her hips, proud of her work. "Shirt off. Underwear, too." *Fuck.* I freeze. "Ben," she says quietly, "safe word."

"What?"

"You heard me. You know what the hell a safe word is."

"Of course, love, but I'm supposed to be asking that of you," I counter.

She lets out a heavy sigh. "I don't want to make you uncomfortable or accidentally hurt you."

"I told you, you could never hurt me."

"Then, clothes off." Layla pulls her shirt over her head, then unclips her sports bra and tosses it to the ground.

"Fuck," I whisper, mostly to myself. She seductively peels off her leggings and knickers and stands before me naked. Her eyes wander down my body, my injury not fazing her. For the first time, I feel like someone sees *me*—not money or a disability.

"If you want help, ask, but you have two minutes before I'm turning that water on—with or without your clothes on."

I strip off my shirt faster than I have in my life and Layla's eyes flare as if I'm the last eclair in the bakery. I hook my fingers into my boxer briefs, hesitate for a moment worried I'm going to wake up and find this was all a dream. I take a deep breath, then drag them down my legs and toss them aside.

"I fucked up." Layla steps into the shower, standing between my legs when I want her straddling me. "The water is going to be cold at first. I'm sorry. I should have turned it on before we got in." She turns on the shower, wincing at the cool water hitting her back.

"Are you okay, love? You don't have to do this."

She glances down at my freshly pierced cock and smirks, lightly licking her lips. "Oh, I'm more than okay. It's just cold, it'll warm up quickly. I'm not going to ask again. Safe word, Ben."

"I don't need a safe word, darling. You do. Come here." I guide her to climb onto my lap, keeping my semi-hard cock between us but not touching, as much as I want her to. "I need to keep you safe from me. I could destroy you, sunshine."

Her fingers slide into my hair and her eyes dart between mine. "Do your worst. I dare you to try and sink me."

Layla will absolutely be mine.

Fucking. Permanently.

18

LAYLA

There's a gorgeous man in my apartment threatening to destroy me... *Am I going to let him?*

I reach behind Ben for my shampoo, squirting a dollop into his hair and replacing the bottle on the shelf. I begin washing his hair, loving how he closes his eyes and sighs when I massage his scalp.

"You don't have to—"

"Shh. I'm working here," I whisper. His cock twitches against me and he winces. While his eyes are closed, I risk a glance between us, confirming his perfect cock is ready to play.

Of course it's perfect, everything about him is. I feel like damn Goldilocks—it's long, but not too long, thick, but not too thick... just right.

I must be staring too long because his voice startles me as he asks, "Like what you see, love?"

"I, um, sorry. Doesn't it hurt? You're hard after getting pierced; that can't feel good."

I move to climb off but Ben grips my thighs and pulls me back to him. Taking my chin between his thumb and fore-finger, he kisses me softly. "Yeah, it fucking hurts," he whis-pers against my lips. "But you're not moving, sunshine."

"I don't want to hurt you."

"It's worth it. Can I see you?" His question confuses me. I look down between us, assuming he means my pussy but he tilts my chin back up with a chuckle. "No. I mean, I want to take you out. I don't intend on seeing anyone else, and I want whatever this is between us to be more than month-long foreplay."

"I don't know," I admit. "Isn't keeping this casual better for both of us?"

"For you, maybe." Ben tucks wet strands of hair behind my ear, his wide, vulnerable eyes darting between mine. "But not for me." He pauses and swallows hard. "I would be a fool if I didn't try for more with you. You're fucking extraordinary, sunshine. I know I don't deserve you, and it's safer if you run far away from me, but I want you to be mine all the same."

"You want to *date* me?"

"Well, yes, that is the general idea. I don't just want that pretty pussy of yours, love."

I shake my head, biting my lip to hide my smile. "But then I won't be able to interview you for my book. Conflict of interest, you know."

"*That's* what you're worried about? I'll find you three billionaires to interview if it means I get to keep you."

"You can keep me until you leave. Deal?"

"I'm going to hold you to that."

Ben tugs me closer to him without care of his fresh piercing. I pull back. "Careful! Last thing we need is Big Ben being injured. Besides, my water is going to turn borderline freezing any minute now. Loofah time, then bed, mister."

"Loofah time?" he asks with a frown.

I grab it from behind him and repeat, "Loofah. Time." Squeezing my orange and lavender body wash concoction I made last week onto the loofah, I lather it with my fingers.

Ben steals the sponge from me and sets it aside. "No reason to get you clean, if I'm just going to get you dirty."

"Not tonight." I snatch it back and proceed to drag it over his shoulders and down his arms. "You haven't even taken me on a proper date, and you think I'm some kind of hussy that's going to climb into bed with you?" I jest and continue to wash his chest.

"Are we not sharing a bed tonight, sunshine? I was hoping you'd sleep naked with me." He reaches between my legs and grazes my clit, forcing a moan from me.

"I feel like I should wear a long-sleeve onesie." The water is now lukewarm and I rush to finish washing him and myself.

"What's the hurry?"

At his question, I'm hyperaware that the water is getting colder by the second. "That's why!"

"Oh, fuck!" I grab the shower extension and quickly hose both of us off as we laugh. I take extra care to make sure I don't get it anywhere near his cock and shut the water off as quickly as I can. Showering together was a terrible idea with his piercing. "Come here," he groans, still every bit the growly, bossy billionaire I was hoping he would be for my book.

While I'm definitely well off for an author, I'm nowhere in the same monetary league as him. I just hope he'll continue to be growly and leave the billionaire at the door.

Damn it! I'm living a real life billionaire romance, aren't I?

Ben grips the nape of my neck and kisses me. I chuckle against his lips as we both remain cold and wet. "We should get out." I climb off him and grab two of my bath sheets. "Room temperature towels. You don't mind, right?" I playfully toss a towel at him and he laughs before drying his face and hair. "No butler to call to warm them. I would've turned on the towel warmer for you, Mr. Fancy Pants, but you were insistent with your 'get in the shower' so, here we are." I quickly dry myself and wrap my towel under my arms and across my breasts to cover up. Drying his hair, he drags the towel down his face, and his sinfully gorgeous blue eyes are on me drying off. "What?"

"Nothing. Well, not nothing. Fuck, do you have any idea how beautiful you are? Never cover up for me."

My cheeks heat and I deflect the praise, "I look like a drowned rat who likes tacos a little too much. But, thank you. Give me a second to throw on some clothes and I'll—"

"I thought I was clear. You're sleeping naked with me tonight, darling."

I roll my eyes. "Fine. I'll put on a robe until we go to bed." He groans. I'm about to grab it when an idea strikes me. "Oh! Do you use crutches at all?"

"From time to time. Why?"

I rush out of the bathroom and into the hallway to my small storage closet. I fling open the door and grab my mother's old crutches that I really should donate at some point, then run back toward the bathroom. Unfortunately, my feet are still slick and slip on my floor. I yelp as they go out from beneath me and I land on my back.

"Layla!" Ben calls from the bathroom. "Are you all right?"

"Nope, I'm a dumbass and ran across laminate floors with wet feet. I'm going to need a minute."

I've left a beautiful man, who is missing half his leg, in my bath-shower hybrid. His prosthetic leg is a good five to eight feet from him, and I'm laying on the floor like a fucking idiot who didn't think to wipe her feet before racing out of the bathroom. There's a thump which sounds like a wet towel being thrown on the ground, a zipper, and an unwrapping of plastic.

"Stay there, I'm coming, love. Just need to wrap my—"

"Doesn't matter. I'm coming, just need a minute." I don't move.

Ben chuckles. "Oh, sunshine, I can guarantee I can make you come in less than a minute. Almost done, then I'll help you up." I lift my head and groan. "What did I say? Stay. There," he growls.

"How the hell are you going to get out of the bathroom, when I know damn well I put your leg—" There's a click and the familiar sound of a prosthetic limb being set into place. During my time working with veterans, many of them had missing arms and legs. The sound takes me back to years ago and I smile to myself. "Please be careful. I know you have it on, but the floor is still slick. We can't both end up on our backs tonight."

He steps into view, fully naked, and leans against the frame of the bathroom door with a smirk. "And why the hell not? I quite enjoy having you on your back, but wouldn't mind you riding me, either." I let out a full belly laugh and he drops to one knee. "Are you hurt? Shall I call a doctor?"

"No, I think I'm fine. Just sore," I wince.

He places one hand on my shoulder and takes my hand with his other. "One inch at a time, love. Don't rush it."

"That's what she said."

He stifles his laugh. "Not the time for jokes. If you can't lift up, I'm calling someone."

"Fine," I sigh.

Ben makes himself an anchor so I can pull myself up. "Slower... There you go... All right, now where does it hurt?"

"Just my back. But I'm sure if I lay down, it'll be fine."

"Can you stand?"

"I think so." He helps me the rest of the way up, abandoning my towel on the floor. In one quick movement, he lifts me bridal-style like he's about to cross a threshold. I wrap my arms tightly around his neck, praying he doesn't drop me. Fucking book boyfriend energy, again—I love and hate it. "You can put me down, I can walk."

"So can I." He carries me into the bedroom and sets me on my bed. "I'll be right back. I need to take care of a few things. I'll grab you a fresh towel but don't you dare move from that spot until I return." His tone is laced with concern and a hint of dominance that entertains my pussy a little too much. I nod and he walks out of the room to who knows where. I lay back on my bed with a sigh.

Ben is gone for several minutes. As much as I want to check in with him, I remain rooted in place as he requested. If I wasn't in so much pain, I would test the possible fun consequences of getting up. When he returns, he has his duffle, the crutches, an ice pack and a towel. He sets down his bag and pulls out a bottle of over-the-counter pain medication from my bathroom and a bottle of water from my fridge.

"What's all this?"

"Let me take care of you." He smirks and hands me the medication and water. "Drink up."

Could I be roofied? Possibly. Nonetheless, I take a little blue pill and four long gulps of water. "Could you find my phone? I think it's in the kitchen."

"Of course." He slips on a pair of boxer briefs he prepped with a pad and heads back out of my room to retrieve my phone. When he returns with it, I text Amanda.

> Just took either naproxen, viagra, or I'm being drugged. Just FYI.

I set my phone down and prop myself onto my elbows. "Is it weird that I want to go to bed so early? I'm normally up until two in the morning writing. I don't have the energy after that run."

"Want to write from bed? I can find your laptop. Are you sure you didn't hit your head? You took quite a fall out there." Concern paints his features. Either he's actually worried, or this is an act and I'm going to meet Jesus in a few hours after what I just took.

My phone buzzes with a text from Amanda before I can respond to him. I can't help my impulsive need to check it.

AMANDA

> Sounds like a good time. Just looked it up. Call a doctor if your ladyboner lasts longer than four hours. Rohypnol isn't typically a little blue pill so I think you're fine. Text me in the morning.

> Tell Ben I'll have Julian send a SWAT team or whoever he has on speed dial if you don't reply by noon tomorrow.

> And thank him for my lobster dinner and far too many whiskey sours.

I giggle and show Ben the text exchange. He laughs and kisses me briefly. "I loved watching you come for me. It's not nearly as sexy if you're sleeping, love." My hand flies to my eyes in embarrassment from what we've done in the past twenty-four hours. He peels my hand away. "No hiding. Now, let's get you to bed. I'll grab your laptop if you want to work, but you should rest." I roll my eyes and scoff. "Oh, and roll your eyes at me again and I won't let you come for a week."

"Consider them unrolled. But you know I have a vibrator. How else do you think I took care of myself before I met you?" I keep my expression as neutral as I can, but a smirk escapes.

"I slept for shit last night, so I'm not going to fight you on this tonight. Tomorrow, all bets are off."

I fling back the covers on one side. "No writing tonight; I can barely keep my eyes open. Hop in."

"Ladies first." Ben kisses my temple and pulls back my covers further. I scoot backward and slide under. He detaches his leg and plugs it in to charge before climbing in next to me. At first, I keep my distance, laying on my side facing him. "Get over here." I move an inch closer. He smiles and brushes my damp hair off my shoulder. "What did I say?"

I move one more inch. I expect him to ask for another but he opts to pull me closer by my lower back and slings my leg over his. He slides his hand up my thigh until he reaches my ass and playfully grips it. I tuck into him as he lays on his back.

"Fuck. How are you the perfect fit, sunshine?" He kisses the top of my head and lightly grazes one of my nipples as he slowly caresses every inch of me.

"Night." I kiss him on the cheek.

He tilts my chin higher and kisses me softly. "Night, love."

I could get used to having him here and bossing me around. I keep forgetting he's leaving soon. And way too attractive to be seen with someone like me. And...

Oh. Fuck. There's a billionaire in my fucking bed.

19

BEN

I wake to the alarm on my phone after what has to be the most restful night of sleep I've had in years. Layla's soft, exquisite body is turned away from me, her back flush against my chest, my hand between her legs cupping her…

Fuck. I must seem like some kind of sex-starved knob! I'm essentially fondling a sleeping woman.

I move my hand up, splaying my fingers on her stomach and bringing her closer. She moans softly and my already hard cock likes the sound a little too much. It hurts worse than anything I've experienced in my life. Part of me feels the pain is justified after everything I've done in the last decade. My karma. I almost destroyed the career of the most incredible woman I've ever known because of my own greed. I don't deserve her.

Kissing her shoulder, I whisper against her smooth skin, "Sorry, sunshine. I need to make a call. I'll be back in a minute." Layla groans something unintelligible and I kiss her neck one more time before turning away from her.

I remove the charging wire for my leg and put it on, snapping it into place. I'll replace the wrapping later. I grab my duffle and phone, carefully walking to the kitchen and setting my bag on the counter. I then head to the washroom to take a piss and clean my piercing. Thankfully, it's not bleeding and I'm able to clean it quickly with the solution the piercer provided. I remove the old protection from my underwear but don't replace it. I feel like it needs to breathe. Then, I make my way back into the kitchen.

I haven't talked to my mum in a week; she doesn't know about Layla. Before ringing her, I pull up my text exchange with Julian to ask about my cousin, Jack, and the upcoming archeological dig we are trying to fund, only to find two missed messages from him.

> **JULIAN**
>
> What the fuck? Amanda said you're at Layla's?
>
> I thought you agreed to stay the hell away from her!

Bollocks. I thought Amanda was joking when she told Layla she'd contact Julian. There's no way I could stay away from her if I tried. If I thought Amanda was serious, I would've offered her more than dinner and my flat.

Glancing at the open door to her bedroom for a moment, I can't help wondering if there's some alternate reality or past life where we knew each other. The pull I have toward her is indescribable.

> Sod off, Jules.

Of all the women you could chase after, you chose my wife's friend? She's the human equivalent of a damn rainbow. What the fuck is wrong with you?

I don't reply; I can deal with his overprotective bullshit later. He won't be in any mood to discuss a Scottish castle when he's miffed at me. I swipe and tap on my contacts and click on *Mum*, hoping she might have an answer.

"Benedict, how are you?"

I blow out a long breath. "I'm all right." I am *not* all right. I'm falling hard for a woman I shouldn't. "Dove right into work as soon as I got here. How was your week?"

"Ben, you can cut the shit. I saw the photographs. She's very pretty."

My brows pinch together. "What photos?"

"The ones where you were out with Julian and his wife. How is he, by the way? I haven't seen him in ages."

"Since the wedding," I agree.

"Well, marriage looks good on him. They're such a handsome couple and Rebecca is lovely."

"Yes, they are." I sigh. While I'm happy for my friend, I know what's coming next.

"So, tell me about Layla Thorne."

Ah, there it is. She'll be planning the wedding by month's end.

"I'd rather not discuss this right now," I grit out, keeping my voice low to not wake Layla.

What is there to say? We met two nights ago and now I'm contemplating restructuring my entire company because of her? I pierced my cock because I needed to ensure I wouldn't fuck her? She's the most extraordinary woman I've had the pleasure of kissing? I stole her purse so I could spend more time with her?

"I raised you better than this. I have to learn that my son has a new woman in his life—who doesn't look like she was picked out of a catalogue—from a tabloid photograph? You like this one, I can tell."

I let out a defeated sigh. "Yes, Mum, I like this one." *More than like, I'm obsessed with her after knowing her for a week. Bloody hell. What's wrong with me?* "Now, will you drop it? I was calling to inquire about—"

"It's settled. No need to worry yourself. I funded it myself. Well, most of it."

A weight lifts off my chest. "When will Jack get to begin his work at the site?"

"Next month. Cameron is going to join him." The smile in her voice has my own lips turning up. "There was an additional donor who helped fund the project. Her only stipulation was that she could be at the site. If we find another investor, we should make sure they are there to keep an eye on things. There's something about her I don't entirely trust. Who knew archaeology was so expensive? It's only a shovel and bones."

"You know very well that it's more than that, Mum." Jack has to fund his writing and I can't have my name on it or it could jeopardise his research. I haven't made friends in academia, especially in Scotland. On the contrary, I bought out two of their primary journal publications and subsequently made enemies. If there isn't another investor, I'm thankful my cousin, Cam, will be there.

"I was only kidding. He's thrilled to begin."

"All right, Mum, I apologise for the short call but I have an important meeting to attend shortly." *Between Layla's thighs.*

"Call soon, Benedict. Next time, don't let me learn of your relationships through online photographs."

"I won't," I laugh. "I'm off."

"I love you."

"Love you, too, Mum."

I hang up, toss my phone onto the counter, and rush back to find Layla curled up under the sheets. I sit on the side of the bed and trace my fingers up and down her naked back, wanting to memorise every inch of her and loving the feel of her soft skin prickling with goosepimples after each swipe. She shudders and turns to face me, slowly opening her eyes.

"Good morning. How was your call?"

"Mum had good news for me." I detach my leg and set it beside the bed before joining her under her duvet. "I didn't mean to wake you. Are you still tired?"

"No." She shakes her head with a beaming smile. "I should get up and start breakfast soon. Sundays call for mimosas! Are you hungry?"

"You have no idea."

I take her chin in my hand and kiss her. I start slow, parting her lips just enough to take her bottom lip between my teeth. The sigh she lets out is music to my ears. I pepper kisses along her jaw to just below her ear and down her neck, breathing in the familiar scent of orange and lavender that I've come to enjoy so much.

I climb on top of her, settling between her legs. She instinctively wraps them around me and my cock aches to be inside her. I push through the pain, wanting her more than I care about my own comfort. I kiss her neck and suck hard, branding her as mine and not giving a flying fuck who might see it. As I graze my teeth against the dark pink mark, she arches into me and moans. She's already wet, making my boxer briefs damp.

"Fuck," I groan and pull my cock an inch away from her.

Layla gasps. "Shit. Are you okay? Did I hurt you?"

I bury my face in the crook of her neck and chuckle. Layla tries to get up but I grip both her hands, interlacing our fingers and placing our joined hands above her head.

"No, sunshine. You're fucking perfect. My cock isn't wrapped, I forgot to replace the napkin, and, well, you're wet, love. Don't worry about me. You can get up and make breakfast after I've had mine."

"You're so fucking cliché," she giggles.

I kiss her collarbone, her chest, and take my time teasing each of her barbell pierced nipples. I draw them into my mouth one at a time; grazing my teeth as I swirl my tongue. Her fingers tangle in my hair as she lifts her hips, seeking more.

"Patience, sunshine. I have all morning, and I want to enjoy myself." I release her hands and slide mine down her body, kissing past her stomach until I reach just above her pussy.

"Please," she begs and lets out a desperate moan.

"Fuck, I love to hear you beg. But if you interrupt me again, I'll taste you for hours, and never let you come. Be my good girl, so I can take my time exploring every inch of you."

"What about you?" She bites her lip.

"What did I say, sunshine? This is your final warning; I don't mind taming the little brat in you, if need be." I lick up her cunt, making her gasp, then tease her with a kiss just above her clit. "You're mine to do with as I please, darling. You're going to come five times for me this morning. Only after I take a fifth from you will I let you rest."

She whimpers, nodding. I can't help my smirk; I'm going to have too much fun with her in a month when I can finally be inside her.

As promised, I take my time; drawing firm, slow circles around her clit and tracing her entrance. I press two fingers inside her and curl, finding the spot I know will have her coming for me quickly. I can't help myself; I lower my mouth to her pussy, licking a couple of times around her clit before sucking hard. She gasps as I drive my fingers deeper, massaging inside her. It dawns on me that we have matching 'his and hers' barbell piercings. I play with hers in my mouth and huff a laugh; the vibration has her clenching around my fingers. I let out a purposeful moan to give her additional stimulation. She's so tight and wet, sheer heaven and *fucking mine.*

Layla comes hard and fast for me, screaming my name. All at once, I'm overwhelmed with the need to claim her, own her. I'm consumed by my desire and bite down on her clit, enough that I could possibly hurt her. I normally keep my sexual needs to myself, but I let myself slip just now.

I pull back. "Fuck, I'm sorry, I—"

"Why are you talking? Do it again," she pleads.

I kiss her now sensitive clit and whisper, "I don't want to hurt you."

"I said do it again, Ben."

A growl erupts from my chest, and my desire to let go of all inhibitions takes over. I spread her wide to feast on her again, her glistening cunt ready and waiting for me. I'm pulling five from her this morning. Period. "Safe word, Layla."

"I don't need one," she breathes.

I spread her wider, making her wince. "I'll want to test your limits. I can't do that if I could possibly hurt you."

"Fine. Um, *Brexit*."

I lower my head, laughing, then lift it to find her head back against her pillow, hand over her eyes. "Layla," I say softly. "Never hide from me unless we're playing. Eyes on me, love." She props herself onto her elbows to look at me. "If I'm too rough, you have to tell me, okay?"

"Okay," she replies with a nod.

"Where is the infamous vibrator you've been alluding to?"

Layla laughs and opens up her bedside table, handing me a yellow clit vibrator. "This one is my favourite."

A sly smirk spreads across my face. "Oh, sunshine. It had to be yellow, didn't it?"

"Would you rather it be red?"

"Keep up with that smart mouth of yours and your arse will be."

Her eyes widen but she hides a smile. "Promise?"

"My darling, you think you can test me?" I turn the vibrator on the highest setting and place it against her clit. She screams a moan and falls back against the bed, gripping the sheets. I flip her onto her stomach and lift her arse in the air with her face pressed against the pillow, giving me a beautiful view of her dripping cunt. I replace the vibrator on her clit and rub her arse twice before I lift my palm and bring it back down with a crack. Her yelp quickly becomes a moan and I massage the fresh, pink mark I left. "You need another? I want to hear you beg for it."

"Please," she moans.

"Please, what, love?"

"Again."

"That's my girl." I spank her again, then drive two fingers inside her wet pussy, but resist taking a bite of her perfectly round arse. My cock is leaking without touching it. I was warned not to have sex or masturbate for a month, but they said nothing about coming from the sight of marking the most beautiful woman I've ever met as my own. The pain is excruciating but I'm intent on continuing.

"I'm close."

"I know, love." I add a third finger, making her gasp. "You're doing so well, taking your punishment like a good girl. When you come, I'm going to fuck you harder with my fingers to take another from you." Her whimpers fill the room. "You can take it, beautiful." I know she's on the edge as she arches her back and grinds against my hand. "That's it, just like that. Come for me."

Her second orgasm lasts longer than the first. I continue the same pace with more pressure, prolonging it. She's close to a third, but I'd rather have her come on my face. Desperate to taste her again, I slowly remove my fingers, sucking them clean, and press a soft kiss to her lower back. "That only counts as two. Three more, sunshine. Then, you can rest."

"I—"

There's an opening and closing of Layla's front door, followed by, "Layla-love, I brought breakfast!" from an unfamiliar voice.

Bloody Hell.

"Fuck," Layla squeals, "what the hell is she doing here?"

Shit, shit, shit! I can't fucking move. I'm still mid-orgasm with my face in a pillow and a delicious man playing with my pussy because, for some reason, he thinks it's a good time while his cock heals. Not exactly how I'd like my mother to find me, no matter how progressive she is.

"One second! I'm coming!" I yell to the living area.

"Oh, you will be," Ben snickers.

"Don't you dare start. I know, I walked into that one," I whisper-shout to him. "Put on some pants."

"Oh, no, darling. I told you five. You owe me three more." He bites his lip as his eyes darken. Maybe just one more…

No! Mom's in the damn kitchen! No more secret sexytime with the billionaire.

Ben climbs on top of me, bringing his face within an inch of mine. "You're choice, sunshine. Just know if I don't take three from you right now, I'll take six later and I'll make you work for it."

"There's no time." I close the distance and kiss him, keeping it chaste until his thumb grazes one of my nipples and a stray moan escapes me. I claw at his back and he growls into my mouth in response, which only encourages me to let him play for a moment longer.

There's a knock at my open bedroom door. "There you are, I— Oh. Sorry, sweetheart, I didn't know you had company."

"Fuck!" I try to scramble out from under him but it takes an extra moment as I attempt to simultaneously cover up. "Mom, what are you doing here?"

"I brought breakfast, but I can go." She glances at his leg and back to me before wheeling out of the room.

"No, it's okay. I didn't know you were coming for Sunday mimosas. Let me get dressed and I'll be right out."

Ben lays on his side, propped up and resting his head on his fist, looking far too proud of himself. I glare at him as I shimmy out of bed. Mom wheels out of the room and once she's out of earshot, he asks, "So, what's for breakfast?"

"You're not staying." I throw open my dresser drawers, searching for something to wear that will keep his hands off me. I settle on a pair of black leggings and a shirt that says "Pun Always Intended."

"And why not?"

I spin in place and his gaze changes from playful to something dark I can't quite put my finger on. If given the opportunity, he would pin me down and have his way with me… again. And again. And again. I put on my bralette and shirt. As I'm tugging my leggings up, I ask, "What are your plans for the day?"

"No plans, other than staying another night with you."

"You're not staying over tonight."

"Then I'll stay until sunset," he counters.

"Ben," I warn.

"You said you're mine until I need to leave to go back home. Why wouldn't I want to spend every available moment I have with you?"

While I want him here, it's awkward as fuck with my mother dropping by. "Fine," I concede. "You can stay for breakfast, but then you have to go."

"Can I take you out tonight?"

"You're worse than Julian," I mutter. He moves to the edge of the bed to adjust his leg wrapping and I notice a dark mark on his underwear. "Did you forget a pad? You, uh." I gesture to his cock.

He glances down. "Fuck, I forgot but... that's not blood from my piercing, that's from you, darling."

"From me?" I frown.

"Well, it's half you and half me. I nearly came and you're entirely to blame."

I bite my lip to keep from laughing. "Well, you should change."

Ben nods toward the door. "Go see your mum. I'll be out shortly." I press a kiss to his cheek and turn to leave my bedroom, but he grips my wrist and pulls me to him. "Not so fast, sunshine."

"Yes?" I place my hands on his shoulders and stand between his legs.

"Can I take you out tonight? You didn't answer me." He presses his lips to the inside of my wrist, not breaking eye contact.

"Maybe." I bend to kiss him. "Get dressed." As I right my posture, he playfully swats at my ass. My pussy is satisfied, my ass is sore, and my nipples are standing at attention. I should've put on a real bra. Of course, of all the days my mom had to drop by today.

I make my way to the kitchen where she's unloading groceries into my fridge. "Hey, Mom."

"Who's the new guy?" She looks around the fridge door with a quirked eyebrow, eyeing me suspiciously.

"Ben. We're…" *What are we doing?* "Dating… ish. And before you say anything, yes, I met a stranger from the internet."

Mom rolls her eyes and laughs, continuing in the fridge. I have a feeling she watched some home organization show and is about to spend too much money on clear plastic bins for my fridge.

"How the hell did you meet a publishing giant online?" Her voice is laced with a firm, accusatory tone.

I sigh. "I was researching a book and we started talking… Hold on, how do you know he's in publishing?"

"He's Benedict Turner, is he not? Everyone knows who he

is. How many one-legged billionaires are there in the world? Are you living under a rock?"

"No." *Yes.*

She doesn't look up from the fridge reorganization. "He's not a good man, sweetheart. I hope you're being careful. You're an author, how on earth did you get involved with a man like him?"

"Well, he's friends with Julian and Becca." It's not entirely a lie, he *is* friends with Julian. "One thing led to another and now we're—"

"Good morning," Ben chimes in, saving me from an explanation.

My hand flies to my chest. "For the love, where did you come from?"

"Do you really want me to answer that?" he playfully asks, biting his lip. Mom peeks around the fridge, eyeing him suspiciously.

"Ben, this is my mother, Jennifer. Mom, this is Ben."

"My apologies. I wasn't aware Layla expected company this morning. I'll see myself out."

As he reaches for his phone and bag, Mom insists, "Nonsense. I texted her only an hour ago that I was planning on stopping by. I didn't hear back, but I assumed she was still asleep. Please, stay for breakfast." She gestures for him to take a seat at my kitchen table. "Nothing fancy, just bagels we top with avocado and gruyere cheese, turkey sausage, and mimosas."

"Sounds lovely. I'd love to stay, if Layla doesn't mind." He looks to me for permission.

"Sure, I don't mind," I answer nervously, knowing the inquisition will continue from my mom, and now he'll be the brunt of it.

Ben winks and makes his way to the kitchen as my mom closes the fridge. "Anything I can help with?"

Mom glances at his legs and back to his face. "I can manage. But if you poured me a mimosa, I wouldn't be opposed—mostly champagne with a splash of orange juice for color. It's the only sugar I'm allowing myself today."

"Is there any other way?" he chuckles.

Ben takes the champagne and orange juice out of the fridge. I watch intently as he reaches to my top cabinet and retrieves three stemless wine glasses.

"Mimosas, Ben. The champagne glasses are to the left." I gesture to the stemless champagne glasses on the top shelf.

He shrugs. "No one is driving, I presume. Why not enjoy a larger glass?"

"That's the spirit," Mom adds. Since when is she Team Ben? "Do you mind grabbing the cutting board and a knife, Layla-love?" She lifts the lowered counter extension I had installed for her and sets it in place as I bend to rummage under my cabinet for a cutting board. Ben slaps me on the ass as he walks past and I yelp. Mom turns around. "Everything okay?"

"Yep, totally fine." I right myself and whisper-shout to Ben, "Really, *Brexit?*"

Ben's eyes widen. He glances at my mother, who isn't looking in our direction, then back to me. Once he closes the distance between us, he insists, "I didn't mean anything by it, I'm so sorry, sunshine. Won't happen again." He wraps me in a tight hug and kisses the top of my head, whispering into my hair, "I promise."

"You better let it happen again, just not when she's here, okay?" For someone so well-mannered, he doesn't seem to understand basic etiquette for meeting parents.

"Understood." He releases me and returns to the mimosas. He pours the Champagne between the three glasses and tops them with juice, handing Mom hers first that is significantly less orange than ours. I always make sure to have low-carb bubbly on hand for her sporadic visits, and am glad she's not consuming too much sugar.

"A man who knows how to follow directions," she says into her glass as she takes a few sips of her drink. Ben smirks and hands me mine.

We continue making breakfast and I set our 'basic bitch' breakfast at my kitchen table. Ben makes a fresh batch of mimosas in a carafe so we can top ours off if we'd like. He also brings over two cans of sparkling water. Leaning in, he whispers, "In case she doesn't want any more sugar," and kisses me on the cheek. The sweet gesture makes my heart swell.

I feel like Becca when she was dating Julian. She didn't know about his financial situation, making simple dinners for him, mortified to learn he's a billionaire. He was spending a lot of time in her small New York apartment, eating pot roast or enchiladas. I'm now feeling slightly embarrassed, offering turkey sausage and bagels. While it's my favorite breakfast, I'm sure he has an on-staff chef to make whatever he pleases.

I'm comfortable financially, only because my money is tied up in various investments. Harriet's father, Dylan, set it up for me. If I play my cards right, I won't have to worry about money ever again, but I still live a semi-minimalist lifestyle.

Mom fills the silence by telling me all about her recent trip to Scotland. Ben perks up, sharing with my mom that his cousin is an archaeologist and lives there. I'm embarrassed to admit I didn't know archaeologists are *not* the same as paleontologists, as my mother pointed out. To be fair, his stories would be far more interesting if his cousin dug up dinosaur bones.

During the entirety of breakfast, Ben's hand never leaves my thigh. He swipes his thumb back and forth, and while it doesn't feel sexual, it still lights me up inside.

I'm lost in thought when Ben grips my thigh and I'm brought back to reality. I only hear the tail end of my mother saying, "...conflict of interest?"

"I'm sorry, I didn't catch that. I was, uh, thinking about something I need to write," I lie. "What did you say?"

"I was just asking Ben if you two seeing each other is the best idea, since he bought the company you're published under."

"Oh, uh—"

"My lawyers have already drafted up a contract. I will not oversee the direct hiring or firing of anyone who touches her books. I'll be signing it tomorrow when I return to the office."

I turn to face him. "When were you going to tell me?"

"We…" He looks between my mother and I, lowering his voice, "We haven't exactly had time to discuss it." I suck in a breath and he returns his attention to Mom. "Rest assured, I cannot and will not interfere with your daughter's career."

My mother is about to respond when there's a knock at the door. We all look toward the noise. Ben stands and insists, "I've got it," and checks my peephole before opening it.

"I should really have a key while I'm here, don't you think? You're alive! No roofie!" Amanda exclaims as she practically skips inside. "And… Jennifer? When did you get into town?" She takes a seat at the table next to Mom without invitation, giving her a half-hug.

"Late last night. What about you?"

"Julian flew me in a couple days ago to watch over this one." Amanda gestures with her thumb toward me. "Where are you staying?"

"A hotel downtown because I didn't want to wake Layla. Seems I managed to anyway." Mom gives a knowing look.

Amanda lets out a full laugh. "Did you walk in on them? That was me yesterday. You should've called me! I stayed at Benny-boo's last night. Swanky as hell penthouse apartment; easily would've accommodated both of us and a harem of forty men." Ben gets up to bring Amanda a glass and pours her a mimosa. "Thank you."

Ben tops off mine and offers to my mother but she declines. He then leans in to kiss my temple, refilling my glass. "I'm going to head out so you can enjoy your company, but I'll see you tonight." He rights his posture. "It was a pleasure meeting you," he addresses my mother, then Amanda, "I take it I won't be expecting anything unusual when I return to the flat?"

"Oh, it's worse than that scene in *The Hangover*. Pretty sure there was a tiger when I woke up and everything." Amanda keeps a neutral expression as she sips her drink.

Ben scoffs. "Is that all? I expected more from you." He winks and adds, "Have a wonderful rest of your morning, ladies."

He retrieves his bag and phone, then his key from Amanda —which she reluctantly gives up. As soon as my front door clicks shut, Amanda jumps right in, "Start talking."

21

BEN

Thinking back to my conversation with Julian last week, I question everything I knew about dating, relationships, and... *love*. He asked if I've ever been in love and I lied. I've had a few serious girlfriends, but I was never in love with any of them. One week was all it took for my entire world to be turned on its head. While I don't believe I'm in love with Layla, I most definitely will be if I continue spending time with her.

I adore Layla. After we've spent countless hours on the phone talking about everything and nothing, I feel comfortable telling her anything. The connection I have with her is unlike anything I've ever known. When she walked into that restaurant, my heart stopped and she absolutely captivated me.

There's no question that she's stunning. No, that doesn't even begin to describe her devastating beauty.

It's more than her enchanting hazel eyes that always find mine or her sinful figure that beckons me to touch her.

Layla disarms me with a single look in my direction, as if she sees *me* and accepts my imperfections. She makes me want to be a man worthy of her.

I'm certainly not… at least not yet.

We only just met, but I know with all my being that there is something extraordinary about Layla. I can't help my incessant need to spend every single moment with her in my presence—even if it means I have perpetual blue balls for the next thirty-something days.

I would drag her down to hell and make her my queen, if only it wouldn't destroy her light.

On the drive to my flat downtown, I place an order for three bouquets—one for Layla, one for her mum, and one for Amanda—to be delivered to Layla later this afternoon. Once I'm back at my place that lacks the same character Layla's does, I turn on my laptop and pull up my email to message one of the acquisitions managers who oversees the Kipling merger.

To: Dennis Jones
From: Benedict Turner
Subject: Kipling Merger

Dennis,

Tomorrow morning, please see me in my office at 8 a.m. to discuss the consolidation of three of the Kipling offices.

Regards,

Benedict Turner, CEO
Turner Publishing

My mouse hovers over 'send' but I can't bring myself to press it. Consolidating the three locations is the most lucrative and follows my typical routine when acquiring a new publishing house.

Perhaps my sunshine has had more of an effect on me than I thought?

I adjust my draft.

To: Dennis Jones
CC: Ryan Morgan
From: Benedict Turner
Subject: Kipling Expansion

Dennis,

Do not respond to or address this email over the weekend. Monday morning, please see me in my office at 8 a.m. to discuss expansion of three of the Kipling offices.

Additionally, Ryan, please book the conference room for 9 a.m. and include all involved parties, especially Roger.

Regards,

Benedict Turner, CEO
Turner Publishing

I don't press send, choosing to leave it for later, and turn off my laptop. I can't make this big of a decision without additional research. I blow out a long breath and take note of the flat.

Amanda used the guest bedroom, but otherwise there isn't a single item out of place. I hate it how sterile the space is. Not only is Layla not here, there's no warmth. As I look around the kitchen, I spot a torn piece of paper taped to the fridge door.

Ben's-A-Dick,
Hurt Layla and I'll castrate you.
xoxo,
Amanda
P.S. I'm not kidding. I will literally remove that
pierced peen of yours and feed it to a raccoon.

I don't know Amanda well, but I don't doubt that she's serious. I assume Layla told her about my piercing, but I would never do anything to intentionally hurt Layla. Certainly nothing that would warrant castration. As Julian pointed out, Layla's a fucking rainbow—rare and full of colour. She exudes a positivity that I could never attempt to replicate.

The part of me that felt envy for Julian has diminished. While Becca is an incredible woman, she's not Layla. I've been gone from her flat for less than an hour and I already miss her. Since I didn't get to finish what I started earlier this morning, I order an item to be delivered to her within the hour. I'm nothing if not a man of my word.

Forty-five minutes later, my phone rings and *Sunshine* lights up the screen. I do my best to contain my excitement as I answer, "Well, hello, love."

"What did you send me?" she sings.

"Open it up and find out."

There's a rustling of packaging. "Ben," she squeaks, "why did you send me a vibrator?"

"Wear it tonight." I attempt to keep my tone playful but it comes out as a growl. The idea of her wearing the clit vibrator I sent while I control the remote has my cock pressing against my— "*Fuck.*"

"Ben? Are you okay? What's wrong?"

"Nothing," I manage with a groan I can't hold in. "I'm fine. Be ready at six, I'm picking you up. Don't forget the remote, sunshine… Actually, I'll be there to retrieve it from you within the half-hour. Make sure it's paired properly or I'll test it out myself."

I need to see her.

"I dare you." I fucking hate brats, but I love… *like* when she challenges me.

"Are Amanda and your mum still there?"

"Yes, why?"

"Then I hope you don't mind them seeing me bend you over and claiming that delicious cunt of yours in front of them."

She gasps. "You wouldn't."

"Try me, love. I told you I'm taking five from you this morning. I never specified how or when." There's silence on the end and muffled voices. "Layla, are you still there?"

"Oh, yes, sorry. I'm here." She clears her throat, then whispers, "Don't make me use my safe word. If you drop by, I'll give you the remote but that's all. I'll see you tonight."

"Shall I send Ryan to retrieve it, instead?" I would never, but want to see her reaction,

"No," she squeals. "Absolutely not. Highly inappropriate, *Benedict.*" I hate my name, but from her lips, I'd listen to it all day.

"I'll be there soon."

We hang up, and about thirty minutes later, I arrive at her building. A nervousness overtakes me, despite there being nothing to be nervous about. I greet the new doorman I hired earlier today and press the button for her flat.

"Hello?"

"Just me, love."

"Come on up," she says with a smile in her voice. Layla buzzes me into the building and I approach the elevator, where a second security officer is standing guard. He asks for her flat number and name before allowing me to ride the lift. Despite them both being on my payroll, I appreciate them not automatically granting me access to her flat.

When I approach her door, I'm hesitant, the same nervousness from before causing my stomach to tie in knots. I knock twice and she answers almost immediately.

Without greeting, I ask, "Are they still here?"

"Amanda—"

I storm in, take her face in my hands and kiss her without care if anyone might see me. Layla sighs the moment our lips touch and I pull her to me by her lower back. She lets me own this small piece of her as she allows me to taste and tease, exploring her mouth. A voice clears behind her and Layla reluctantly pulls away, sighing in disappointment.

"Sorry, I was trying to tell you. Amanda is still here. Mom went to the store."

"Hi, book daddy," Amanda chimes in. "Don't mind me over here, boyfriendless and vibratorless. Feel free to send me one next time. I'll put it to good use." I know what Layla and I have is new, but Amanda implying I'm Layla's 'boyfriend' has me seriously considering not going home to Canterbury.

Layla shuts her eyes tight, shaking her head. "She was here when I opened it… and while I was on the phone with you."

"At least it wasn't your mum," I jest, wrapping her in my arms and kissing the top of her head. I whisper into her hair, "I'll take what's mine and be on my way"

"What's yours? Oh, the remote. Right." She pulls away to grab it but I keep her close. "I can't get it if I'm stuck in my doorway making out with you." I carefully wrap my hand around the front of her throat and bring her lips back to mine. She allows me to taste her for the shortest moment before she grips my wrist and pulls back. "Remote, Ben," she laughs.

I clear my throat. "Yes, the remote." Layla walks into the kitchen and returns to me, placing it in my hands. "I'll see you tonight, darling."

She lifts onto her toes and kisses my cheek. "Tonight."

"You're in trouble with a capital 'T,' babes," Amanda teases after Ben leaves.

"You think?" I lean back my head and groan. "Mom already lectured me on this. *He has the worst manners of any British person I've met.*' And don't forget, '*Who openly touches a woman in front of company?*' I get it, he's socially inept, but I don't get what the big deal is. It's temporary. Why can't I have a bit of fun?"

"I saw the way he looks at you and it's *not* casual. He looks like he's going to devour you any moment. Pretty sure if he was a caveman, he'd throw you over his shoulder and haul you off to his abode to have his way with you."

I raise an eyebrow at her. "Isn't that the definition of casual sex?"

"I'll bet he probably has a breeding kink, knocks you up, or tries to mate with you for life. Is the caveman analogy throwing you? Okay, let's try fantasy. A five-hundred-year-old fae shows up at your door, says you're his mate and… Wait, no. That's Julian's schtick. Instalove and fated mates bullshit with Becca. So, I don't have a good one for this, but just know that he's super into you and it sure as fuck doesn't look casual from where I'm standing."

"I barely know him. We met two days ago."

Amanda purses her lips and crosses her arms over her chest. "You saw what happened with Becs. These billionaire men mean business. Think about it: How the fuck did they become billionaires? It wasn't the lottery! They saw something they wanted and took it. You think they look at women differently? Nope. You're something he can acquire, just like all of the companies he buys out. He's set his sights on you. Prepare to be wooed, wined, and dined. It's not like you're fucking for a month with that pierced cock of his."

"How did you kn—"

"Ah-ha! I knew he got it done. Cheeky bastard. I found period pads in his bathroom and you and I are synced up, so there's no way they were yours. It was a guess but thank you for confirming it."

"You're such a bitch," I laugh.

"Takes one to know one. So did you see it?"

The front door opens and my mother struggles to wheel through with two bags of groceries on her lap. Amanda and I rush over to help her.

"Here, let me grab those for you," Amanda offers.

"Thank you. They're heavier than I thought they would be. I always forget I can get so many delicious low-carb goodies at the bakery down the street on my way back here."

"Mom, you should've let one of us go with you."

"I lost my leg, not my arms. I can wheel myself around just fine." Mom always gets defensive about her independence. I get it; I'd be the same way. Her physical therapy didn't go well once they fitted her for a prosthetic leg. We were hopeful but she didn't have the luxury of state-of-the art designs that Ben has.

Amanda and I head into the kitchen to put everything away. Even though I can see everything in the bags, I ask what Mom got at the store in an attempt to lighten the mood.

"Meats and cheeses for a charcuterie board and everything to make tacos."

"Pretty sure Layla's taco was already eaten," Amanda chimes in.

"Amanda!" I smack her shoulder.

"What? Deny that he didn't tongue-fuck you, and I'll take it back."

"Girls, I really don't want to hear about my own daughter being *tongue-fucked* by the hot billionaire."

"Mom!"

"What? Amanda started it." Mom shrugs. "You act as if I haven't read your books or hers. I won't deny he's attractive… for an asshole."

Amanda wraps my mom in a hug around her shoulders. "Can you adopt me?"

"Take the number one spot, Storm, and I'll consider it," Mom chuckles.

"Hello! I'm right here! Number four bestseller for thrillers and number three for fantasy romance. Am I chopped liver?"

Amanda sighs wistfully. "Now that we're basically sisters, I say this with love: Go fuck the hot billionaire. I told Becs the same thing when she was dating Julian. Get it out of your system."

"Okay, that's enough about my daughter having sex, Amanda. Let's have lunch. I feel like my blood sugar is wonky. Don't think for one second that will get you out of telling me all about the hot Scottish man you met in New York."

"There's not much to tell." Amanda shrugs. "It was a hot one-night stand. It would make for one hell of a book for Becs to write! Mild age gap, no names, golden retriever energy with a dirty mouth… Sadly would probably just be a novella, since I'll never see him again. As hot as it was, I'd much rather hear about Ben's pierced dick."

"Amanda!" I shriek.

Mom is about to respond when my intercom buzzes. We all look over and Amanda rushes to it. "Yes?"

"Hi. I'm with Pixie Floral and have a delivery."

Amanda and Mom give me a knowing look, then Amanda lets him up. Several minutes later, there's a knock at my door and this time I answer it. There are three beautiful bouquets: one with white tulips, one with black roses, and one with a combination of red, yellow and orange roses. I sign for them and close the door.

We check the cards. The one with black roses reads:

THOUGHT YOU WOULD APPRECIATE THE BEAUTY IN THESE. I RECEIVED YOUR NOTE AND REST ASSURED NO BEHAVIOUR OF MINE WILL WARRANT THE REACTION YOU SUGGESTED.

—BEN

The note for the white tulips reads:

I KNOW YOU'LL NEVER ACCEPT HELP IF I OFFER. HOWEVER, I HOPE ONE DAY YOU'LL ALLOW ME THE OPPORTUNITY.

—BEN

Finally, the roses have a note that reads:

YOU SAID YOU'RE MINE UNTIL I LEAVE. WHAT IF I NEVER DO, SUNSHINE?

—YOURS

Amanda breaks out in a fit of laughter. "Did I call it, or did I call it? The wooing has begun."

23

BEN

"Please? One hint?" Layla begs.

"Fine, but only one, no more." I pause for dramatic effect. "Americans have it all wrong."

She chews on her lip, repeating my words to herself a couple of times, then lights up and asks, "Soccer?"

"Yes, love. We're going to a *football* match." I pull out two football kits from a bag I stowed in the front seat next to the driver. It feels wrong to wear anything other than West Ham, but I want her to experience her first match with me. "My clue was a little too obvious for you."

Layla squeals with excitement. "Are you serious? Is it as boring as I think it will be? I can't wait! My second guess would've been tea."

Confused, I ask, "You're excited for something you assume is boring?"

"Well, you know what happens when you assume——you

make an ass out of you and me. Or, in your case, an *arse*. What's something you've never tried?"

I look at my driver, then back to Layla. "I'd show you but there's no partition."

"Just tell me then." Layla brings her lips into her mouth for a moment to smother a smile. I lean in and kiss the corner of her lips where a smirk is trying to escape. My hand slides up her thigh, resting where it meets her hip. I resist touching between her legs; it'll only be torture for me.

I trail soft kisses along her jaw and nip at the shell of her ear as I whisper, "I've never shagged in public." She swallows hard and whimpers. "Not just any shag, darling." I press a kiss to her neck. "I'd hunt you. Once I catch you" —I graze my teeth against her soft skin—"I want the whole world to hear me claim you as mine."

"Until you leave," she corrects.

I right myself to look into her bewitching hazel eyes I can never seem to tear myself away from. Meeting Layla was unexpected. I'm supposed to spend a few months here, one in New York, then return home. Why do I suddenly want to throw away the empire I've built for a woman I only just met?

"Even if I do leave, I'm quite certain I'll always be yours, sunshine. What have you done to me?" I ask, mostly to myself.

"I'm pretty sure you and Julian have far more in common than just your obscene mountains of money."

"I apologise, I'm not sure I know what you mean."

"Nevermind, I'm probably reading this all wrong." She blows out a long breath.

About to continue, our driver interrupts, "We'll be there in two minutes. I'll drop you at the front. Send me a text five minutes before you'd like to leave and I'll meet you at the same location. It's a bit busier than usual today, so it might take me a moment to get to you."

"Perfect, tha—"

Layla talks over me, "Take the rest of the night off. I'll see to it that he makes it home safely."

He glances back at me through the rear view mirror. I nod and he returns to driving. I look back to Layla and keep my voice low. "Stay the night with me."

"Oh, no, you can keep your own bed warm tonight. Can't make it a habit of sharing a bed with a hot, broody man every night. Might get attached," she teases with a wink. Her tone is light, but after last night, I'm not sure I want to ever spend another night apart from her.

I kiss her neck and whisper, "It wasn't a question, sunshine. You're staying with me."

We pull up to the stadium and I retrieve my confirmation email to show the steward. I keep Layla's hand in mine, loving the feel of our interlaced fingers as I brush my thumb against hers. I've never been one to enjoy public displays of affection and I know there's a very good chance it could garner media attention, but Layla's worth the risk.

If I'm not careful, I'm going to do exactly as Julian predicted and hurt this beautiful siren.

The attendant scans my pass and we make our way to a lift to the suites. About to press the up button, Layla stops me, covering my other hand with hers. "Do you think we could get regular seats in the stands? You know, have the whole experience? Do people eat hotdogs at games? Or is it something posh like bratwursts?"

"You want to sit in the stands?" I'd gladly give her anything she asked for. I bring her knuckles to my lips and she nods. "Come on."

We walk to guest relations and after speaking to one of the representatives, we keep our suite and add on two seats in the stands behind the bench. At Layla's insistence, before heading to our new seats, we stop for concessions.

"It's a value night! Look at that, we can get two hotdogs, a popcorn, and two bottles of water for twelve bucks. What do you say we get a few of their cheapest beers and make it a party?"

I do my best to hide the disgust on my face. "There is no way I could stomach American beer, love."

"Don't be a *wanker*, Ben! Live a little," she giggles.

I close my eyes and sigh in defeat. "All right, I won't be a spoilsport, sunshine. You win."

It's curious to me that she'd zero in on a discounted option; I know how much money she brings in from her books. There's a story there, but I want to keep things light tonight so I don't ask.

Layla orders for us and attempts to pay. I refuse to let her and thankfully am quicker in retrieving my card than she is. I'm half tempted to steal her handbag, permanently this time. This is our first real date, under no circumstances will I allow her to pay.

We walk down the steps to our seats. There's a good fifteen minutes left before kick-off and Layla fills the time telling me about her childhood and how her father often took her to American football games before he passed. The games she went to sound remarkably close to the football matches back home; the same rowdy fans, same enthusiasm of the crowds, and the same less-than-desirable food options. For years, I've refused to go to an American football game, but if she were to ask, I'd be there without question.

As soon as we're done eating, I discard our rubbish in the bin and return to my girlfr—

She's not my girlfriend. But, fuck, I want her to be.

No, if I have it my way, she'll be my wife one day.

What am I saying? We just met!

This is all Julian's fault.

The game begins and I take a single sip of the poor excuse for beer before switching to water. My hand instinctively takes hers and she offers a beaming smile as she squeezes twice before placing them in her lap. She may not be my girlfriend, or have an official title, but she's mine. At least for now.

The crowd roars as the forward kicks in the first goal of the game. We're all on our feet and Layla is one of the loudest. As we sit back down, I accidentally bump the remote in my pocket. Her wide eyes dart to me, to her lap, then back to me. I hadn't intended on using it in public like this, but the idea of making her stay quite intrigues me. I reach in my pocket to lower the intensity.

"Ben, what are you doing?" she hisses.

I rest my arm behind her on the back of her seat and lean in to whisper, "So, you did wear it, didn't you? You only come when I say you can come, understood?"

Layla tries to focus on the game but every few minutes she squeezes her thighs together. After ten minutes of quiet praises, I finally increase the intensity. Watching her struggle has my cock at attention against my trousers; the pain is excruciating. I press on, determined to build her up, wanting to ruin her, piece by piece. When she touches herself, I want her thinking only of me. I want to consume her thoughts as completely as she has mine.

"Ben," she softly moans.

"You're doing so well, sunshine. Not yet. I know you're close." I lower the intensity.

"No!" Her timing is impeccable and I chuckle; the opposing team was inches from scoring during her outburst.

"Darling, what did I say? You come when I say you can."

"I was right there!"

I tuck her into me and kiss the top of her head, whispering into her hair, "I know. When you come, it'll be on my tongue, in the privacy of the suite I reserved. I don't want anyone hearing your screams but me."

She fists my shirt and turns quickly to press her forehead into my shoulder. Her voice is muffled when she says, "Please, Ben, I can't." I turn up the remote and kiss her hard to muffle her desperate cries. "I'm… Oh shit, I'm…"

She grips my forearm, her nails digging into me as she comes.

"I said to wait, love," I whisper against her lips. I lower the intensity level by level, then turn off her vibrator. "You're never getting this back." I tuck the vibrator remote into my pocket, then slide my hand into her hair, and roughly kiss her.

"Why are you torturing me?" she whimpers, limp beneath my touch.

I chuckle softly. "How do you think I feel, craving you every moment that you're not within arms reach? Wanting a woman I've been warned to stay away from, but would tear down the world to be with, is no easy feat, sunshine."

She pulls back with an almost sad look in her eyes. "Don't stay away from me. Don't listen to Julian, or whoever has been warning you."

"I couldn't if I tried, love." I kiss her, wanting to take it further but I need her to really hear me. As we break apart, I trace her jaw and take her chin in my hand. Bringing her close, a breath apart, I add, "You stole my heart, which I didn't think existed, and decided to take it for a fucking joyride. That is *my* torture, sunshine. If you feel an ounce of what I do, I'll happily buy out every seat in the stands, every football contract, just so I could strip you down and properly pleasure you right here. I don't want another man setting his eyes on your insatiable body. But, if I can't feel your tight cunt wrapped around my cock while we both come, the next best thing would be hearing you scream my name while I take what's mine."

Cheers erupt around us as everyone stands, but we both remain seated. Her eyes dart between mine and I know she feels everything I do. This incredible goddess of a woman in front of me fell like I did. And I'm not leaving her. Fuck the bids and proposals, fuck the companies I've acquired, and fuck everything I've built. I'll give it all up, if it means I can keep her.

"Who are you?" Her eyebrows pinch. "I'm an author, I'm great with words. But you?" She chuckles to herself. "You're the man that every woman reads about in books and touches themselves to."

"I don't just want that pretty, pierced pussy of yours. I want that beautiful mind of yours, too. You want romance? Tell the story of a broken man who falls for a woman he's just met. Tell them our story, love."

"Does it end in a happily ever after? If not, it's a tragedy, not a romance."

I grab her hand and lead her out of the stands. She's protesting about something as I haul her up the steps behind me, but I ignore it. When we reach the top, I pull her to me and ask, "Stay or go? You want to watch the most inconsequential game of footie I've ever seen? I'll gladly finish the game from a private suite where I'm the only one who can hear you scream as you come all over my lap. Or, we can go. Your choice, sunshine."

I can't not touch her. I can't not kiss her. I can't not have her in my arms. I don't care where we are or what we do, her soul is connected to mine in some inexplicable way and I don't ever plan on letting her go.

I'm hers.

"Stay. I'd like to stay." She lightly licks her lips. "But you're not touching me. In fact, I'll be right back." She rushes off to the loo, leaving me dumbfounded. When she returns, she places the small vibrator in my hand, still damp. "Here."

My fucking brat.

I lov— *like* Layla when she's acting up.

"Knickers, love." I hold out my hand expectantly.

She looks around and whispers, "Why do you want my panties?"

"Run along, sunshine." I pocket the vibrator and she walks back to the toilets, glancing back at me a few times. After several minutes, she comes back to me looking quite pleased with herself. "Put them in my pocket."

She does as I asked, leaving her hand in my pocket for a moment longer than necessary. "You're lucky Big Ben is pierced, or we'd get kicked out of here for you fucking me against a wall somewhere."

I firmly grip the front of her delicate neck and she gasps. I swallow her almost cry with my lips on hers and taste every inch of her mouth. Someone taps me on the shoulder. I break away from Layla and turn to face them, my fist clenched—even if I'd never hit a stranger unwarranted.

"Yes?" I growl.

"Sir, this is a family establishment. We'd like to ask that you refrain from…" He glances between Layla and me.

"Of course, my apologies. Mrs. Turner and I will head up to our suite." I quickly walk away from the usher to the suite lifts. Once inside with the door closed behind us, I kiss her once more.

"Mrs. Turner?" Layla whispers to me.

"Only a matter of time, love."

Maybe this isn't Julian's fault. This is all me.

Layla pulls back. "Excuse me?"

"Nothing."

"It's not nothing. You can't joke about things like—"

The door opens. I take her hand, interlacing our fingers, and kiss the back of it. "I don't joke, love."

Is it impulsive to joke about marrying someone I just met? Absolutely. But it's not impulsive to imagine building a life with someone like her.

I lead the way to our suite. We reach the door and, before I swipe the card, I ask, "You sure you don't want to go for a run first?"

The concerned expression she has disappears and is replaced with a smile that makes her nose crinkle and small lines form at the edge of her eyes. "I'd rather do anything else in the whole world." The door closes behind us and I press her against it, one hand on her hip and the other bracing me against the door. "Ben, it's not fair I get to come but you don't. It's why I said you can't touch me."

"You expect me to not touch you, not devour that delicious cunt of yours whenever I please?"

"Yes." Her breath is heavy, eyes pleading. "One month."

"Counter offer. You let me touch you one last time, but you spend every night in my bed until I need to leave for New York."

"You think you can go an entire month without touching me if we're in the same bed?" She lifts an eyebrow but a smile tugs at her lips.

I press my forehead to hers. "I went an entire lifetime without touching you. What's a month?"

24

LAYLA

ALMOST ONE MONTH LATER

With the exception of work, Ben and I have spent the last month practically attached at the hip. He only has another month before he has to leave for New York. Yes, I'm a masochist for agreeing to stay every night with him. He went so far as to set up an office space for me at his apartment with a brand new computer. I've never turned it on.

Most days, I'm back at my apartment or finding places around the city to write. I need color and life to work. His place is stale and feels more like a hotel than a home. It's not conducive to my writing. Having dinner together every night, date nights several times a week, and falling asleep in his arms, keep me here.

True to his word, he made me come in the suite at the soccer game and hasn't touched me since.

It's been twenty-seven days.

The longest twenty-seven days of my life.

Morning routines usually consist of him waking up first because I'm up until 2 a.m. writing. He tries to stay up with me but fails every time. He leaves for work early and every morning I wake up to a fresh pot of coffee he set and a note.

Have a good day, sunshine!

Or…

Take the #1 spot today, love.

Or…

Be ready at 5 p.m. in my favourite black dress.

Today, the note says:

I love you, sunshine.

Wait, what? I'm holding my breath but I can't let it go.

Did Ben tell me he loves me in a fucking note? I look around and behind me, thinking this must be some kind of prank. There's no way he would drop those three little words this way.

I'll admit, I'm in love with him, but I've kept it to myself because I'm scared to death of what it could mean. He's not supposed to stay; we've had the conversation a dozen times.

Tears prick behind my eyes. How could he be so careless with his words?

The front door opens and closes. "Sunshine?" Ben shouts toward the bedroom before spotting me in the kitchen. "Fuck, I'm late." He stalks toward me, wrapping me in his arms.

"What do you mean you're late? It's ten. You're supposed to be at work."

"No, love. I'm supposed to be here." He lifts me up onto the counter by my waist and I squeak in surprise. "It's"— he checks his watch—"Five past ten, which means I'm late. You found it, didn't you?"

"Yes," I admit quietly. My heart beats in my throat.

He brushes a few strands of hair away from my face, tucking them behind my ear. "I had plans to bring you one of those chocolate croissants from the bakery down the street so we could have breakfast but, today of all days, a meeting with Roger ran long. I'm sorry, love." A stray tear escapes my eye and he cups my cheeks, brushing it away with his thumb. "Oh, my beautiful Layla, I'm so sorry. I was going for romantic and fucked up." He kisses my cheek where the tear fell. "I love you. I've been in love with you since the moment I saw you but I couldn't risk scaring you off or losing you."

"You never call me Layla."

Ben chuckles. "I know." He pauses. "I'm so in love with you, sunshine. I'm sorry you had to see it on a piece of parchment and not hear it from me first. I wanted to be here when you found it."

"But you're leaving," I whisper and squeeze my eyes shut, lowering my head to hide my unshed tears. He rests his hands on top of my thighs. It's not sexual; he wants to touch me in some small way.

"Do you love me?"

I open my eyes, lifting my gaze to his. "Yes. That's why it hurts."

"Come to New York with me."

"I have Harriet's wedding in three days."

He sighs. "I'll cancel my meetings so I can go."

"No." I shake my head and brace my hands on his shoulders. "You're expanding two offices, you can't cancel."

"I feel like I have the worst possible timing."

I take his face in my hands, loving the feel of his freshly trimmed beard. "You don't have the wrong timing. It's one weekend away."

"I want you with me, love."

"We stay at your place or mine every night."

"No, that's not what I mean. Move in with me."

"What?" I squeak.

"You heard me. Move in with me, sunshine."

My brows pinch, and he brushes his thumb between them to soften my frown. "I love you. But don't you think that's fast?"

"Do you think I care? You said you're mine until I leave. I intend to hold you to that."

"You're leaving for New York," I counter in jest.

"You know damn well that's not the same. I'm not leaving. I shouldn't tell anyone this, but... I'm selling off my shares of Kipling while I'm there. Roger will be the primary shareholder and plans to make some big changes I don't agree with, but I'll be able to stay in Seattle for at least another year."

What kind of changes? "You want me to move in?"

His bright, rare smile dances on his lips but I kiss it away. He pulls me closer to him until I'm straddling his waist. I can't help myself, wrapping my arms around his neck and kissing him harder.

"Yes," he says between kisses, "if you can tolerate me. I love you, my sunshine."

"I love you, too. But I'm not moving in."

He kisses my forehead. "Think about it?"

"Okay," I concede. "I'll think about it."

The next morning, I receive an email from my apartment building saying the AC is out. With the abnormally warm weather, they recommend that the elderly and those with disabilities find alternative housing for the next forty-eight hours. They will subsidize up to $600 a night for a hotel. I text Ben.

> Did you mess with the air conditioning at my building so I would move in with you?

I chuckle to myself and set my phone on the kitchen island to finish making myself breakfast. Less than a minute later, it rings and Ben's name lights up on the screen.

"Yes?" I answer playfully.

"Do you really think I would sabotage the aircon at your place? Darling, you know I'm known for doing morally orange things, but that would be low. Even for me."

"It was a joke! I was joking, Ben."

"What's going on at your flat?"

I nervously chew on my thumbnail. "I know you always ask for me to stay the night, so I don't want to assume that I can stay, but my apartment doesn't have air conditioning. It's only for one or two days, and I'm leaving for the wedding in a few days anyway so I was—"

"Yes."

"You don't even know what I was going to ask," I laugh.

"Stay with me."

"Are you sure? I don't—"

"Yes. I'll contact your property management to see if I can move things along, but stay as long as you'd like, love."

I sigh and set down the phone, putting it on speaker so I can continue making breakfast. "I'll run to the store to grab a few things. It's really hot out there. How does a cobb salad sound for dinner?"

He growls and I know what's coming next. "Don't you dare."

"No cobb? How about I order some sushi rolls?" I have entirely too much fun messing with him.

"Sunshine," he warns, "if you think for one moment that

I'll allow you to buy a single thing while you're staying with me…"

"How do you intend on stopping me?" I taunt.

"You better hide, love. When I find you, you won't be able to sit for a week."

"Looking forward to it, *darling*." I hang up before he can. I'm playing with fire, but going a month without him touching me has left me feisty and desperate.

I finish making breakfast and head out to the store. It's so humid, I'm sweating after the short two-block walk to the small grocery store. The air conditioning hits me the moment I step inside, and the couple behind me also let out a contented sigh as we walk in.

Grabbing a cart, I meander down a few of the aisles, picking up lettuce, eggs, avocados, tomatoes, crumbled blue cheese, and roquefort—my favorite dressing. I also grab a bottle of his favorite red wine vinaigrette, shredded chicken, and cooked ham for Ben. I've been trying to keep semi-vegetarian but I'd never ask him to, even if he insists he wouldn't mind doing the same.

I make it to the frozen food aisle and add a pint of cookie dough ice cream for me and mint chocolate chip for Ben to the cart. *Who the hell actually eats toothpaste flavored ice cream?* I shake my head and laugh to myself at my weird as fuck boyfriend. Is he my boyfriend? In the month we've been together, we haven't talked about it because we have an expiration date.

It's better this way.

No. No, it's not.

As I'm about to add popsicles to my cart, I notice there are popsicle molds displayed on the freezer door. I could make simple ones with mostly water and a few drops from my food-grade essential oils. Not only would they be refreshing, I could trace the outline of Ben's perfectly sculpted abs with one and…

I shake away the thought. This month of celibacy is messing with my head.

I drop the molds into my cart and grab a few more items. After checking out, I brave the disgusting weather for the two blocks back to Ben's. Once I'm upstairs and unload everything, I order a new swimsuit for me and swim trunks for Ben. There's a pool on the roof of his building that I'm sure is packed like sardines with this heat, but I still want to take a dip at some point.

As I settle in at the desk in the office, I debate turning on his computer. Instead, I take out my laptop and write for a few hours. I've made amazing progress on my billionaire romance and am now nearly halfway done with my first draft.

My character, Tom, is nothing like Ben. He's a ruthless businessman who has no problem destroying everything in his path. Ben claims that's who he is—or at least who he was. All I've seen this past month is him more involved with charities and expanding publishing houses instead of destroying them.

Ben is usually home around six, so I'm startled when I hear the door open and close with a click of a lock a little after four. There's a low chuckle before he yells into the apartment, "Sunshine, you better run."

25

BEN

There's a rustling and a faint *"oh shit"* coming from the office. I can't wipe the smile off my face; she has no idea what she's in for. I got the green light three days ago from both my doctor and my piercer to have sex or masturbate, but I haven't told Layla. I want the first time I'm inside her to be special, not when we're playing.

I give her a head start, footsteps padding down the hall giving her away. I want her to squirm. As I open the refrigerator, I find a few bottles of wine, salad makings, and a small cake. In the freezer, there are two pints of ice cream and homemade ice lollies. I take one out of the mold and taste it—nearly flavourless with a hint of something floral. How she could consume these baffles me.

I can think of a few other uses…

"Sunshine? You have one minute," I shout into the flat.

I take my time stalking toward the bedroom. There is nowhere she could hide from me here, but I enjoy the anticipation all the same. The door is slightly ajar and I slowly open it, stepping inside. Ice lolly in hand, I twirl it in my fingers.

"Darling, it seems you made a trip to the store. I thought I was clear?"

Layla walks out of the ensuite wearing a half-open red silk robe and matching knickers. Her pierced nipples show through the fabric and the need to touch her almost breaks me. Fuck. She's an absolute vision.

"Oh, you were," she replies, lightly licking her lip and tilting her head. "What are you going to do about it?" She spots the ice lolly and her eyes widen as they dart between my hand and my face. "Oh, no," she whispers.

"Oh, yes. On the bed, love." I place it between my teeth to free my hand and remove my belt as I close the distance between us. She sits on the edge of the bed, wrists together, ready for me. I work quickly to bind her wrists, pulling her hands up and nudging her back onto the bed. She laughs but quickly stops as soon as I remove the ice lolly from my mouth and trace it along her collarbone.

"Please touch me." The desperation in her voice is fucking delicious.

"Are you ready for your punishment?"

"Yes," she breathes.

I lick up the droplets left behind on her neck. "Good girl. For someone who listens so well, you're quite the brat sometimes. I'm not going to let you come, love. Are you sure you want me to touch you?" I move the ice lower, into the valley between her full tits. Unable to help myself, I take one of her peaked nipples in my mouth, obsessed with the moans she elicits when I play with her piercings. "Fuck, I missed you."

"How can you miss me? We spend almost every night together."

I nip at her and she yelps. "Don't get smart with me, sunshine. You know what I mean." I move the lolly lower, until it's melted a trail down her stomach to an inch above her pussy. I kiss down her body, loving her small shivers from the melted ice. "Spread your legs for me."

"You're not putting that inside me," she snaps.

"I hadn't planned on it, but now that you mention it…" I bite the inside of her thigh and rip down her knickers. Teasing her cunt, I swirl the ice around her clit, but don't push in.

"Fuck, that's cold."

"Well, my love, if you hadn't done the exact opposite of what I asked, you'd have my warm mouth instead."

I push it inside her, just an inch. She's so wet for me, but she's tight. I take my time. I'd love nothing more than to have my cock buried deep inside her—but not like this. I press in another inch.

"It's too much," she whimpers.

The ice is melting quickly and I push in another two inches. "You can take it, love."

"I promise, I'll never buy anything ever again!"

I'm done playing and tug gently to remove it from her, wanting the feeling of her around my fingers. It won't budge. "Darling, you need to stop clenching."

"I'm not."

I try again. "I'm serious, you need to let go, love."

"I swear, I'm not clenching. Is it… Did you just get a popsicle stuck in my pussy?" Layla chuckles and while it's normally music to my ears, I'm genuinely concerned about this being inside her.

"This is no laughing matter. Yes, I do believe it's stuck. I'm not going to pull, I don't want to hurt you."

"Why is this our life? Last month, we were walked in on a million times, now you get ice stuck inside me?" She's in a fit of giggles. I kiss them away and reach up to unbuckle the belt holding her wrists.

"I'm sorry. Wait, maybe if I…"

Moving down her body, I press soft kisses until I'm between her legs to lick around the ice. Thankfully, after only a few swipes of my tongue, it's free. I remove it, and after a long suck of it in my mouth, I make my way to the ensuite to toss it in the sink. Fuck, she tastes too fucking good.

When I return to Layla, she's still spread wide for me, hands over her eyes. "Sunshine, look at me." Her head pops up and she finally removes her hand from her face. I unbutton my shirt and toss it to the ground. She closes her legs, embarrassment painting her features, but I push them open again. "I love when you hide from me, but right now I want to see all of you. It's been far too long since I've properly tasted you. I know I promised I wouldn't touch you until you could touch me, but I'm about to break that promise."

"It's only a few more weeks, right? That's nothing. I can—"

I lick up her slit and draw her clit piercing in my mouth; biting down just enough to make her grip the sheets and scream my name. I want her to come hard and fast for me; I can take my time with her later. Like clockwork, in just under a minute, she's my good fucking girl and coming on my tongue, her back arched off the bed. I lap up every last drop of her, slowing my pace to help her come down from her orgasm.

"That was," she says breathlessly.

Layla jolts up, grabs the back of my neck, and kisses me. It's not sweet or slow, it's messy and full of fire. I'll never get enough of her when she's like this.

"Fuck, I missed that mouth. Are you hungry? We can have an early dinner. Maybe cool off in the pool after?" she offers.

"If you think for one moment I'll allow anyone but me to see that incredible body of yours, you have another think coming."

She scoffs, squaring her shoulders. "It's only a swimsuit! It isn't as if it's *knickers*. Come on, I'm starving after what you just did to me."

"You know I'll never say no to you."

Her smile doesn't leave as she gives me a quick peck on the lips. "I know. The minute you're healed, you're in trouble."

26

LAYLA

He did say no to me.

Last night, we had dinner together but after his incessant growling about the pool, we decided to stay in and watch a movie instead. After one too many glasses of wine, I nearly jumped him like some kind of jungle cat in heat. It was all for naught, he still said no. As my wine buzz wore off, we fell asleep together like any other night.

I wake up wrapped in Ben's arms. He kisses my bare shoulder and pulls me tighter, whispering, "Morning, love."

"What time is it?" I check the alarm clock. "*Shit!* You're late! It's nine forty-five. You were supposed to be gone hours ago."

"I'm taking the day off."

I turn in his arms. "Since when? You didn't say anything last night."

"Must've slipped my mind whist tongue-fucking you." He kisses me and rolls me onto my back, settling between my legs. "I wanted to spend the day with you before I head to New York."

I'm not sure if his piercing has healed properly yet. I don't ask, he doesn't tell. At this point, I'm actually nervous to have sex with him. What if it's bad? What if *I'm* bad? The anticipation is almost too much.

Ben kisses down my neck to my shoulder. "We should do something fun today."

"I was going to head back to my place at some point and pack for the wedding." My words are breathless. "With the AC out in the building, it'll have to wait for tonight. It's pushing triple digits out there. Maybe we can go somewhere indoors?"

"We can stay here. I have a brilliant idea for how to pass the time: you can ride my face, and I can see how many times I can make you come before you're begging for my cock."

"I doubt Big Ben is healed."

Ben groans and pulls up my tank top, exposing my breasts. "Why must you wear clothes to bed?" He swirls his tongue around one of my nipples before taking the piercing between his teeth. I can't help the moan that escapes me.

"We shouldn't do this if you can't... *ah!*" He bites down hard and pinches my other nipple with the same force.

"You were saying?"

As he moves down my body, his beard scratches my stomach, kissing lower until his mouth is just above my panties.

My fingers tangle into his hair, my body begging for more. Last night wasn't enough.

"I need to taste you, sunshine," he growls. In one swift movement, he rips off my panties and tosses them to the ground.

"Ben," I warn, even if it comes out like a plea. "We're not having sex."

"You're right." He spreads my legs wider. "It's not going to be a quick shag, darling. I'm going to make love to you all morning and most of the afternoon. A little this evening and late into the night."

I'm about to protest but he's faster, burying his face between my legs and sucking my clit. I can't seem to catch my breath; I crave his touch. I instinctively grind against his mouth, seeking more friction. I can't fight him, nor do I want to. It's been a month since we even took a shower together, and the last time I saw that perfect cock of his.

Twenty-eight days to be exact... *not that I'm counting.*

He slowly presses two fingers inside me. "Why are you so tight, love?" he asks between licks. "Haven't you been touching yourself the past month?"

"No," I whisper.

"No?" He stops his movements, keeping his fingers deep inside me.

I prop myself onto my elbows to look at him. "Why did you stop?"

"You haven't come in a month, except last night? Even by yourself?"

I shake my head. "No. I told you. I wouldn't until—"

He drives his fingers deeper and slides up my body until our faces are less than an inch apart. "I'm hopelessly in love with you, sunshine, but when you say things like that... Fuck, I don't know if I can be gentle."

"Then, don't be." It's risky, but Ben would never hurt me.

"Oh, darling, be careful what you ask for." Ben kisses my neck and picks up the pace thrusting his fingers deep inside me with more pressure. He groans against me, "Fuck, you feel too good."

"Ben, I need you." The words escape me and it takes me a moment to realize what I've asked of him. "I'm sorry. I know we ca—" He swallows my defense with a searing kiss that I feel all the way to my toes. "We can't," I finally finish, muffled by his lips on mine.

He pulls back to look at me and admits, "We can, but I need to be careful. You can't hurt me, love. I'm healed enough, we just have to take it slow." I brush the hair off his forehead and swipe away the worried look from between his brows. His expression softens, looking more like my Ben.

"We have to use condoms." I blurt out, probably ruining the moment. "Sorry, it's just that I'm not on birth control or anything."

"Fuck, why did you have to tell me that?" he growls.

My face falls. "Oh. Is that a deal breaker?"

"No." He buries his face in the crook of my neck, grazing his teeth against my skin. "Darling, I don't know how to say this, but I'd love nothing more than to come inside you over and over until your belly is swollen with my child. But, I've been told to use a condom the first few times with my piercing. No knocking you up tonight."

"Did you just say 'knock me up?'" I attempt to make light of it. "How very un-British of you! Shouldn't it be something about me in a 'delicate condition?'"

He grinds his length against my clit and I stifle a moan. "My darling, I try to be romantic and you shut down. I try to explain to you what turns me on and you jest. Now, all I want to do is bend you over and punish you until your cunt is dripping for me. But not this time. This time, you're going to give me every piece of you, but I'll put you back together when we're done. There are condoms in the top drawer. Grab one," he commands.

I reach over to open the drawer, but can't quite reach the box. "A little difficult with you on top of me."

Ben takes one out of the box, tearing it open with his teeth, then hands it to me. "Your choice, love. How do you want me to take you?"

"On your back. Sit against the pillows and headboard."

He kisses my cheek and chuckles. "You know I prefer to be in control, love."

"Hush. Let me have this one time, then you can have your way with me."

Ben laughs and climbs off me to sit with his back against the headboard. I slide the condom onto his thick cock, taking time to admire his healed piercing. I've never been one to enjoy blowjobs but my mouth is watering at the sight of him. Knowing I can't wrap my mouth around him for at least another month is a special kind of torture. I climb on top of him and line up his cock with my entrance.

"Are you sure about this?" he asks cautiously. "We can wait if you want to— *Bloody hell.*" I lower myself onto him, inch by inch.

"Shit! Did I hurt you?" I fucked this all up; we should've waited.

Ben slides his hands up my thighs to my hips and pulls me further down onto him. "No, sunshine. Quite the opposite. You're fucking perfection." I try to lift up but he holds me in place. "Not yet. I need a moment to savor the feeling of being inside you." He thrusts into me while grinding my hips against his. I steady myself, holding onto his shoulders as I gasp at the fullness, afraid to move. "You okay, love?"

"Yes. It's just a lot." I can't bring myself to tell him that it's not only having him inside me for the first time. I'm over-whelmed; feeling cherished and adored for probably the first time in my life.

I thought I'd been in love with other men. I was wrong. Meeting Ben has changed my idea of what love is. He looks at me as if I'm his everything. For all the times I teased Becca when she fell hard and fast for Julian, being in Ben's arms has me wondering if soulmates actually exist.

"I know," he whispers and wraps his arms tighter around me, softly kissing every inch of me within reach. I rock back and forth; he's hitting exactly where I need him. If I keep the same pace, I'll be coming in minutes. "You're mine, sunshine. From this day forward, my name will be the only one that you'll scream as you come."

"Ben, I—"

"No, love. You're not going to rationalize this." He thrusts harder up into me. "Show me you belong to me, as much as I belong to you."

I reply without hesitation, "I'm yours." At my admission, he growls and grips the back of my neck, kissing me deeply. It's not rushed, he takes his time tasting and teasing me, as if he's trying to commit this moment to memory. He doesn't slow his punishing thrusts and I can't hold on much longer. "I'm close."

"I know, darling. You're going to wait for me. I want to feel you pulsing around my cock as I come." He rolls me onto my back, still inside me. "But make no mistake, I'm nowhere near done with you. I want you fucking spent."

"Fuck, I'm co—" Ben kisses me hard, swallowing my words as my orgasm washes over me in waves. He pushes deep inside me for three more thrusts before finding his own release. Our breaths are heavy, but so is the air between us. When I finally find my voice, I admit, "It wasn't just words or something hot to say during sex. I'm yours, Ben, even if it's just temporary."

Ben chuckles against my neck. "Darling, you're the most extraordinary woman I've met in my life. None of this is temporary." He rolls us to our sides, still inside me. Our faces less than an inch apart, he says softly, "I don't deserve you or your love, but I want both all the same. I'd sacrifice every ounce of pleasure I've ever known, if it meant I got to keep you as mine. You're my forever, sunshine."

"What do you mean 'your forever?'"

"You're coming back to England with me, or I'm staying here. Either way, I'm yours."

My heart's caught in my throat, unable to breathe. "You're staying? Really staying? Not just for a year?"

"Or you're going. Your choice." He presses his forehead to mine. "I'm not going to lose you. I... can't lose you."

"You're staying?" I repeat, mostly to myself, as if saying the words over and over again will make them feel more real.

"Yes," he laughs. "If you'll have me, I'll make it happen."

How could I not? Tears prick behind my eyes as I nod fervently.

"If you can love a monster, I promise I'll love you until my last breath."

He kisses me but I stop him with my hands on his chest and move him back an inch. "Ben, stop. You can't say things like that."

"I swear, if you dare compare me to Julian again..."

"No," I laugh. "Nothing to do with him. You can't call yourself a monster. You're the furthest thing from it."

"I warned you that I'd destroy you, love. Have I succeeded? You think I'm something I'm not."

"You're not a monster, or a villain, no matter how many times you insist you are." I lift my hand to cup his cheek. "Come to the wedding with me? Please? You can meet me there."

"You want me to go with you?"

"Yes," I laugh. "Just maybe have better manners than when you met my mother."

"I've apologized no less than a hundred times for that!"

"Well, you should come, bad manners and all. Unless you want hot eligible bachelors hitting on me?"

That should do the trick.

"What time? I might be able to charter a flight from New York. It's in Napa, right?" We both wince as he pulls out of me. Ben slowly removes the condom and ties it off. "I'm going to toss this and we can discuss—*Fuck!*"

"What? Is your piercing all right? Shit, I knew we should've waited."

"No, my cock is fine... This isn't." He holds up the condom. There's a small hole the size of the ball of his piercing, his cum seeping out.

Ben grabs one of his crutches leaning to the side of the bed and heads into the ensuite to discard the condom. When he returns, worry paints his pale face.

As he climbs back into bed, he wraps me in his arms. "I'm so sorry, love." He kisses the top of my head. "I hope you know I didn't mean for that to happen. Fuck, I'm so sorry. Let me know what you need."

"I can pick up a morning-after pill at the pharmacy later." I snuggle closer to him, sighing against his chest. "Sorry to disappoint you, no one's getting *knocked up* today."

Ben laughs and I feel it everywhere. "I'm not disappointed, but you'd make a great mum one day."

"Is it weird we're talking about this?"

"Why?" He tilts my chin to look at him. "I can't imagine myself being with anyone else. I *will* marry you one day. And if you ever want children, we'll be sure to practice loads before it happens." I kiss him softly, careful not to take it further. "When you're ready, I'm ready. I love you, my sunshine."

I smile against his lips. "I love you, too."

Thump-thump. Thump-thump. Thump-thump.

"Ben, look at me. What's wrong?"

I fucking knew this would happen. I turned my back for one minute and things went tits up. I don't regret spending the day with Layla, but it came at a price. She's saying something to me but I don't hear any of it. My heartbeat drowns out her words and my mind is racing faster than the horse I bet on last month.

Layla rubs my thigh to get my attention and I finally glance up at her from my phone. "I'm sorry, what did you say?"

"You look like you're about to kill someone. I'm impressed the vein in your forehead hasn't popped. What's wrong?"

"I have to go." I move away from her to quickly wrap and attach my leg.

"Okay. When will you be back?"

I check my watch—it's 7 p.m. It'll be faster to try and catch a late night flight than to charter one. "I won't. I'll be at the wedding but I have to take care of this." I slide my hand into her hair, kiss her softly, and whisper against her lips, "I'm sorry."

"What are you sorry for?" She turns off the movie I was admittedly half watching as we both stand from the couch. "Ben, talk to me."

"Darling, I would if I could. Just know if I don't leave now... I'm sorry. Please, stay here and allow my driver to take you to the airport tomorrow." I wrap my arms around her; this is all my fault. "I'll see you Saturday. I love you."

Layla holds me tighter. "I love you, too."

Those three small words have my heart bursting out of my chest.

I release her, grab my luggage, and head for the door, glancing back at my beautiful goddess before stepping out. Hopefully, not for the last time.

The entire flight, I'm a bloody wreck. Layla has tried calling and texting me but I'm sure she won't want to talk to me after today. How I could lose so much in one day baffles me.

I'm focused on my emails when Ryan taps me on the shoulder. "Hey, Captain. When we get back, should we head to your flat in London or your home in Canterbury? I can make the arrangements."

"We aren't going home yet." I won't be scared off that easily. "We need to solve this in New York."

"After everything, are you still planning on staying here in America?" It's a loaded question. If Layla still wants me after all of this, I want to be wherever she is.

"We'll see."

Ryan's brows pinch together. "You love her, why would you not fight for her?"

"It's none of your business," I snap, then take a deep breath. "I'm sorry. That was uncalled for. Yes. I love her. More than I've loved anyone. But it's not that simple. Love doesn't conquer all like it does in her books."

This is my karma—losing the love of my life.

Spending the night without Ben feels wrong. I would stay at my place tonight but the air conditioning still hasn't been fixed. The bed is cold and I can't sleep. I grab my laptop from the office and bring it to bed with me; I should at least get some writing done. It's a better alternative to staring at my phone that's not ringing or doom-scrolling social media.

Ben won't return my calls or texts. If he's on a flight, he likely has in-flight Wi-Fi so he should be able to answer or at least message me back. All of this has left me confused and anxious. Not wanting to waste this feeling that is honestly foreign to me, I choose to pour it into my work.

The third act break-up is my favorite. As an author and avid reader of romance, I know it has to end in a happily ever after, but the possibility that it couldn't keeps me on edge wondering what will happen next.

Is this my third act break-up with Ben?

More like a first act break-up. We only lasted a month.

I'm reading too much into it.

I dive into the meat of the chapter. My billionaire is stuck in a miscommunication trope—she thinks he cheated but he only has eyes for her. The poor guy got caught with a woman throwing herself at him. It wasn't his fault, he pushed her away. My protagonist is a fucking idiot, but I love writing the ridiculous storyline all the same.

I fall asleep with my laptop open, waking up a few hours later. Checking my phone, there's still no contact from Ben.

Something's wrong; he was so upset before he left. It seems work related but all I saw was a text from Ryan saying, "It's happening." Nothing scares Ben—it's not an exaggeration, he's fearless. Two little words from his assistant had him in full panic-mode.

With the time difference, there's no way I'll hear from Ben tonight. I take a melatonin gummy and pray sleep finds me.

"It's been twelve hours, Becs! Are you sure Julian hasn't heard from him? It's like he's ghosted me."

Phone glued to my ear, I'm pacing Ben's bedroom, passing the time before I need to leave for the airport. I can't stand still—something about inertia… or whatever it is about things in motion. That's me. I should've paid more attention in science electives in college.

"Layla-love. It's fine," she laughs. "You're not Emma, and even if you were, it'll set you up for the hottest second chance romance I've ever heard in my life. If only she'd let me write her story."

"This isn't the time to make jokes! Wait... What are you talking about?"

"Emma, Harriet's mom."

"How have I not heard about this before? What do you mean they had a second chance romance? Emma and Dylan are basically marriage goals."

Becca laughs hysterically. "They are, aren't they? And people say my husband is amazing." She sighs wistfully. "Dylan is *obsessed* with her. You'll have to ask Emma the whole story but..." She lowers her voice. "He totally ghosted her in her twenties."

I gasp. "No. That's unforgivable!"

"Says the woman who claims to be ghosted," Becca deadpans.

"How could he do that? I've seen the way he looks at her! I mean, it was only once when I had to meet with him to go over my investment portfolio. But still! He's so in love with her. How could he do that?"

"Men are fucking idiots. But moral of the story, even though he fucked up, she forgave him and now they're living an epilogue ending."

"Says the woman living her own," I scoff. "Ben said he'll see me at the wedding but he won't return my calls and now I feel like some kind of desperate slut throwing myself at a man after a one night stand."

"Layla!" she screeches. "One night stand? Did you finally have sex? What about his *situation?*"

I stop my pacing. "Julian is listening, isn't he?"

"Hi, Layla," Julian says nonchalantly, as if he didn't just hear me say I slept with his friend. Fuck, this is mortifying.

"Hey, Julian. So, um, how much of that did you hear?" I wince.

"He didn't listen to me when I told him to stay away from you," he sighs. "I haven't heard from him but once this month—he's been avoiding me. He told me that he wouldn't hurt you but… Layla, he's not a good guy. I love him like a brother, but he has done some fucked up things in his life. Hell, he can't even invest in his cousin's project because he's made so many enemies. Ben destroys careers. Be careful." Julian pauses. "Sorry, ladies, I have a call I need to take." He then says quietly to Becca but I still hear, "Please talk some sense into her?"

Thanks, Julian.

None of this sounds like my Ben. I know he's a ruthless businessman, but who the hell pierces their dick to stay away from a woman? Maybe I've turned a blind eye to the red flags?

He was completely inappropriate when my mom was here.

I'm pretty sure he hid my purse at the bar the first time we met. How else did he find it so quickly?

We don't talk about his work, only mine.

We have sex for the first time and he disappears twenty-four hours later?

Maybe Ben was telling the truth and will indeed ruin me? He said he's done awful things—like destroying companies —but how could that hurt me?

He could've left for New York early. He could be here. He could be back in England... I feel like I'm trapped in a damn children's book called "Where's Ben?"

"I'll be careful," I assure Becca, rolling my eyes despite her and Julian not seeing it. "I'll see you guys later. I should head to the airport soon."

"Call me if you need anything," Becca says cautiously.

"Thanks."

I hang up and take a deep breath; this can't be how Ben and I end. I didn't imagine the last month. It happened. I was there.

Ben, where the fuck are you?

LAYLA

I fly often and don't get nervous—my anxiety isn't from travel, it's from my sort-of-boyfriend. While he said he loves me, claimed he wants to marry me one day, and even asked me to move in, the last look he gave me before walking out the door was pained, as if it might be the last time we ever see each other. It's ridiculous, but I know what I saw.

Maybe Julian is right and he's up to something awful or about to do something unforgivable.

It's a quick flight to California but I may as well get some writing done. I'm about to send an email to my alpha reader, Jamie, when I spot one from Ben. I quickly click on it.

To: Layla Thorne
From: Benedict Turner
Subject: Cancellation of Upcoming Release

Ms. Thorne,

Due to the recent merger between Kipling and Turner, we regret to inform you your upcoming title *Last Reward* will no longer be published. Your agent and any affected parties will be contacted to discuss the cancellation of your contract. All current titles will be removed within the next ninety days.

Should you have any questions, please reach out to your representation.

Regards,

Benedict Turner, CEO
Turner Publishing

My blood runs cold. Time stops. A hundred other clichés for what I'm feeling rush through me.

What the actual fuck? This can't be real. Except there are no less than two dozen other emails from author friends of mine who received the same boilerplate email. Heat creeps up my neck and, if I wasn't in public, I would chuck my laptop across the damn airplane. How could he do this to me? To other authors? Did the last month mean nothing to him?

"If you grip your laptop any tighter, it'll snap in half," the man to my right chuckles. He has a thick, almost-British accent. Maybe Irish?

I'm in no mood for a laugh. I'm fucking furious, and his sexy accent reminding me of Ben just pisses me off more. As I finally glance over, he's actually quite attractive. He's a little older than me with tattoos painting his forearms like Ben. His emerald green eyes are beautiful, but Ben's blue eyes pierce your soul with one look.

No! Ben's a dick. Stop thinking about Ben's ocean eyes, sexy tats, and sinfully hot accent.

My seatmate is wearing a simple wedding band, so unless he's a creepy cheater, I'm probably fine making small talk without worrying about him hitting on me.

I take a moment to collect myself and sigh, "Sorry, I just got bad news."

"That's unfortunate. Shall we have a drink and wallow in your sorrows together?"

He signals for the flight attendant, who approaches imme-diately. "How may I help you, Mr. Beck?" She has a sweet southern accent that makes my anger soften.

"Ms. Kristina, I'd love a whiskey on the rocks, if it isn't any trouble. My friend here would like a—" He turns to me. "What would you like, love?" Him calling that makes my heart drop to my stomach.

"I'll have what he's having," I reply.

"I'll be right back with those."

Once she walks away, he smiles and asks, "A whiskey drinker, too? Just like my partner." *Oh, he's gay!* I breathe a sigh of relief, grateful for a seatmate who won't hit on me. "There's an incredible distillery in Delasnia that makes a delicious vanilla-infused whiskey. It's her favorite."

Did he just say 'her?' Crap.

"Oh, I'm more of a margarita girl. Just didn't want to bother her with making two different drinks."

The flight attendant returns in record time and hands one to each of us, then scurries off. "Well, margarita girl, what's this bad news we're toasting to?" I clink my glass against his and take a long gulp, finishing the two shots of whiskey in one go. "Slow down there, it's a marathon, not a sprint."

I shake my head and take a deep breath. "My book was canceled by my publisher boyfriend."

"I'm sorry." He's mid-sip when I speak nearly chokes on his whiskey. "Did you say publisher boyfriend?" I nod. "Are you by chance an author?" I nod again. "Bloody hell, that sounds incredibly complicated. Though, I'm not one to talk. My not-wife was my boss for a short time."

"Not-wife?" I gesture at his wedding ring and he spins it with his thumb with a wide smile. "I don't mean to pry but is this a poly situation? Like, you have two? Or…"

He laughs heartily. "Never. No, we never wanted to get married. She's the love of my life. I'm hers as much as she's mine, and we don't need a piece of paper to prove that. So, what's with your bloke and this book not being published?"

"I don't know." I shrug. "I got an email from him that had me spiraling. He left late last night to deal with something at work and now I have this bullsh— *garbage* email. He won't return my calls." I blow out a long breath. "Sorry, word vomit."

"It's fine, I'm used to it. My best friend would put you to shame with her topic jumping when she's excited." He signals to our flight attendant and points to me, then shakes his glass, indicating I need a refill. "In any case, he sounds like a twat."

I chuckle. "Yeah, Ben's a dick. Anyway, I'm flying in for a wedding and he said he's going to be there. After this? I hope he isn't."

"I'm actually an event planner, mostly weddings. I assure you, the majority of them have drama. My favorite was when a groom was outed for sleeping with the bride's mum. Gave us all a laugh. If he does show, it will be one of a hundred things the wedding planner will diffuse. We're used to it."

"I don't want to cause any drama on Harriet's big day," I sigh.

"Harriet?" He stills. "What's her last name?"

"Don't take this the wrong way, but we don't know each other and I feel weird telling you. She's also an author but she's marrying someone who is kind of high profile in sports. I'm sorry." I bite my lip nervously.

He chuckles. "Well, I didn't properly introduce myself. I'm Tyler Beck. Sounds a lot like you're referring to Harriet and Robbie. There aren't many other authors marrying third basemen this weekend. I'm their wedding planner. Or rather, my mate Ethan is, and I'm assisting for day-of coordination."

Our flight attendant returns with another whiskey. This time, instead of finishing in one gulp, I heed Tyler's advice and take small sips. "You're kidding?" I laugh into my glass.

"No, I've known the Alexanders for years. Ethan is retired from event planning, but because it's his best friend's daughter getting married, he insisted he plan it."

Tyler takes a drink and pulls up a picture of him with two men I don't recognize, but Emma's husband, Dylan, has his arm around Robbie. In return, I show him a picture of Harriet and I at a book convention last year.

"Small world," he laughs.

"How did you meet them?"

"Harriet and I met a few years ago. We're not super close, but my friend's husband did the audiobooks for her YA fantasy series and I beta read for her. She introduced me to her father, Dylan, who's now my financial planner. I'm also signed under her mom's agency. But that's the extent of it... Now that I say it out loud, it's a little incestuous."

"You're right, it is indeed a small world," he laughs. "Well, I wouldn't worry about this Ben of yours. I've tossed men out of weddings in the past, and have no issue doing it again."

Tyler and I chat for the remainder of the flight and I feel much better having someone else in my corner who knows what's happening with Ben. Between Amanda—who has no issue putting someone in their place—and my new friend Tyler, I'm all set.

When we land in San Francisco, Robbie is here to pick me up; I assured them I would take a rideshare, but they insisted. Amanda's flight arrived an hour ago and is waiting with him near baggage claim.

While I walk with Tyler through the airport, I text my friend, Jamie.

> Up for destroying a publishing giant? Last Reward has been axed, along with hundreds of other titles.

JAMIE

Say less. I'm in.

Tyler slings his duffle over his shoulder. "Well, love, it's been a pleasure. I'll be seeing you tomorrow." He winks and I wave goodbye as he walks to the exit, calling over his shoulder, "Come find me if you need me to rough someone up."

When I reach baggage claim, Amanda wraps me in a tight hug and whispers, "Thank fuck you're here. If I had to hear another word about his *mi cielo*, I'd throw up."

"What the hell is a *mi cielo?*"

She releases me and sighs. "It's Robbie's adorable pet name for Harriet. It means darling, or sweetheart, or something. I don't know. I had to use the online translator; I took German, not Spanish, in high school. A single girl can only handle so much of it. Between you, Becca, and now Robbie, I'm capped out on the cute nicknames."

"Fair enough," I chuckle.

"As soon as we get your bags, do you mind if we get a late lunch with Harriet? She's still downtown meeting with her agent. Something about a last minute book emergency. It'll be the last time I see her before the wedding," Robbie pipes up.

Robbie is adorable—a love-sick puppy, obsessed with Harriet. I don't know their whole story, only that he waited years for her and passed up huge baseball contracts to stay close to her. I don't follow baseball, but he's supposedly one of the top third basemen in the country.

"Of course," I reply, then ask Amanda, who is frowning at her phone, "What time is the bachelorette party?"

"What? Sorry. My phone was still on airplane mode and I have a billion emails, including this one. What the fuck is going on?" Amanda hands me her phone, showing me an email that looks identical to mine. "Maybe that's what Harriet is freaking out about."

"Shit. You, too?" I say out loud to myself, then turn to Robbie, "Did Harriet also get an email from Turner or Kipling Publishing today?"

Robbie shrugs. "I have no idea. All I know is she was upset and rushed off after checking her email. She mentioned something about how Becca had the right idea, but I have no idea what that means or what she was talking about. When she talks about the business side of writing, I usually tune out," he winces.

"At least you read her books," Amanda laughs.

"Shit, my phone was on silent!" I unclick the button on my phone. All at once, it's vibrating and lighting up like some kind of fancy vibrator. "Fuck! I can't even click onto my email app, there are too many notifications popping up!" I turn it on silent again and sift through the notifications to show my email to Amanda and Robbie. "See, I got one while I was on the plane. I also had emails from other authors asking if I got the email."

"Motherfucker," Robbie seethes. "Your asshole boyfriend canceled your contracts? That has to be why Harriet was freaking out this morning." He takes out his phone to call her. "Baby, was your contract for your book canceled?... Yeah, Amanda and Layla got the emails, too... Does your mom know?... Okay, we'll be there as soon as we grab Layla's bags... Love you." He hangs up and looks at me and Amanda with wide eyes. "Harriet's, too."

"There has to be an explanation for this. It's *Ben*," Amanda offers.

"What explanation?" I throw my arms wide. "My boyfriend-*ish* fucked me over; fucked all of us over."

"Something's weird." Amanda keeps scrolling her phone as she tries to make sense of it. "Think about it. He saved you from the first round of cuts, he saved me after mine was already cut, why now? Shit, I thought Julian was fucking love-drunk when it came to Becca. Ben is like Julian, but so much worse. He's hotter, though, because he has an accent."

"Julian warned me Ben's not a good guy. Apparently, he's the morally gray billionaire I hoped he would be, after all. Except this isn't just morally gray, he's the damn villain," I groan. "Why did I have to fall for the bad guy? Ben's a dick, indeed."

Amanda scoffs. "You've read too many of my romantic suspense books. He's not a book boyfriend, Layla. Text him. I'm sure there's a perfectly acceptable reason for this fucked up situation. Don't jump to conclusions and become some kind of cliché miscommunication trope. You know I hate those." Amanda crosses her arms over her chest.

The turnstile for baggage begins moving, drawing our attention to it.

"Message Ben." Robbie's jaw tics. "I'll grab your bags. What do they look like?"

"There's just one. Yellow, hard shell with a black tag, should be easy to spot."

He stalks over to wait with the rest of the travelers for my luggage. I check my voicemails, texts, and emails. None from Ben, except the one destroying my career. After drafting and deleting three times, I settle on a text to send.

> Got the email. You have some explaining to do.

I pocket my phone. When I look up, Amanda's trying to hide a smile. "What? There's nothing funny about this," I snap. My voice is harsher than I intend it to be, but today has been too much.

"You sure about that, love?" a deep, sexy voice purrs behind me.

"Ben," I whisper and whip around to face him. I instinctively wrap my arms around his middle, but pull back and hit his chest. He chuckles in response. "What the fuck? Why haven't you answered your phone? And why did you cancel my book?"

He holds me tighter. "Do you really think I would do anything to hurt you?"

"She did," Amanda chimes in. "So, book daddy, great to see you, but what the hell is going on?"

NOT HER VILLAIN   257

Robbie joins us with my suitcase. "Is this him?" I nod. "You think you can show up here, after what you did to my fiancée?"

"Yes, I canceled the contracts," Ben admits.

"What did you just say?" Amanda asks. "You just said you wouldn't do anything to hurt her, then one-eighty it, admitting you eighty-sixed our contracts. Shit, that's too many numbers. I'm not a math person. Anyway, I'm out here defending you, and you actually did it? Thanks for making me look like an asshole."

"Have you talked to your agents?" Amanda and I shake our heads. Ben nods with a smirk. "Maybe start there. Trust me when I say you won't want to be around for what is about to happen." Ben brushes my cheek with his thumb, cupping my neck. He lowers his voice, so only I can hear, "I had to protect you and the other authors."

"Protect us from what? International bestselling success? What did you do?" I seethe.

"What needed to be done."

Amanda's eyes narrow at me. "Let me get this straight. You, on purpose, removed us from your catalogue?"

"That's correct. Your agent agreed it was the best course of action to avoid bad publicity around your titles. Unless you're of the mindset that any press is good press, in which case, feel free to remain under the Turner Publishing umbrella." I look around. "Is there some place more private we can discuss this?"

"Harriet will want to hear this, too. Can it wait until we meet up with her?"

"You must be Robbie. My apologies for not introducing myself earlier. I'm Ben, Layla's…" *What are we?*

"Lover," Amanda finishes.

Layla chokes on her own air. "Amanda!"

"What?" Amanda shrugs. "Beats *boyfriend-ish.*"

"Boyfriend-ish?" I ask Layla, unable to contain my amusement.

"We never talked about it," she replies through gritted teeth. "And I'm still furious with you."

"Why don't you and I drive together and discuss why you're so angry with me, while my face is between your legs?" I whisper low enough that no one else can hear.

"Well, on that note, things just got weird." Amanda claps her hands together once. "Robbie-boy, let's go see *mi cielo*. Those two can ride together." Robbie rolls his eyes at her terrible misuse of his pet name. She then addresses me, "So help me, if you try to screw me over…"

"We'll see you shortly." I guide Layla by the small of her back toward the airport bar, wheeling her luggage behind me. Once out of earshot, I stop her in her tracks. "Sunshine, I'm sorry. I hope you can forgive me."

"Are you going to hide my suitcase and then magically find it?" Her voice is still ice cold.

I laugh once. "What are you talking about?"

"Did you, or did you not, hide my purse the first time we met?"

I school my expression and carefully answer her question, "I didn't hide it." *Not a lie, I threw it in the bin.* "What is this about?"

"Right, well"—she looks around, then gestures behind us —"the exit is that way."

"I want to talk to you before we go."

Layla clucks her tongue. "Why should I believe anything you have to say? My book is no longer going to be published and the rest will be pulled. Do you even fucking understand what that means for me, Ben? It's the end of my career. Doesn't that matter to you?"

"Do you trust me?"

"I don't know," she replies quietly, her eyes darting between mine. "I'm pissed at you. You could've called or texted. Instead, you just show up here after you send me an email telling me my book and my career are fucked. What about the hundreds of other authors?"

I lean in, brushing my cheek against hers to whisper, "Why is it, love, that when you get plucky like this, I want to bend you over right here, not caring who might see us?" She sucks in a breath. "It's been less than a day, but I already miss the taste of you and your moans when I'm marking you."

"You wouldn't dare."

"Wouldn't I?" I slide my hand around her waist to her lower back and pull her flush to me. "There is nothing I wouldn't do to hear you scream my name as you come. I have the means to burn down the world, and would, if it meant I could ensure your pleasure, darling."

"This isn't about sex, Ben," she sighs. "You fucked with my livelihood."

"Come have a drink with me and I'll explain what I can."

Layla lifts her chin and her eyes narrow. "So you can get me drunk and have your way with me? I don't think so." She pauses. "What are you even doing here? I thought you had meetings all day and couldn't come until tomorrow?"

"I have a meeting with a literary agency in an hour." I trust Layla, of course, but I need to keep this quiet for now. As soon as things are final, I can tell her everything.

"Fine, but no sex. One drink. No more. I'm still pissed." I smile at my small win, despite her being furious with me. She continues, "I have to check in at the hotel and get ready for tonight."

My face falls. "What's tonight?"

"Bachelorette party," Layla replies with a mischievous grin. I can't help the growl that escapes me. She laughs and insists, "It'll be fine. No need to go all caveman on me. I'll be a good girl and only go home with someone if they are extremely hot. Maybe I'll upgrade to a *boyfriend-ish* with a Scottish accent… *Or* maybe I'll find someone who doesn't cancel publishing contracts."

Fuck. That.

I grab her hand and head to the ticket counter. "Two first class tickets to anywhere."

"Sir, you'll need to be a little more specific. I can't just—"

I slap my credit card on the counter. "Anywhere."

"Ben, I can't. The wedding is tomorrow and you just told me you have an appointment downtown."

The attendant types on her computer to search for the next flight. While I wait, I take out my phone and confirm I can move my meeting an extra hour. The attendant finds me a flight and hands us our tickets.

Layla attempts to let go of my hand but I don't allow it. "Ben, where do you think you're going? I still have my bag."

"True." We walk back to the luggage claim and approach the attendants. "Could you please have this mailed to my address?" I give him my address and a thousand dollars in cash, which the man insists is too much, and we leave before he puts up too much of a fight.

"No," Layla protests. "I need my things for the wedding." The last word gives me pause. Why do I want to steal her away and marry her right now? It's irrational to even consider it, but I'd happily marry Layla today if she'd have me.

"You can last a day without them. I'll buy you anything you might require," I counter.

She doesn't fight me again and we make our way to airport security, bypassing the line—one of the perks of flying commercial first class. The other is access to the VIP lounge. Security at the airport is always a pain in my arse; they usually have to do a thorough check of my leg to make sure I'm not transporting something and it's humiliating. There was one instance where I had to remove it completely and they wouldn't allow me to do it in the privacy of an office. Thankfully, the TSA agents don't give me any trouble today.

Once through security, I locate the lounge for the airline. There are small, quiet rooms for travelers to work in; it'll do in a pinch. We check in and I'm able to reserve one for the next hour.

Layla hasn't said a word since the luggage handoff. The moment the door closes behind us, she finally breaks her silence. Looking away, she asks softly, "What are we doing here?"

I take her face in my hands. "I didn't bring you here for a shag, sunshine. Though, the thought crossed my mind." She remains unamused. I can't have her going to a hen do while things are unsettled like this; it'll drive me mad with jealousy. "If you're going tonight, I need us to be okay. I'll be a jealous arsehole all night if there's a chance, even for one moment, someone other than me might touch you, or worse, that you'll let them because you're cross with me. So, let me have it. Yell at me, if you must, but when you walk out of here, I need to know you still…" My stomach drops and I can't get the words out.

"That I still what?" Her eyes search mine.

I close my eyes tight and rest my forehead on hers. "Love me."

"Without trust, how can I?" Layla takes a deep breath. I hold mine as she fists my shirt. "In one day, you managed to destroy my publishing career. I don't know if I can forgive that, no matter how noble your intentions."

I have to tell her. It's the only way I have a shot at keeping her.

"Call your agent. See if she can patch you in to Emma Alexander. Put it on speaker."

"What does Harriet's mother have to do with this?"

I pull back. "Call. At least this way, I'm not in breach of contract."

"Okay…" Layla takes a seat in one of the lounge chairs and reaches in her purse to retrieve her phone. As she calls, I sit in the chair beside her.

"Layla?"

"Hi, Melissa," Layla sighs.

"I'm so glad you called." Melissa sighs with relief. "I'm sure you saw the email. Please know it's not what it looks like. They are finalizing details today but it will be all in place by Monday at the latest."

"What will be in place?" Layla asks, her brow furrowed. Her voice sounds tired, like it might break.

I cut in quickly. "Melissa, this is Benedict Turner. Could you connect us with Mrs. Alexander, please?"

"Oh, yes, of course. One moment." The line is silent while Layla eyes me suspiciously.

"Ben. I saw you moved back our meeting. Is everything all right?" Emma asks.

"Yes, I'm here with Layla and, for personal reasons, I'd like to request that you explain a brief overview of what transpired so I'm not in breach of my NDA."

Emma laughs. "I can't say I'm surprised. Hi, Layla. I'm sorry I can't include contractual information for legal reasons, but I'm in the process of expanding my agency to include publishing. We currently handle representation, editing, and are otherwise considered full-service. Dylan has been pushing me to add on a publication division since I became President. I was approached by Ben this morning, and now that dream is about to become a reality."

"I'm sorry, I'm not following. Why am I no longer under Kipling, I mean, Turner?" Layla asks.

"There were some issues that I cannot discuss, but you know I have my authors' best interest when I make decisions. I could not in good conscience allow you to stay with your publisher. I was able to buy out the contract for you and two hundred other authors at Ben's request," Emma explains. "Well, I should say it was more of a demand than a request. Ben, you have far too much in common with my husband. Hope you don't mind me saying that you two are a little too growly for your own good."

Layla looks to me. "So, you're expanding Emma's agency?"

"I cannot confirm or deny, but I can say that they want your publishing contract. Your books will still be published, including your backlist." I wrap an arm around her to keep her close. "Details are being sorted out. Emma and Melissa will be in contact to finalize the details. I'm not privy to those, nor do I want to be." Layla nods with understanding. "Sunshine, I'd never do anything to hurt you, I hope you know that."

"Okay, well, if that'll be all, I should go. The minute pet names are involved, that's my cue to hang up."

"Thank you, Emma," I laugh. "I'll be there shortly."

"Take your time. Harriet left to have lunch with Amanda and Robbie. Dylan and Julian will be here soon. If you need more time, we can start without you, Ben, and catch you up. Layla, I hope you know this conversation is highly sensitive and confidential. I'll be sending you an electronic NDA. Please sign and return as soon as possible. If I don't receive it within the hour, I'll need to terminate your contract."

Layla's eyes are impossibly wide. "Um, yes, of course. Send it right now. Thank you."

"Great, see you soon."

Emma hangs up and Layla pockets her phone. She chews on her lip and after what feels like eternity finally asks, "You did this for me?"

"Darling, I don't mince my words. While I've never been in love with anyone before, I'm in love with you. I saw an opportunity to fix things and I had to try. If I told you, it could've jeopardized everything. I'm sorry."

"Hold on, you've never been in love before?" she asks with a chuckle. The shaky fear in her voice is gone now, filling me with relief. "I don't believe you."

Now is as good of a time as any to admit everything. "I thought I had. There were a few I had strong feelings for, even told them I loved them. But it was nothing like this." I rake a hand through my hair. "I don't think anyone has truly seen me the way you do."

"Ben," she breathes.

"No. We don't pity, remember?"

"It's not pity, it's surprise. I had no idea. I'm sorry I jumped to conclusions earlier, but you know how it looked, right?"

"I do, love. I'm so sorry. Come here." She stands and perches on my left leg. "I love you. I can't explain it. If you feel even a tenth of what I feel for you, I could die a happy man. I'd do anything to ensure your happiness."

"I don't think I deserve you." She kisses me, and it takes everything in me not to push for more; I need this moment of softness from her. "I love you a hell of a lot more than a tenth," she whispers against my lips. "I'm so in love with you, my morally orange man."

I laugh but my heart swells at her words. "I am most defi-nitely not a good man, but I promise I won't keep things from you again."

Except the handbag. That stays between me and the bin.

Layla pulls back an inch and I instantly miss her lips on mine. "You don't by chance have condoms with you?"

While I dreamt about being inside her for a month, nothing came close to the real thing. If we had condoms, I would absolutely sink myself in her and break another fucking one right here in this airport. We've only had a twenty-five percent success rate of them remaining intact because of my piercing.

"Oh, my beautiful, magnificent sunshine." I take one of her hands and kiss her palm. "I don't need to be inside you to know you're mine. I'll see you later tonight when I can properly fuck you. Until then, knowing we're all right is enough for me."

"Maybe for you." She lightly licks her lips. "But not for me."

31

LAYLA

"Darling, we're not shagging in the airport," Ben laughs.

"Why the hell not? No one would know. Come on, let's have some fun." I palm his cock over his clothes, careful to avoid the tip.

"*Fuck*. I don't have condoms. If I did, I would've been buried inside you at baggage claim, without caring who might see or hear us." I begin to climb off his lap but he pulls me back down. "Not so fast, sunshine. Don't get any ideas. If you want to play, you can wait for the hotel."

Oh, I have ideas. I'm going to mount this beautiful man right now until he comes, then I'm going to destroy whoever is responsible for this whole mess. "Just give me a second, I'm going to use the restroom," I lie.

Ben groans. "I don't think so. You're going to return with a condom. I'll have no choice but to fuck you right here and we'll be banned from the airport. You can wait, love."

"What if I'm quiet?" I whisper, leaning in to nip at his earlobe. I don't want to be quiet. Something about the risk of getting caught excites me.

Ben grips the front of my throat as his mouth crashes into mine. There's nothing gentle about how he's claiming me. He pulls me closer to him, but I need more. I get up and straddle him, instinctively grinding against him, and feel him hardening beneath me. I try to kiss him again, missing him owning every part of me, but he tugs on my hair, exposing my neck.

He nips gently below my ear and groans, "Darling, you couldn't be quiet if you tried." A whimper escapes me when he pulls back and asks, "What's going on? This isn't like you. Don't get me wrong, I adore you being up for anything, but you were livid a few minutes ago." He cups my cheek and I cover his hand with mine. "You know we can't do this."

"I could use a distraction," I admit.

"A distraction is reading a book, not fucking in an airport, love."

"Whatever happened to you not saying no to me?"

I reconsider what I'm asking for a moment. He's right, I did do a bit of a U-turn after finding out what happened, but I desperately need to feel something other than sad, angry, or frustrated. I don't handle stress well and want to forget everything that's happened.

Ben concedes with a sigh, "Fine, you have three minutes. If you can't find a condom in three minutes, we're leaving." I've never stood so fast in my life. "I'm setting a timer. Run, sunshine. Clock's ticking. If I have to come and find you, know that it will end with you being bent over and both of us on the no-fly list."

"Your threats sound like a good time, so perhaps I should wait outside the room until the timer goes off."

"I never said I'd fuck you, just that I'd bend you over. You won't be sitting for a month by the time I'm done marking that beautiful arse of yours." *And just like that, I'm wet.* "Two minutes. Tick. Tock."

"Shit!" I squeak and run out of the room to find one of the lounge attendants. There are two men and a woman—the woman is probably my best bet. My palms sweaty, I approach her. "Excuse me, do you know where one might purchase"—I lower my voice—"a condom?"

The woman speaks just above a whisper. "You came in with Mr. Turner?" I nod and she looks around. "If you get caught, you didn't get it from me."

"Thank you," I whisper-shout as she discreetly hands me a condom from a drawer. There's no point in using one from a birth control standpoint, but with his new piercing, we need to use protection for at least another month. I need to look into something for myself. I can't take a morning-after pill every day.

As I walk away, she adds, "That is one hot man. If I was ten years younger, I would climb him myself. Have fun!"

Oh, I intend to.

I rush back to the room with fourteen seconds to spare. "Well, looks like sex in the airport is on the menu after all." I hold up the condom between my middle and forefingers.

"Bloody hell, you actually found one." Ben shakes his head and stands, taking it from me and tossing it onto the small table. "Only for you, sunshine, would I risk being kicked out of an international airport." He takes my face in his hands and kisses me. When he pulls back too quickly, I whimper. His lips are a breath away from mine as he insists, "You're going to do exactly as I ask, or you're not going to come. Are we clear, love?"

I nod and trace my fingers up his back. "Yes." He doesn't close the distance and the anticipation is too much.

"Yes, what?"

"Yes… *Captain?*" I can't contain my amusement.

"Captain? Have you been talking to Ryan?"

I lift onto my toes to kiss him again, laughing against his lips. "He told me the whole thing a week ago."

"Bloody hell, I'm not a fucking pirate," he chuckles and backs me up against the wall. "Hands against the wall, love." I turn in his arms and do as he demands. He runs his hands down my sides, gripping my hips. "You're fucking perfection, even with that smart mouth of yours."

I glance over my shoulder. "What are you going to do? Make me walk the plank?" He playfully bites my shoulder and I relish the sting, craving more. "Fine, no plank."

"What am I going to do with you?" Ben bends down on one knee, carefully takes off one of my shoes, and pulls down my leggings and panties, leaving them around the other ankle. He palms my ass and slides his hands up and down my thighs, torturously slow. "I want to mark every inch; claim you as mine." I let out a whimper. "Oh, sunshine, you love the idea of me marking you, don't you? Shall I use my teeth or hands? Or would you rather I fill you, so you can feel me dripping down these beautiful thighs of yours for the rest of the afternoon?"

"Why would you make me choose?"

He stands and wraps his arm around my middle, pulling my back flush with his chest. I lean the back of my head against him, loving the feeling of being in his arms as he kisses my neck with his beard scratching against my skin. His hand slowly wanders lower until he's between my legs; the feather-light touch is torture.

"Ben," I whimper as he circles his middle finger around my clit.

"Spread your legs for me." I do as he asks and he dips two fingers inside me, curling them to hit right where I need him. "Fuck, I love that you're already wet for me," he growls into my neck, driving his fingers deeper as grazes his teeth against my the side of my throat. "Is this enough of a *distraction* for you, sunshine?"

"No."

Ben chuckles and nips at my ear. "Good."

He removes his fingers and steps back, bringing them to his mouth to suck them clean. As I glance behind me, he unbuckles his belt, his eyes never leaving mine. He catches me biting my lip and his brow lifts, but continues unfastening his pants.

"Keep looking at me like that and you're not going to the party tonight."

"Oh no, whatever will we do?" I tease.

"I'm half tempted to fuck that pretty mouth of yours, piercing be damned." Ben slides his slacks and boxer briefs down to his knees, then rolls on the condom. My mouth waters at the thought of being on my knees for him. "This isn't going to be gentle or slow. I want you dripping for me the rest of the day, thinking about how I'm going to take you tonight when I have proper time to play with that delicious cunt of mine."

"Yours? Last time I checked, you don't have a pussy, Ben." I know he's going to snap any minute now. I can't wait. I love when he gets possessive of me.

Ben grips my hair and pulls back, kissing me hard as he slides his cock between my legs. It rubs against my clit, eliciting a moan from me. Slowly pushing inside me, he whispers, "This pussy is mine, love. When you come, your screams belong to me, too."

"I thought you said you weren't going to be gentle."

"There's a difference between pleasurable pain and hurting you. I'll never hurt you. Spread your legs wider for me." He reaches around and grips my inner thigh, pulling until my knee hits the wall. "Hold it there, just like that."

Ben pushes in and out of me torturously slow, whispering sweet praises. He reaches up to hold one of my hands on the wall while his other arm wraps around my waist to steady me. His thrusts become deeper and harder as he maintains his punishing pace. I'm winding tighter and tighter, ready to come on his command.

"Fuck, you're exquisite, taking my cock like this. I know you're close, love. Let go for me," he growls and sucks hard on my neck, pulling me closer to him. I fall apart at his words, stifling my moans as I come. While it isn't the mind-blowing orgasms he's given me before, my legs are weak and my entire body is buzzing. I sag against him. "I'm not done with you, darling," he purrs.

I'm breathless but manage, "I don't think I could handle another, not here at least." I clench my pussy around him and hold, hoping it will be his undoing. After only two more thrusts, he comes, and the condom breaks, filling me. True to his word, he didn't hurt me; I'm absolutely spent.

"Sunshine, I think we tore another one," he chuckles, then nips at my shoulder.

We shouldn't be here, and definitely shouldn't have had sex in a fucking airport, but I've cycled through a rollercoaster of emotions in the last twenty-four hours. I needed his hands on me. I needed *him*.

Ben slowly pulls out of me and discards the condom. Still braced against the wall, my head hangs back as I catch my breath. I hear the buckling of his belt behind me but I can hardly move. I'm startled when he reaches his hand between my legs and presses two fingers in my pussy.

"This stays inside you, darling. I told you, I want you to feel me the rest of the day."

"Are you *trying* to knock me up?"

He removes his fingers, turns me around until my back is against the wall. "The minute you're ready to be a mum, absolutely. Until then, we should look into another form of birth control. You can't be taking the emergency one every time a condom breaks." I nod slowly, chewing on my lip. He tilts my chin between until my gaze meets his. "Layla, I love you. But we can't make a habit of having sex in an airport, either."

"I know." I huff a small laugh. "I just needed it to be you and me for a minute after everything that happened today." A pang of guilt settles in my stomach. As amazing as it was, I shouldn't have pushed for this.

He kisses me sweetly, a stark contrast to what we just did. "What do you want? Name it and it's yours. I will burn it all to ashes, if that's what you wish."

"I want to destroy whoever had you in such a hurry to leave," I reply confidently, then lick his fingers clean. He groans as I savor the taste—a mix of the two of us. "I want them to pay for what they did."

"That's my job, not yours. I can't let this corrupt you. I won't let it." Ben falls to his knees to pull up my leggings and panties, then slips on my shoe.

"What if they hurt you in the process?"

"I won't go down with the ship, love." He chuckles. "You jest that I'm a pirate; I suppose I've been a pirate for far too long. But, I'd never let anything happen to either of us. Allow me the pleasure of taking care of the crocodile."

Too late, Ben. I won't rest until they get what they deserve.

32

BEN

I crave Layla, even though I was inside her moments ago. It isn't just sex—which is the best of my life. The temptation to touch her, feel her, and the need to have her close to me, is absolute torture. I have a constant, inexplicable ache in my chest that no antacid could ever fix. The yearning I have for her is unbearable, even with her right in front of me.

"You have a meeting and I have a bachelorette party to get ready for." Layla brushes the hair off my forehead. I close my eyes, leaning into her touch. She brings me peace like nothing else I've experienced. At the same time, I want to mark her as mine for the world to see before she leaves for the evening.

I take her hand and kiss the inside of her palm. "I'm not loving that you'll be attending a hen do. I'd much rather take you out tonight myself."

She smiles brightly, assuring me I have nothing to worry about. "You're so British. Hen do? It's a *bachelorette party*,

Ben. I'll come back to you all liquored up from too many margaritas, but don't worry, I'll be on my best behavior."

Before I can respond, there's a knock at the door. "Mr. Turner, shall I renew the hour for you to continue your… *work?*" Layla covers her mouth to stifle her laugh.

"We'll be right out," I yell to the door, then lower my voice to Layla, "What's so funny, love?"

She shuts her eyes and crinkles her nose. "That's who gave me the condom."

"Oh, fuck," I laugh. "Well, we should be off, then. Otherwise, we'll end up on the no-fly list."

I still can't believe we fucked in an airport. I'm not an impulsive man but all bets are off when it comes to her. I check the room to ensure we didn't leave anything behind and exit quickly. Layla takes my hand, weaving her fingers with mine, and I bring her knuckles to my lips as I tell her, "I love you."

She sighs. "I'm sorry. We shouldn't have done that. I just—"

"I know, sunshine. You don't need to explain." I have an unexplainable urge to take her away from here, back to England with me. Better yet, I want to whisk her off to Gretna Green and make her mine permanently.

What am I saying? I need to clean up this mess first before I even consider it.

Mum would love her, though.

"So, who was responsible for all of this?" Layla asks as we make our way to the exit.

I take out my phone to message my driver to let him know we are a few minutes out. While typing one-handed, I reply, "Kipling," without much thought to the ramifications. Realisation hits me, and I fumble, "Shit, I mean, I don't know who is responsible." The lie is sour on my tongue. I promised I would be honest with her, but I can't discuss this with her. Not yet. Not until everything I've put in motion is finalised. I have some of the best men and women in the business taking care of it, one wrong move and it could all be in jeopardy.

We make our way out of the airport and something doesn't feel right with Layla. She was upset earlier—which is understandable. A lot happened. This feels darker. The wheels are turning and I'm worried she might be trying to solve this on her own.

The ride to Emma's office is quiet. Layla spends most of her time looking out the window, tapping her fingers on her lap. Every time I ask, she insists she's only thinking. It doesn't take a genius to figure out she's lying to me.

The office is a beautiful corner building downtown— twelve stories high with tall windows. It looks as if it was built in the early 1900s. Unlike most buildings, this one is a forty-five degree angle to accommodate a side street. It reminds me of some of the buildings in London and makes me miss home.

I don't visit San Francisco often. This has to be the third time I've been here in ten years. It has the same fast-paced feel that New York has, with fewer taxis. I don't know that I could ever live here, it doesn't have the same charm home does.

Layla's silent on the lift ride eight floors to Emma's office. I'm genuinely worried about her; she hasn't spoken more than ten words to me since we shagged at the airport. It was a mistake, especially after everything that happened. I just hope I can fix this, too.

The lift doors open and Layla pulls her hand away as we're greeted by a receptionist. "Sunshine, they know we're together," I quietly assure her.

"I'd like to meet with my agent, Ms. Birch, while Mr. Turner is in his meeting," she tells the fresh-faced receptionist, avoiding my gaze.

"Yes, of course, Ms. Thorne. Please have a seat, and I'll let Ms. Birch and Mrs. Alexander know you've arrived."

Once out of earshot, I ask Layla, "What's wrong, love?"

I attempt to take her hand but she swats mine away. It's like the first night we met, but exponentially worse. I want to protect her from all of this and wasn't lying when I said I would burn down the world for her. There's nothing I wouldn't do for her.

How things change in a month…

"Everything's fine, I—"

"Mrs. Alexander will see you now," the receptionist announces.

I cup Layla's cheek and kiss her softly, but she doesn't kiss me back with the same fire I'm accustomed to. While I don't expect her to stick her tongue down my throat, she isn't melting into me, either. I don't push for more, but with her going out tonight, I'm worried she could be pulling back from me or having second thoughts about us. As much as I hate to leave her like this, I have to meet with Emma, or all of this was for nothing. Trust, once broken, is hard to repair. I can fix this whole mess and we can move on from it, together.

"I'd love for you to wait for me, but if you want to leave, call my driver and they'll take you to the hotel." I retrieve my phone and type out a message to her with the driver's information. "I'll be done in an hour." I kiss her temple and stand to follow the receptionist to Emma's office. I glance back and Layla's typing out a message on her phone. Hopefully it's Amanda, Becca, or her mum.

I enter Emma's office, which is remarkably similar to mine. There are dark wood accents, bookcases overflowing with books, and two dark brown leather chairs across from hers.

"Ben. Have a seat." Emma stands and gestures to one of the leather chairs. She rounds her desk and shakes my hand before sitting in the other. It's quite informal, taking me by surprise. We sit and she hands me a folder. "Julian, Dylan, and legal will be here in twenty. They'll meet us in the conference room, but I wanted to speak with you privately first."

"If it is regarding the merger, it should wait until all parties are present," I insist.

"This is personal. I need to ask a favor."

"Is my multi-billion dollar investment not enough?" I jest.

Emma huffs a laugh. "I'm hoping you'll help me move Harriet's contract to another company. Mine has represented her since she first published, but I don't want there to be any conflict of interest having her published here under my new department."

"I see." I nod in understanding. "In that case, I'd like to ask that Layla's contract be revoked from your agency. While there aren't many options outside of my umbrella of companies, I don't want my funding to have any impact on her success."

Emma's nostrils flair once. "You're not representing her, so that'll be between my agency and her." All pleasantries are gone; I've offended her with my request. Though, she's right, it's up to Layla. "There's already a target on her back, as well as Amanda and Harriet's, since they're no longer under Kipling and we have a personal connection. The remaining authors will be an easy transition."

"Perhaps I didn't properly explain. Layla will be my wife, and I want to ensure her merits are not associated with my wealth. Her books are brilliant and I never want anyone to think that I had anything to do with it."

Emma's eyes are wide, but soft. "Congratulations. I didn't know you were engaged. That explains a lot."

"Oh, we're not engaged." My face falls at my admission. "I just meant one day. I need to protect her from, well, me."

She smiles and shakes her head with a small laugh. "I get it. My husband was the same way when I took over the company and our daughter started writing. So, I'll leave it to Layla. We'll be transparent with her so she can make an informed decision. Should she want to leave, we'll void her contract without penalty."

There's a knock at the door and Emma addresses them. Julian and Dylan are here early and waiting in the conference room. My legal representation should be here shortly and we leave Emma's office to meet them.

As we pass the waiting area, Layla's no longer there, likely already in her meeting with her agent. I open the door to the conference room for Emma to walk in and she whispers, "Last chance to run."

There's no reason to run. This is bigger than business. This is Layla and I'll protect her at all costs.

33

LAYLA

"So, tell me, what's going on with you and that tall drink of water in Emma's office?" Melissa eyes me suspiciously and drums her nails on her desk.

"Ben and I are... I don't know what we are," I sigh. "That's not why I'm here. I need your help. I need to destroy Kipling, so I need you to restore my contract."

Her drumming stops. "I'm sorry, what?"

"I love Ben. Truly, I do. But the only way that Roger will get what's coming to him is if I take down his company from the inside."

Melissa frowns. "I'm not following."

I tell Melissa about the phone conversation I had at the airport with Emma and Ben, as well as Ben's slip up. She's the only one I can discuss this with, being under my NDA. I need to talk this through with someone who isn't Ben, and it's not like a therapist could help in this situation;

despite desperately needing to talk to one with my emotions being a jumbled mess today.

Ben has something up his sleeve, but I can do this without him. I can't wait around for his white knight plan to come to fruition. Roger's the reason hundreds of authors are without contracts; he has to pay.

"In the end, I want to remove myself from Alexander, Turner, Kipling... all of it. Becca had the right idea going independent and I want to do the same. But first, I want to take down Kipling. The easiest way to do that is to destroy profitability. I can spend the next year ensuring that my books tank and not hurt Emma's company." It isn't the best plan, but it will ensure Roger pays financially for what he did.

"What about Benedict Turner? Taking down a publishing house that was just acquired by your new boyfriend won't hurt only Kipling, it'll hurt Turner too."

Ben still has shares for Kipling, he just isn't the primary stakeholder anymore. If I take down Kipling, it will hurt Ben financially. However, for a man worth $75 billion, he can stand to lose a few. Roger could still walk away with millions, if not billions. I just hope Ben cut ties sooner rather than later—easier to hurt Roger if he's by himself. I have to isolate him so I can ruin his life the way he did all of those authors' careers.

"Okay, I'll have legal see what they can do. We'll reinstate the Kipling-Turner contract and you can go on your villain spree. Just know there's a target on Ben's back for taking three big authors from Kipling. Just... be careful." Melissa smirks, which is all the confirmation I need that this is a brilliant plan.

Or a complete disaster.

Probably a disaster.

Everything is in place, except for having Jamie put out some bad PR for Kipling.

Fuck, I forgot about Jamie. She still thinks Ben is responsible for all of this. I'll need to let her in on what I'm up to and put a stop to the guerrilla warfare she has planned against Ben.

"I need to make a call." I stand abruptly to leave.

"Layla, wait, what's going on? We should talk about logistics for *Last Reward*," Melissa calls after me.

I continue to the door. When I reach it, I turn and reply, "There's something I need to take care of. Please, find a way to keep my publishing contracts. But only for a year. Sorry, I need to go."

Rushing out of the office, I pass by their conference room with floor to ceiling windows. Ben, Dylan, Julian, and Emma, in addition to a few men and women in suits I don't recognize, are sitting around the long mahogany table. Ben and I lock eyes as I keep walking. I mouth "I'm sorry" and continue to the elevator. I know there's a ninety percent chance he'll chase after me.

I press the down button what feels like fifty times. "Come on," I mutter to myself.

I close my eyes when I feel the familiar scratch of Ben's beard on my neck. He kisses me once just below my ear and whispers, "Where do you think you're going, sunshine?"

My heart aches and stomach drops. I can't tell him. I can't tell him that I'm planning that could hurt him. I also can't tell him that I regret having sex earlier. I shouldn't have pushed him to do that in a damn airport just because I was going through some sort of mental breakdown.

"I'm sorry." They're the only words I can get out.

Ben turns me to face him. "Why? What's wrong? You've been off since we left the airport."

"It's nothing," I lie.

"Come to the meeting with me. I'm sure they could use an author's opinion." He rubs the back of his neck. "I'm investing to expand her company. Julian's throwing money at it as well for audiobook production."

"I'm going to fuck over Roger," I blurt out, covering my mouth as the words fly from it.

"And how do you expect to do that, darling?" he chuckles. "I told you, I have it handled."

"I'm sorry, I have to go before—" The elevator doors open.

"Before what?"

"Before I change my mind, Ben. I'm sorry. I have to go."

I take a step toward the elevator but he snakes an arm around my middle and pulls me until my back is flush with him. I take a deep breath, instantly regretting it; he always smells so good. I swear it's cedar or pine… a damn forest. It's my kryptonite.

"You're not going anywhere until we talk through this," he growls.

I swallow hard. "There's nothing to talk about. I'm going to take down the man responsible for hurting my friends' careers. But first, I need to talk to Jamie." I turn in his arms and place my hands on his chest. If he moves any closer, he'll kiss me and I'll never be able to go through with this. "Fuck. I have the bachelorette party tonight." I fist his shirt and press my forehead against his chest. He wraps his arms around me and guilt washes over me. "I'm sorry."

"You keep apologizing, but there's nothing you could do that would ever make me see you differently, love." He rests his chin on the top of my head and sighs. "You don't make a very good morally gray heroine. Let's fix this together, okay? I don't want you getting hurt in the crossfire between me and Kipling."

"I literally just told you I'm trying to actively destroy him, which could hurt you, and you're trying to protect me?" I glance up at him. My favorite wide grin that he so rarely shows beams back at me.

"Darling, you couldn't hurt me." I feel like I should be offended, but it's hard to be upset when he's, well, him. "After the wedding, come to England with me. For a few weeks, or a month."

"Are… are you leaving?"

He pulls me tighter, which just solidifies his answer. "Yes, but only while the lawyers sort everything out. I don't want to be here when it all comes to pass. But, if you don't come with me, I won't go."

I contemplate it for a moment; I can write from anywhere. I'd be with Ben, and he claims he'll be cleaning up this mess. It feels like a win-win, but something is holding me back. It could be the fact that I've known this man for a month and…

We've only known each other for a month.

"You should go. I'll stay here. Roger needs to pay for what he's done and I have a lot of big changes coming in the next year that I'll need to hire staff for."

"Wherever you are, I am, love. I'm not leaving without you. If you're really intent on ruining Roger, then allow me the pleasure of doing it." Ben tilts my chin and brings my lips to his for a chaste kiss. I melt, my body both on fire and a puddle at his touch. "I won't allow this to break you, harden you, or make you anything less than my sunshine. I don't care what you did that you need to fix. I'll fix it. I've been doing this for the better part of the last decade, let me do this for you."

"I'm just so"—I sigh deeply—"angry."

"I know, love. Come to the meeting with me and we'll sort out your 'evil mastermind plot gone wrong,' after."

He takes my hand and begins walking back to the conference room but I remain rooted in place. "About that," I say, chewing on my lip. "I'm going independent in a year. Having me there would be a conflict of interest, or something."

With a wide smile, he asks, "When did this happen?"

"You're a little too happy." I eye him suspiciously. "I thought you might be upset that I'm considering following in Becca's footsteps."

"I was hoping you would find another agency and publisher. I don't want anyone to think that my wealth has anything to do with your success or talent. I'm sure Becca can connect you with some incredible people in the indie world. I couldn't be more pleased with this outcome, sunshine."

"Pleased with this outcome?" I can't help but smile.

"I am, but that shouldn't come as a surprise. Are we all right? Or will I need to chase you?"

My cheeks heat and I swallow hard. "What do you mean 'chase me?'"

He leans in, his beard scratching my cheek as he whispers, "There is nowhere you could run that I wouldn't find you. Go to the hotel and get ready for the party tonight. You should be long gone before I arrive. If I find you there, expect to attend with my handprint on your arse."

"So, what I'm hearing is that I should just stay in tonight?" I tease.

"I'm not fucking you tonight, darling. But I'm capable of doing far worse."

If I have it my way, I'm going to spend the rest of my life with this man, if only to find out exactly how bad 'far worse' is.

34

BEN

After Layla left, Melissa approached Emma and I to let us in on Layla's plans. I have to hand it to her, she continues to surprise me. No matter how much I protested, they agreed to keep her contract intact with Kipling, which expires in a month. They also agreed to not renew the contract for a year, as Layla requested.

When I originally pulled her contract, it was with the intention that she could work with Emma. Things have changed, now that I'm investing more than I anticipated in her new publishing division. Layla's name would be tied to mine; her becoming an independent author is the best possible option at the moment. Even so, if she stays with Roger while I'm in the process of dismantling his company, she'll be collateral damage.

Layla isn't a wolf in sheep's clothing—she's just a sheep. A magnificent sheep, but a sheep nonetheless. There's no way she could take down Roger. I appreciate her wanting to right a wrong, but she doesn't have the means or the business knowledge to destroy him. Not like I do. She'll only get hurt.

Emma's team offered me a small workroom to send emails and make a few calls. It's eerily similar to the one I was in earlier today with Layla at the airport. I'm flooded with flashbacks of her against the wall, stifling her moans so we wouldn't get caught. My cock twitches in my trousers and I shake the thoughts away. I should've said no, especially after everything that happened. It's another perfect example of how I'm incapable of thinking rationally when I'm around her.

A few hours of work later, Layla's hen do is likely in full swing and she should no longer be at the hotel. I think back to the first time I laid eyes on her. If she's wearing those trousers that may as well be painted on... The thought of another man touching her, or so much as looking at her, has me seething with jealousy. I reign it in and resist the urge to message her.

I officially have no self-control, and begin typing, "What are you wearing tonight, love?" but then delete and opt for a safer option.

> Hope you're having fun with the girls.

I close out my laptop and pack it in my tote, slinging it over my shoulder as I head for the door. My phone vibrates in my pocket. Hoping it's Layla, I quickly retrieve it, only to find an emergency message from Ryan.

> RYAN
> Check your socials, Captain. It's bad.

Fuck. What now?

I open an app and type in my name as a hashtag. There are hundreds of posts originating from Kipling about their parting with Layla, due to an "inappropriate working relationship" with me. This has to be retaliation for bringing over hundreds of authors, or him finding out about my investing in another publisher. I slam the phone down on the table with enough force to crack the screen. For a moment, a smirk tugs at my lips as I think about Layla's phone debacle the first night we met. My amusement fades quickly as I realise I'm a fucking idiot and can't call her.

Rushing out of the office with phone in hand, I find the receptionist from earlier. She's packing her bag to leave for the evening and startles when she spots me sprinting down the hall toward her. My leg aches; I forgot to take my medication, but any discomfort I'm feeling is overshadowed by my fear that Layla's career could be tarnished because of me.

"Mr. Turner, is everything all right?"

"No. I need to contact Layla Thorne, but my mobile is, um…" I show her the shattered screen.

"Oh, yes, of course. While I can't give out her personal number, I can call her from the office line."

I should be grateful she's gatekeeping Layla's information, but being in a pinch, I don't have time to deal with this. "It's an emergency."

She dials the number but it goes to voicemail. She then tries Emma, who picks up on the third ring. "Hi, Mrs. Alexander, I'm so sorry for calling so late with your daughter getting married tomorrow, but could you contact Ms. Thorne? Mr. Turner has an emergency and needs to reach her." Nodding, she replies to Emma, "Thank you. Here he is."

"Emma?"

"What's going on, Ben? I just saw a ton of book drama all over social media. I was going to call but I figured you were doing damage control."

"I need to talk to Layla."

Emma sighs. "She's at the bachelorette, so her phone is probably on silent or was confiscated by one of the girls. They are at the Waterfront on the pier for dinner, but please don't make a scene."

"Understood. Thank you."

We hang up and I rush to the lift. Once inside, it feels like eternity for the numbers to drop from the eighth floor, leaving me with my thoughts for far too long. I hate this; all of this. There's no reason why Roger should go after Layla and I. We've been dating for… No. This isn't dating. She's mine. Admittedly, I've never been in love before, but that doesn't negate how completely my heart belongs to her.

I took extra legal steps to ensure I wouldn't come within a thousand miles of her books. It was all for naught.

As I make my way downstairs and out to the street, I realize I never rang my driver. I don't have his number memorised, leaving me with only one option. A taxi. I shudder for a moment, since I can't recall the last time I needed to rely on transportation without a private driver. It can't be worse than a commercial flight, right? I hail a taxi on the corner and one pulls up almost immediately. I get in, cringing when I breathe in the scent of stale cigar smoke and sweat.

You're doing this for Layla.

I give the gentleman the restaurant name, and twenty minutes later, we arrive. The walk down the pier gives me time to rehearse what I'm going to say to Layla. The last thing I need is for this to become one more reason she could walk away from me. I should take her away from here until the press dies down. Julian had to be away from Becca when things became complicated, but there's no reason I can't go back home *with* Layla and shield her from the bad press.

The restaurant has a decent view of the bay and would actually make a romantic place to propose to someone at night with the city lights in the background.

There's a thought…

No, you twat, she's not going to marry you after knowing you for a month.

I'm greeted by the hostess, who shows me to their table. When Layla is in view, I stop her and insist I'll make it on my own the rest of the way. She returns to the host stand and I stuff my hands in my pockets, lean against the doorframe to the dining room, and take a moment to appreciate Layla in her element with the four other women.

She's sitting with Amanda to her right and a younger woman, who must be Harriet, on her left. They're all wearing black sashes, except for Harriet's, which is white. They are laughing hysterically at something Becca is saying. The fifth woman is younger than Harriet with dark rimmed glasses and raven black hair, standing out amongst the other women. She spots me first and nudges Harriet, who then whispers to Layla.

When Layla's eyes meet mine, her laughter ceases immediately, replaced with a wide smile. She gets up from her chair and rushes over to me, wrapping her arms around my middle. "What are you doing here? Don't you have work or"—she gasps—"are you skipping your run tonight for little ol' me?"

"How much have you had to drink, love?"

She doesn't answer, instead lifting onto the balls of her feet and kissing my cheek. Fuck, I want to haul her over my shoulder and take her home.

She's home.

I grip her chin and bring her lips to mine. She tastes like lime and reposado tequila. While I'm not fond of margaritas, I'm in love with the way she tastes after one. I whisper, "You're coming home with me."

"We can't go back to Seattle yet, the wedding is tomorrow night," she chuckles. Her laughter makes me feel lighter, but also has me resigned to my decision.

"I meant *my* home, sunshine. Come home with me. I would steal you away tonight, but I know how much you've been looking forward to the weekend. We can leave Sunday morning."

She pulls back. "Hold on, what do you mean 'your home?'"

As I'm about to reply, Amanda yells across the restaurant, "Do I need to make good on my promise, Ben's A Di—" Becca's hand clamps over Amanda's mouth. Layla hides herself, gripping the lapels of my jacket and pressing her forehead to my chest.

While I love when she's wearing her favourite black heels, I love that she's in flats even more, making her the perfect height to tuck under my chin. "Come back home with me. One month, just until the contract is up."

Layla breathes deeply and replies, "I'm too buzzed to wrap my mind around it."

"You don't have to decide right now, but... please consider it. I want to protect you from the fallout."

Becca calls out, "Ben, come have a drink with us!" Layla lifts her head and, with a grin, takes my hand and drags me over to the table. She offers her chair and sits sideways on my left leg, which I'm grateful for. There's still a dull ache in my right but if I'm able to get back to the hotel within the next hour or two, I'll be fine. Still, I take the opportunity to keep my arm around her. Not touching her feels wrong, especially since her demeanor is a stark contrast to earlier. She's my relaxed sunshine, not my vengeful temptress.

"One drink, *darling*," Layla giggles then lowers her voice so only I can hear, "If you need to *Brexit*, let me know."

"I'll have a dark rum, neat."

"Gross," Harriet says, nose turned up. "What are you, a pirate? I mean, I suppose it's better than a gin and tonic like my parents drink. Who the fuck drinks liquid pine trees?" She shudders but signals for the waiter. "Have you eaten? We just finished but haven't had dessert."

I don't take my eyes off Layla as I reply to Harriet, "I haven't eaten, but I'm certain what I want isn't on the menu." There are a few gasps and an "ope" from

Amanda. I finally look at Harriet. "I'm fine with the rum, thank you."

"Shit, and I thought Robbie was a Casanova. Look at you walking in here with your perfectly tailored suit, hot English accent, trying to sweep my friend off her feet," Harriet laughs into her glass.

The waiter comes by and takes my order. I discreetly hand him my card to cover their tab, since it's the least I can do after everything. The woman across from us finally introduces herself, "I don't think we've met. I'm Lizzy, Harriet's sister." She waves, which I'm grateful for because to shake her hand would require me to let go of Layla, and I have no intention of doing so.

"Benedict, but please, call me Ben."

"He's our 'book daddy' for the foreseeable future," Amanda clarifies with a smirk.

"Oh! You're the one that got my sister out of her contract. All right, he can stay," Lizzy laughs.

"Of course he can stay," Layla insists. "But only for a drink. After that, he needs to leave before he tries to convince me to move to England for a month."

Becca chokes on her drink mid-sip. "I'm sorry, what?"

"Well, that's enough inquisition for the night." I pat Layla's thigh. "I should get going. You ladies have fun tonight."

Layla leans in, her cheek brushing mine as she whispers, "Wherever you are, so am I."

"You're drunk, love."

"You missed your nightly run to be here. Must be a big deal." She nips once at my ear; I can't help the groan that comes from deep in my chest. "I'll come home to England, if you take me to the hotel right now."

"I told you earlier, I'm not fucking you, sunshine." *What am I saying? If she unbuckled my belt, I'd take her right on this table.*

"I don't need your cock to come, *love*," she teases. You have a perfectly good mouth." Layla pulls back, biting her lip. If I don't get out of here, this is going to be an airport lounge situation all over again.

The waiter drops off the round of drinks and I finish mine in three long gulps, savouring the burn. Harriet mutters, "Damn pirate."

"Have fun with the girls, I'll meet you back at the hotel. If you still want to leave in the morning, we'll be on the first flight. Do you have your passport?" She shakes her head. "We'll stop in Seattle first."

There's a gasp at the table. Layla and I turn. "What an asshole!" Harriet huffs, looking at her phone.

Bollocks.

"What is it?" Layla asks, pulling away from me. I keep my hand firmly placed around her waist. If they're seeing what I think they are, I don't need Layla having a similar reaction to earlier. And I sure as hell don't need her trying to convince me to run off to the bathroom for a quick shag. I'd say yes, I know I would.

The waiter approaches, leans in and keeps his voice low. "Sir, there are six men with cameras out front asking about you. Should you and your friends need to leave, may I suggest the back door?"

Fuck.

Layla heard him as well and asks, "Why would there be paparazzi?"

"Because of this," Harriet slides her phone across the table with one of the posts that has now made mainstream media. I have to hand it to Roger, he moves quickly.

"When did this come out?" Layla zooms in and scrolls on Harriet's phone.

"That's why I'm here, love."

"To take me away to England," Layla finishes.

I tuck her stray strands of hair behind her ear as she continues reading, and reply softly, "Yes."

"Let's go." Layla stands abruptly while the girls and I stare at her dumbfounded. "I'm not going to ruin Harriet's wedding. Let's leave tonight."

"Sunshine." I take her hand in mine and brush a kiss to her knuckles. "We—"

"We'll walk out front together publicly, so Harriet can enjoy her bachelorette party, and we'll leave for Seattle tonight. I'll grab my things and, in the morning, we head home." Layla then addresses Harriet, "I'm so sorry, I didn't mean to ruin your party or your wedding."

"Well, the best wedding present you could give me would be fucking up Roger's life. So, make that happen and we'll call it even," Harriet says with a wink. She raises her drink in a toast, her smile never wavering, even though I'm sure she's disappointed.

"Deal," Layla replies. Her beaming smile that has been missing for most of the past two days has briefly returned, but it falls when she turns back to me. "I'm so sorry, for everything."

"You tried to be the morally grey villain, darling. It doesn't suit you."

Layla kisses me on the cheek and whispers, "Orange. But you're right."

I chuckle softly. "Come on, let's get you home."

Layla says goodbye to her friends and we leave the restaurant with my arm around her shoulder and hers around my waist. Through the flashes and questions from the paparazzi, Layla holds her head high, proud to be with me.

I open the limo door, kiss her temple, and whisper, "I love you. I'm going to fix this."

"Want to give them something to write about?" She cups my cheek and kisses me deeply. The lights flash brighter and part of me loves that the world will see she's mine. I press a final kiss to her palm and help her inside the car.

While this didn't work out the way I thought it would, I'd be lying if I said I wasn't elated that she'll be running away with me. Even if it's only for a month.

35

LAYLA

I don't plan on coming back. Not because Ben would keep me captive on the other side of the world. I want to be with him, wherever he is. He's sacrificed so much for me. If things work out in the coming months, I wouldn't hesitate to stay with him. How could I not? I'd be a fool to walk away from someone like Ben. He challenges me, encourages my writing—even if he joked that it's vampire smut once—and I love spending time with him. In and out of the bedroom.

The ride to the hotel is quiet, but Ben hasn't let go of my hand since we left the restaurant. Harriet insisted we take the limo back to the hotel and that her uncle, Ethan, would be there to greet us. I remember Tyler from my flight mentioning he was helping Ethan with the wedding. My heart hurts that it has come to this; getting her family involved.

It feels as if Ben and I have traded places a dozen times in the past couple of days, and I hate that he's lost in thought, not sharing. I break the silence and ask, "Are you angry with me?"

He pierces me with a heated gaze. "Quite the opposite. I could never be cross with you, love. I'm… I don't want to scare you with what I was thinking."

"Tell me." I turn my body to face him completely. "I can take it."

"Trust me, you don't want to know." He brings our joined hands up to his lips, his eyes never leaving mine.

"Well, now I really want to know!" I laugh.

"You, my love, are absolutely breathtaking. It took everything in me to keep my hands to myself tonight. We'll leave it at that. It's the last thing I should be thinking about with all that's transpired today."

"Transpired? Oh, you mean the airport sex," I wince. "I'm sorry about that. I know we shouldn't have done it, it was just a stress response, and—"

"No," he growls. I don't think I've been growled at this much in my life. It's both sexy and unnerving. His eyes darken and mine widen in response.

"No? I just want to apologize for—"

"I said no. You are not apologizing for a single moment we've spent together. Meeting you was happenstance, and I certainly didn't expect to fall in love with someone as incredible as you. I know you shouldn't love me; I'm a difficult man to love. And, yes, shagging in an airport was careless. But do not, under any circumstances, apologize."

My chest warms at his words. For someone who claims he's never been in love, he loves deeply, unconditionally, and with his whole heart. "Fine, I won't apologize," I say softly. "But will you please tell me what has you so wound up?"

"Today was absolute shit. I've spent years destroying lives and never thought twice about it, but now someone is trying to destroy yours." He shakes his head. "He's going to pay for what he's done, but right now none of that matters."

Confused, I ask, "Why doesn't it?"

"I can't explain it." He leans his head back against the seat, closes his eyes, and sighs. "I can't have you looking at me differently."

I click the button for the privacy screen and climb onto his lap, straddling him. I don't intend for it to be sexual; he's retreating when I need him to hear me. His hands rub up my thighs, then grip my ass, pulling me closer. As I take his face in my hands, his eyes finally meet mine. "Unless you're going to tell me that you've burned down a rainforest, or murdered a dolphin, I don't think there's anything that would make me see you differently. What has you so distracted you don't care about taking down Roger?'

"You, love. I want to protect you from everything, which is hard to do when all I want to do is…" The blue from his eyes is nearly gone, his nostrils slightly flared, and his jaw ticks twice.

I swallow hard and ask, "Is what?" Ben shakes his head so I press again, "What do you want to do?" I keep my voice low. If I'm not careful, he'll strip me down right here, but I might be misreading this. It could be he's only worried about me getting hurt by the recent press.

"There are things I've thought about, fantasized about, that would have you reconsidering being with me," he says carefully. "I'm worried when you figure it out…"

"I'm not going anywhere. Tell me." My heart is thumping loudly with anticipation. I'm certain he's going to reveal some sort of kink he hasn't shared with me yet, and all I can do is hope I'll be into it. "Would it help if I shared something with you first?"

What I'm about to tell him could unleash something in him, so I'm careful with my words. I fist his jacket and close the distance until our lips are less than an inch apart. He sighs, "You don't ha—"

I kiss him to end his protest, but I need him to hear me more than I want to taste the rum lingering on his lips. When I pull back, I give him the eye contact he craves, even if it makes me nervous.

"I love you. Not by accident, not on a whim… on purpose. I love you, even knowing there's darkness in you. You would never hurt me, so I'm not worried about telling you that I want you to mark every part of me as yours." A rumble comes from his chest and his jaw clenches. I lean in to whisper beside his ear, "I want to feel the sting on my ass when I sit down the next morning. I want bite marks I have to hide with long pants and conservative shirts; light bruises that remind me I belong to you. I want you to take from me until I have nothing left to give. Not just in bed. I'm yours, Ben. So, tell me, what could possibly have me looking at you differently, when I know you want the same thing?"

"I don't just want to claim you, darling. I want the whole fucking world to know you're mine… permanently."

36

BEN

"What do you mean permanently?" Layla laughs and the levity is much needed after what she confessed. "Is this not a cosy romantic comedy? I didn't sign up for a dark romance, Ben. Actual enslavement and kidnapping is off the table."

Before I can respond, our driver announces over the stereo system that we'll be arriving in a few moments. Layla climbs off my lap, leaving my aching cock behind. Her admission couldn't have come at a worse time. All I want to do is worship and brand every inch of her.

We pull up to the hotel and walk inside. I check with the front desk to inquire about my medication being dropped off by a courier. Thankfully, it has been. I open the package, take out the bottle, and discard the envelope. Removing two pills, I swallow them without water. Layla rubs my back, her worried brow giving her away.

"I'll be all right in twenty minutes, love."

A well-dressed man with dark blond hair and immaculately groomed beard approaches us. "Benedict? Layla? So glad to meet you both at last. Ethan Barlowe." He offers Layla his hand, holding an Old Fashioned in the other. "Well, I hope you don't mind me saying, red suits you," he tells Layla. She blushes and I ball my fist at my side, stifling a groan. He chuckles, telling me, "Relax, Red Flag, I was referring to you." He shakes my hand with a firm grip. "So, who's ready to clean up a mess?"

Ethan leads us to the hotel bar that's void of a single patron. Layla notices as well and asks, "Where is everyone?"

"Your beau isn't the only one with money to throw around," he laughs, waving his hand dismissively. "Figured we wanted privacy for this. We have an hour."

Moments after sitting, a dark rum and a margarita are placed in front of Layla and me. Layla questions, "How did you…"

"It's my job; I've been an event planner for nearly twenty-five years. I do my research, especially with high profile clients and their guest lists. My wife will be here shortly to answer any legal questions you might have, but in the meantime, let's discuss you two attending Harriet's wedding."

"We aren't," I insist. "We're leaving tomorrow."

"I'm sure your PR team has advised you to stay out of the spotlight, but I wanted to make you an offer that will help you and Harriet. I've known her since she was a teenager and we're not going to make a spectacle of her wedding." He takes a sip of his drink and looks to Layla. "While your boyfriend could buy a small country, we'll have professional baseball players, a few actors, and of course Julian, in attendance. Hell, one of the event planners is a damn prince."

Layla gasps. "A prince? Shit, maybe I should have written a royal romance instead?" I playfully pinch her side and she laughs.

"You've met him actually. Eddie, or I believe he introduced himself to you as Tyler."

"Tyler? Tyler Beck?" Layla asks and Ethan nods. "I met him on the plane here."

"Well, he's a sort-of prince. Edmund walked away from all of it and now he runs my company. He would be planning this wedding himself, but I insisted I do it. Harriet is family."

"So, what does the wedding have to do with us?" Layla hasn't touched her drink, keeping her hand on my thigh since we sat down. While I want to interject, more than that, I want her to have a moment to process everything and make decisions without me. I place my hand over hers and squeeze, not letting go.

"My wife helped Julian out of an incident a few years back. I'm sure you're privy to the details, and if not, he'll need to tell you. We need your help just as he needed ours. The wedding isn't only two people in love getting married, it's also doubling as an opportunity for Harriet to have positive publicity given that shit hit the fan with a certain book giant."

Layla rushes to my defence, "It wasn't Ben's fault." I rest my arm behind her and rub my thumb back and forth on her shoulder. She turns to me in response. "What? It's not."

"It is, love. This whole thing never would've happened if I hadn't tried to buy out Kipling."

"*Anyway*," Ethan interrupts, annoyed. "You'll find the guest list is small but includes family as well as A-list celebrities. Your presence will help Harriet, and we can ensure that staged shots are taken, to change the narrative that's circulating in the press about you two. And, in turn, it will help Harriet."

"I'm not comfortable posing for photos." Layla crosses her arms over her chest and sits back in her chair.

"No one is asking you to fake anything," Ethan chuckles to himself. "Trust me, I've been there, and learned the hard way that secrets always come out. I only mean that we'll make sure flattering photos are taken and purposefully leaked. You not coming to the wedding looks bad for Harriet, as well as Emma, as if what you two are doing is shameful. A united front is best. Emma's my best friend of nearly three decades. I'm asking both professionally and personally that you consider this for her and her daughter."

Layla nods in understanding. "So, if we attend, it won't hurt Harriet?"

"Correct. Her being associated with Ben as things stand right now most certainly will, though. We need to show that nothing is amiss between the two of you and Harriet." Ethan's face lights up as he looks behind us.

A woman sits next to Layla with dark brown hair and crimson lipstick that's a similar shade to what Layla's wearing. She hangs her tote on the back of her chair and sighs. "All right, who's the billionaire I'm bailing out of trouble today?"

"Hey, princess." Ethan wraps his arm around her and kisses her temple. "Turner's situation is nothing like Julian's. He probably already has some plan to buy out the western hemisphere and it'll resolve itself. But from a PR standpoint, what do we need to ensure that tomorrow goes smoothly for Harriet?"

"Hi, I'm Melanie." She shakes both Layla's and my hands. "Don't mind my husband; he gets a bit growly when it comes to family. I assure you, everything is in order on my end. The paparazzi you encountered earlier have been paid off and all photographers tomorrow for the wedding were personally vetted by Ethan."

"Could you send their information to my assistant? I'll want to do a follow up."

"Of course," she replies with a curt nod. "I'll also send along the media information for tomorrow."

Layla turns to me. "Are you okay if we stay?"

"Whatever you want, love."

"Well, that was way too fucking easy," Melanie laughs. "Sorry, it's late and I get a little sweary after hours. Here's my contact information, should you need anything between now and tomorrow evening. Please try to keep things PG here and at the wedding." She hands Layla her card. "I should get going, I promised my friends I'd meet them for a quick drink tonight." Melanie stands and Ethan joins her. "Oh, no, you're not coming, it's buffalo plaid night."

"You mean like those awful pyjamas you have?" I ask Layla.

Melanie answers for her, "The very same. Layla, you want to join us?"

"Oh, no. I have plans."

"Why can't I come?" Ethan scoffs. "Sage will just drink you under the table again."

Melanie addresses Layla and I. "He's full of shit. Have a good night you two. See you tomorrow." She kisses Ethan and seeing the two of them leaves an ache in my chest. They have to be somewhere in their mid-to-late forties. Is this how Layla and I will be in a decade?

"I'm going to walk her out. Here's my contact information, if you need anything for the wedding. Or, you know, if you need me to plan your own ceremony one day." He winks and walks his wife out of the hotel.

Layla looks off into the distance in thought for a few moments before turning to me and asking, "What did you mean by permanent, earlier?"

"What do you think I meant?"

She turns to face me. "I'm being serious."

"So am I," I insist.

"Then, answer me. What did you mean?" she asks again.

The question leaves me vulnerable but I ask anyway, "Do you love me?"

"Yes," she replies confidently.

"When you think about the future, five years from now, ten, twenty-five, do you see me in it?"

Layla chews on her lip, taking longer than I'd like to respond. I'm afraid she's about to say no when she laughs softly and replies, "Yes."

"Then, it shouldn't come as a shock that I want to spend the rest of my life with you."

"Ben, we've only been together a—"

"Month," I finish. "I know, and I don't fucking care. That's where I stand. If I had a ring on me, I'd be on one knee right now."

"You would not," she scoffs.

"Perhaps not literally, seeing as I'm in a bit of pain, but yes, I absolutely would ask you to marry me."

"That's ridiculous. You hate pineapple on pizza. What would we do on Friday night when I want to order in and the pizza place has one pizza available and they don't let you split toppings?" She tries her hardest to hide her smile but fails as the side of her mouth turns up and a soft laugh escapes her.

"In that extremely unlikely situation, you would get a pineapple pizza and I would order from another restaurant. Try again."

"Fine." She lifts her chin. "You drink tea with milk."

"You drink white mochas. Your point?"

Layla gasps. "They're delicious."

"So is tea," I retort.

Her eyes narrow. "You watch the wrong football."

"You, my love, watch the wrong football. There isn't even a foot except at kickoff. Nice try, though."

Layla groans but a smirk continues to tug at her lips. "You snore."

"I do not."

"Okay, fine, you don't."

"Are you out of reasons yet, sunshine?" I take a sip of my rum, awaiting her response.

"You have terrible meet-the-parents etiquette."

"I do," I admit.

"You don't deny it? You were awkward as fuck around my mom."

"You tease about how I acted with your mum, but I've never met anyone's parents before."

Layla's eyes widen in shock. "Come again?"

"You heard me. I've never met anyone's mum before."

"Never?"

"Never."

She pauses but then says softly, "I'm sorry, I didn't know."

"What have I said about apologies? There's no reason for you to be sorry. I know I was a bit of an arse, but I hope I can rectify it in the near future. She won't accept my help, though."

I explain to her that, after her mum left, I contacted her to replace her prosthetic with a higher end one. She refused but my offer put me in her good graces. At least for now.

What I don't tell Layla is last week I asked her mum for permission to propose, when the time comes. She told me if I dared to hurt her daughter, she would sic Amanda on me. I'm not sure what it is about Amanda, but I'm actually more concerned about her approval than Jennifer's when it comes to Layla. Needless to say, neither think I deserve Layla. They're both right, obviously, but I intend to marry her anyway.

"What do you say we get a good night's sleep? It's been a long day for both of us and tomorrow will be even longer," I offer.

"Small problem. I don't have any clothes. I had to buy these, since someone sent my baggage back to his place in Seattle." She cocks an eyebrow.

"Fuck, I'm sorry, I completely forgot. I'll order something for—"

"Not so fast, mister. I'll order my own clothes. We're not having another dress fiasco. We should probably get you a new phone, too. As hot as it is when you get growly and possessive, maybe next time don't destroy the only way you have to contact me."

"Come here." I slide my hand into her hair and bring her in for a slow, languid kiss.

"Are you sure you want to spend forever with me? I'm quite the handful," she teases.

I refuse to stop kissing her, managing between kisses, "You're mine, sunshine. I am absolutely spending forever with you. But no matter how successful you are, no matter how much money you have, you will not under any circumstances pay for a single fucking thing from this point forward. Is that understood?"

"What if I—"

"No, love." I pull back and her eyes dart between mine in question. "When I say you're mine, I mean it, in every sense of the word. Mine to love and mine to take care of. Period. End of discussion."

"Hard to enforce that when you don't have a phone." She shrugs.

"Someone is going to have difficulty sitting tomorrow."

Layla smiles brightly. "Promise?"

37

BEN

Last night, I stayed true to my word even though it took everything in me to keep my hands to myself. This morning, with her wrapped in my arms, is an entirely different story. Laying on our sides with her back pressed to my chest, I kiss her bare shoulder and she stirs, grinding against me.

"Darling, if you do that again, I'm going to fuck this beautiful arse." I grip a fistful and she giggles.

"Promise?" she echoes from last night sleepily, then rubs against me again.

I rip down her knickers and toss them to the floor. "I let you get away with your smart mouth last night, love. Not this morning."

"Too bad you're out of condoms," she yawns. *Shit.* "Just enter me bare. I know you want to, but only if the doctor gave you the green light. Don't want to hurt pierced Big Ben. Oh, and maybe no butt stuff? There will be a lot of sitting today at the wedding."

I don't know whether or not to take her seriously. "If I do, I'm going to fill you over and over so you feel me all fucking day." I splay my hand across her soft stomach, allowing myself a moment to fantasise about her carrying my child. I can't bring myself to admit it to her quite yet.

Her hand covers mine, lacing our fingers together. "I know what you're thinking."

"I assure you, you don't."

"Yes, I do." She lets go of my hand and reaches back between us, palming my cock. I bite down on her shoulder to hold back a moan. "I saw how you looked at me when I told you I had to go to the pharmacy for birth control, and how you're not the least bit upset when the condoms break."

Fuck. She knows.

Filled with stupid hope that she'll say she wants this as much as I do, I dare to ask, "What would happen if I made love to you all morning and you didn't go to the pharmacy later?" While I've always loved testing the line between pleasure and pain, Layla has embraced it. This, however, is newer territory for us.

Layla turns in my arms, frowning. "I'm not going to be your 'baby mama,' Ben. Is it hot to think about? Sure. But I'm not going to risk getting knocked up by a hot billion-aire, only to end up raising a child on my own."

"You'd be able to prove it was mine, so in a twisted world where we don't live happily ever after, you know I would take care of you."

"Money doesn't buy happiness. You, of all people, should understand that."

"You're right." I wrap her tightly in my arms and she sighs against me. "After the wedding, I still want to take you back home until everything is settled. If only for a month. But while we are there, what if we… Layla, I want to marry you."

"You just want to marry me so you can put a bun in my oven," she laughs.

I pull back and tilt her chin to look at me. "No, love. As much as I love the idea of us making something—instead of me destroying everything I touch—if you never want children, then we won't. This is about you and me. I was serious last night, I intend to spend the rest of my life with you, with or without the little nippers."

"For someone who is typically over-the-top romantic, this has to be the worst engagement ever performed. Who proposes to a woman after ripping off her panties, threatening to fuck her ass, then admitting he loves the idea of knocking her up? No, Ben, I will not marry you if you're proposing to me half naked with your cock sandwiched between us."

I bark out a laugh. "Darling, I didn't mean it as a proposal."

"Yes you did. You literally just said that while we are in England you want to marry me. Sounds to me a hell of a lot like a proposal." She shifts away from me and attempts to change the subject, "Are you hungry? Because I'm starving. What do you say we grab breakfast and pretend we never had this conversation?"

Wrapping an arm around her middle, I pull her back to me. "Not so fast. We can have breakfast in bed."

"Someone will still have to get up and grab the room service. I don't think you'll appreciate me opening the door half naked, seeing as you're all territorial today. *You're mine, grrr.*"

"No, love. I'm having you for breakfast." She laughs but it's cut short when I command, "On your back." I slide between her legs, my boxer briefs the only thing keeping me from slipping inside her. "You can tease all you want, but it doesn't change the fact that I intend to spend the rest of my days proving I'm worthy of you."

Layla wraps her legs around me. I savour the sting of her nails raking my back, pulling me closer. "You said you would ruin me," she whispers. "You succeeded. There will never be anyone else. You know I'm yours, I just like it when you get growly."

I bury my face in the crook of her neck, attempting to hold in my laughter. "What am I going to do with you?"

"You can start by taking off my top."

"I quite like this top, though." I slide my hand under it and cup her breast, swiping my thumb over her taut nipple. I tug on the piercing enough to elicit a sweet moan from her. She arches her back and I move lower, biting gently on her nipple through her satin tank. Fuck, I love to see her squirm. Her fingers tangle in my hair as I do the same to the other. As I lift her shirt enough to expose her bare stomach, I pepper kisses lower until I'm inches from her wet pussy. "How much time do I have?"

"What?" she asks breathlessly.

"How much time before we have to get ready?"

"Um, a few hours, I think."

I move lower, flicking my tongue around her clit piercing. She gasps and grips the sheets. "Not nearly enough time for me to do what I want with you."

"You can't tongue-fuck me for hours, Ben."

"You can't tell me what I can and cannot do with *my* pussy, sunshine. If I want to edge you for hours as punishment for your smart mouth, then that's what I'll do."

"Edge me?" she shrieks and props herself up on her elbows. "That's so fucked up."

I nip at the inside of her thigh. "Then be my good girl and let me take care of you properly, without interruption."

"Okay, Daddy." As soon as the word is out, she slaps her hand over her mouth.

I still. "What did you just say?"

Her eyes wide, she doesn't move her hand as she shakes her head. I take her clit between my teeth and suck hard. She screams out, grabs a pillow, and presses it against her face to muffle it.

"Want to try that again, love? What did you just call me?"

"Nothing. I didn't call you anything," she replies into the pillow.

"Darling, I'm going to ask you one last time. What did you call me?"

Layla removes the pillow and winces. "Daddy? But it was a joke I didn't—"

"Call me that again and I will absolutely put a baby in you, understood?"

She bites her lip, "Yes… *Daddy.*" I groan, slip off my underwear, and move my way up her body. "Oh shit! I was kidding, I'm sorry!" Her laughter fills the room and I can't help my smile.

"No, you're not the least bit sorry. And what have I said about apologising?" I tease her slick pussy with the tip of cock, testing her entrance but not pushing in, then grind my length against her clit.

"Ben," she moans.

"I want to feel you coming around my cock with nothing between us, but say the word, and I'll slip on trousers and buy condoms right this moment. Your choice, love."

"They break anyway."

Layla cups her fingers behind my neck and pulls me in to kiss her. I take my time exploring her mouth as her tongue sweeps across mine. While I ache to be inside her, to roughly claim her, I need to be careful. I allow myself to indulge in the fantasy that she won't run off for emergency contraception this afternoon, even if I don't voice it aloud.

I slip my cock inside her with ease. She's warm, wet, and tight; fucking perfection. I'm not going to last long. I push in to the hilt, making her gasp. Our kisses remain unrushed as she gives herself to me. I remain deep inside her, unmoving, wanting to memorise how it feels to have her this close to me. I slowly pull out and she whimpers into my mouth.

I pause to check in, "Is this okay? Are you?"

"More than okay. It's just a lot."

I kiss her again, whispering against her lips, "I know."

As I continue moving in and out of her, deeper each time, she kisses me harder. There will never be another woman in my life. This is the last woman I'll kiss, the last I'll fuck, the last and only one I'll love.

"I love you," she whispers, and those three little words unleash something in me. I don't quicken my pace, I don't drive harder into her, I make love to my future wife. I'm hers, and she's mine.

Her pussy tightens around me; she's close. "Let go for me, sunshine."

There's a knock at the door and we both groan.

"Sod off," I yell to the door. I don't care who the fuck it is, they are not stealing this moment from me.

"Sorry to interrupt the fuck fest! Will one of you check your damn phones?" Amanda yells back before there are retreating footsteps.

"You are *not* checking your phone," I growl to Layla.

"Fuck, I was so close!" she whines in disappointment.

I roll onto my back and pull her on top of me, remaining inside her. Her hair falls to one side of her shoulder, and I take advantage, gripping a fistful at the base of her neck to pull her closer. I lick up her throat and nip at her jaw, making her whimper. "Take what's yours, love. I want you to make a mess all over my cock."

Layla sits back, holding herself up with her hands on my chest. As she slides onto me, I rock her back and forth deeper onto my cock. She arches her back and moves her hands behind her to rest on my thighs, continuing to ride me. I reach between us and circle my thumb around her swollen clit, quickening her gasps and moans. I can take my time with her later but right now I need to own her pleasure. She's a fucking vision.

I tug on her piercing, knowing it will be her undoing. She cries out my name and I sit up, balancing with one hand behind me to wrap my other arm around her. As I pull her closer to me, I capture her screams with my mouth on hers. Her pussy pulses around me, and I kiss her harder, thrusting into her until I come undone. It takes me a moment to catch my breath as I fill her.

Having her with nothing between us is unlike anything I've experienced. I can blame it on the piercing, but it's as if Layla was meant to be mine, a missing piece to a puzzle that I went my entire life without. I want to remain inside her, desperate to hold on to the fantasy that one day she'll be my wife, pregnant with my child.

I shake away the thoughts and shift to pull her off of me, but she sits down further onto my cock. "Don't," she manages as she catches her breath.

"Don't what?"

"Don't pull out, Ben. I'll make a trip this afternoon, but for right now, we can pretend I'm not going to."

"You don't have—"

"It's okay, but… one of us has to be responsible."

"Fuck, I love you," I chuckle.

"I love you, too." She smiles, takes my face in her hands, and roughly kisses me.

I lay back and wrap both of my arms around her, never wanting to let go.

Mine.

38

LAYLA

Ben and I rinse off, then take a long, hot bath. Sitting in the tub with his arms wrapped around me and the jets massaging us, I'm the most relaxed I've been for the past few days. He can't seem to keep his hands off me—more than usual—making me feel loved and adored.

"We should get out, sunshine. Amanda said something about checking our phones earlier and neither of us ever did."

"True, but you did tell me not to check it."

Ben playfully pinches my side. "That was while I was inside you."

"I know," I laugh. "Fine, I'm starving anyway, after what you just did to me." He nips at my shoulder. "What? Deny that you didn't just ruin me for all other men."

He growls because... it's Ben. I've become accustomed to his possessive groans when it comes to me. I expect nothing less.

I try to get out of the tub but he pulls me back to him. "Five more minutes."

"You said we needed to get out! And we're already prunes."

The large bath is more of a hot tub and isn't handicap accessible like mine—there's no door and Ben has to lift up onto the edge and pivot his body to get out. Thankfully, there's a handrail to the side he's able to use to balance.

I dry us off and help him put on his leg. Every time I do, he looks at me with so much sadness and guilt. Assisting him doesn't bother me; he's never asked and he can do it himself. I do it because I want to. He fought me on it for weeks but finally gave in when I was a bitch and stole his prosthetic leg until he let me help him—a victory I'm not entirely proud of, but I needed him to know he's not alone and I'm here.

When I finally check my phone, I find several missed calls from Becca and a few texts from Amanda.

AMANDA

Stop shagging the hot billionaire and come to breakfast.

Fine, keep shagging the hot billionaire but come to lunch.

I'm going to keep saying shag until you text me back, bitch. It's way more fun than saying fuck.

Girl, you need to eat something besides a dick.

Ben peers over my shoulder and chuckles. "That was the big emergency?"

"It appears so. I need to stop fucking a hot billionaire. And eat, I guess." I shrug.

"Darling, tell your friend I can fuck you whenever, wherever, and however I like. But she's right, you should eat something, and you don't drink nearly enough water."

I feign shock. "I do too drink enough water."

"Coffee and energy drinks aren't water, love." Ben kisses my temple and pulls out clothes from one of the bags delivered late last night.

"Shit, I hope mine fit," I mutter to myself.

"What was that?" he asks, slipping on a fresh pair of boxer briefs.

"Nothing." I look through a few of the bags until I find the yellow knee-length skirt and gray sleeveless silk blouse. It's high cut to my collarbone and has a cute tie to the side—perfect for a late summer wedding.

I quickly get dressed. As I'm about to head to the bathroom to put on my makeup and fix my hair, Ben wraps his arms around me from behind and kisses my shoulder. His beard scratches me, making me laugh. I fucking love when he's sweet and affectionate like this.

"You're so beautiful," he whispers against my skin.

"I have to get ready." I turn my head and he kisses me softly. He pushes for more but I wriggle out of his hold and saunter off to the bathroom. "The wedding starts in a few hours and neither of us have eaten. Damn, I would love some tacos."

"Tacos? Don't tempt me, sunshine," he calls. "I'll bend you

over right now and have your delicious cunt for an appetizer."

"You're not eating *my* taco, Ben," I deadpan as I put in my earrings. "I want *actual* tacos. They're so much better here in California than back home."

"Shall we find a tequila bar that serves them?"

"Oooh yes! A margarita sounds amazing. Can you look one up while I get ready?"

Ben slips on his shoes and asks, "Should I check with Julian to see if they'd like to join us?"

"Probably a good idea. You're less likely to get handsy in front of your friend." I wink, returning to the vanity to finish prepping for tonight.

Tacos were as amazing as I expected and the margarita with a little extra orange liqueur was by far one of the best I've had in years. Ben teased that I have an obsession with all things orange; he's not wrong.

During the ride to the wedding, I feel lighter than I have in a while. Ethan called right before we left to assure us that everything was in order and that there's nothing to worry about from a media perspective.

While my stress level is nearly zero, I've been daydreaming about things Ben said to me today: the almost proposal, his near admission to having a breeding kink, how he insists he wants to spend the rest of his life with me. It's ridiculous, especially since we've known each other for such a short time, but I fell hard and fast for my morally orange billionaire. The last word sours in my gut. He only brings up money when I attempt to pay for things, but I'm not sure I like the idea of marrying into so much wealth.

I have my own money. Dylan has helped me turn the millions I've earned from my books into a comfortable nest egg I could live on for the rest of my life. I don't need a mansion or penthouse suite in a posh part of town.

It dawns on me that I know nothing about where he lives. He's told me story after story of his childhood, his college years—or uni, as he calls it—and even a sprinkling here and there about how he got into prosthetics and publishing. I never asked and he never shared about where he lives, and yet, here I am contemplating moving across the world for him.

"Penny for your thoughts, sunshine?" I'm pulled from my spiral as he brings our joined hands to his lips.

"I was just thinking: I know nothing about where you live."

"Shall I pull up a map for you?" he laughs.

"Don't be a smart ass, you know what I mean," I huff

"You know I'm from Canterbury."

"Yes, but is it a house, an apartment, a mansion the size of a village?"

"I have a small estate on the outskirts."

I eye him suspiciously. "Define small. How many bedrooms?"

"Eight."

"Eight?" I shriek. "Why would you need eight bedrooms?"

He shrugs. "I liked the property, so I bought it. Got it for a steal."

"Let me guess, ten-point-eight million?"

"No," he laughs. "Just shy of six-point-two."

"That's so gross." I shake my head.

Ben squeezes my hand. "It's big enough for visitors to not be on top of one another, has floor to ceiling windows in the common area, and I love that there are gardens and a small pond."

"Fuck. It's Pemberley, isn't it? This is some Jane Austen shit. You're going to go for a swim and walk out of a lake like a hotter Colin Firth ready to ravage me, aren't you?"

He keeps his voice low so our driver can't hear him. "If I wanted to ravage you, I wouldn't need to bring you home to do so. I'm no Darcy, love. I would take you right here." I bark a small, unattractive laugh. "Doubt me? Test me and I'll have that skirt hiked up and over your arse in three seconds." I suck in a breath. "But it would be a lie to say I haven't fantasized about taking you back to our home, tying you to our bed, with your head hanging over the edge, and fucking your throat while I place a vibrator between your legs. All so I can feel your moans and whimpers on my cock as you come." I swallow hard and he kisses my neck.

Did he say 'our' home? 'Our' bed?

"You're a lot of talk, Mr. Turner." A groan comes from deep within his chest. I bite my lip to keep from smiling. "Was it something I said?"

"Shall I have the driver turn around?"

"No," I reply softly, "we need to go."

My breath hitches as Ben peppers kisses up my neck to my jaw, then pulls back. "Have it your way, love. You're the one who chose to wear the vibrator tonight."

"You're the one who bought it and insisted I wear it today, even though we have one at my place. But I still have the remote," I sing as I pull it out of my bag and wave it like a winning lotto ticket. He snatches it from my hand and stuffs it in his pocket. "Ben," I squeak. "No!"

"I think we could use some fun tonight. I'll be hanging onto this for safe keeping." He pats his pocket. "Now, what do you say I kiss that red lipstick right off you and allow photos of us to surface, so everyone knows you're mine?"

"Too bad I paid top drugstore dollars for the kiss-proof one."

"Kiss-proof? We'll see about that, sunshine."

I've never been a fan of weddings. The pomp and circumstance, the over-the-top expenses for a one-day event, the faux happiness when everyone is stressed. I can think of no less than a thousand better ways to spend my time.

Harriet's wedding is small, but crowded with couples who are genuinely in love. In the front by the altar, Emma is fixing her husband's boutonniere. He appears less than thrilled to be here, which is expected with him giving away his eldest daughter, but when he looks at Emma, it's as if she is his whole world.

Julian and Becca are nowhere to be found—they're either late or have found a dark corner somewhere. Just as I can't stay away from Layla, he can't keep his hands to himself with his wife.

There's a man with his long hair tied up and muscular build, his arms wrapped around a short brunette. She has a service dog to her right, which is unexpected and I can't help my smile. Next to them is a tall blonde woman with a cane wearing a headset who appears to be working today, but the man she's with is whispering something to her, making her blush. Ethan and Melanie are seated with their children as he kisses her temple and pulls her closer.

There's so much love in the air, it's infectious.

Not a single one of them is faking it. This is what the books talk about, the same books I worked hard to pull from the shelves for so many years.

I never thought I would have what they have. I truly believed if I married, it would be for convenience, not for love. I'd find a model or actress who needed me for my money, and I would use her to keep the media off my arse about settling down.

Now, when I think about my future, I only see Layla. Even back when I thought she was an inexperienced author on a fact finding mission for an upcoming novel, there was always something about her. She's different, special... and mine.

It's a small gathering, only thirty or forty chairs set for guests. We find two seats toward the back on the bride's side of the aisle. I rest my arm on the back of her chair, and Layla leans into me, resting her head on my shoulder. These past few days have been exhausting, to say the least. I can't wait to bring her home and get back to my routine, except it feels wrong to return to what I've done for years.

I think back to Layla and her ridiculous questionnaire, asking me about charities, and I'd love to help more people like her mum. While she might not be able to handle a leg like mine, she deserves something far better than what she's using. The charities I support aren't doing enough. Perhaps it's time for me to start my own.

As I blink back to reality, Layla is deep in conversation with Amanda sitting to her right. I'm not entirely sure when she sat down or what they're talking about. I reach into my pocket to take out my phone. I must've accidentally brushed against the remote for Layla's vibrator because a quiet squeak comes from her and there's a faint buzzing sound against the wooden chair. Layla's nails dig into my thigh and I quickly retrieve the remote to turn it off.

I lean down to whisper, "Sorry, love. T'was an accident."

"It was *not* an accident," she seethes through gritted teeth.

"I promise." I pull her closer and kiss her temple.

"You two are worse than Julian and Becca. At least when I sit next to them, I don't have to hear a vibrator go off." Amanda crosses her arms and leans back in her seat. "When does this start? I could use a drink."

The girls continue talking and I bide the time scrolling my phone. I finally get a good look at some of the recent paparazzi photos. Six photos in, I spot one of Roger in handcuffs, and I smile to myself. Everything I set in motion has come to fruition. Not only did they finally take him down for mild insider trading, he was caught with his secretary in my office, fucking her on my desk. Money may not buy happiness, but it can buy the best private investigators in the business. Thankfully, I have no plans on returning to the Seattle office, or that desk, unless Layla wants me to.

With Roger facing criminal charges, the only hurdles are Layla still being under contract with Kipling and negative press swirling around our relationship. If Ethan's right, we can spin it just right and it'll be seen as a sweet, workplace romance.

Phones around us begin buzzing and chiming with news alerts. Layla doesn't check hers, but Amanda takes out her phone to see her notifications. She gasps, "Layla-love, did you see this?" She scrolls twice as they read together. "Ben's A Dick, did you do this?"

"As if I'd tell you with that nickname you've saddled me with," I chuckle.

Layla chews on her lip as she reads. "Someone has to tell Harriet, but she's getting ready."

I glance up and Emma is covering her mouth as she shows her phone to Dylan. I point them out to Layla and assure her Harriet's mother would take care of it.

The seats begin to fill and, after a few minutes of murmurs and whispers, the priest announces the ceremony is about to begin.

The wedding was beautiful. Harriet and Robbie are young but he's clearly smitten with her. Though I only met him briefly at the airport, I can appreciate how protective he is of her. There's much to celebrate today and I'm grateful to have had a front row seat to all of it.

"I can't believe you missed buffalo plaid night! It was the best one yet," the shorter brunette from earlier, who I have come to know as Charlotte, coos, her service dog sitting attentively at her side.

"I know, I brought my pants and everything, but there was an… *incident*. At the airport. And again last night," Layla carefully replies and I nearly choke on my drink. "Sounds like you all had an amazing time."

"There was no incident," I insist. "It was my fault."

Layla side-eyes me. "At least you didn't hide my purse this time."

"For the umpteenth time, I didn't hide it!" I protest, then mumble into my glass, "I threw it away."

"What was that?"

"Nothing," I reply with a shrug.

Charlotte giggles. "Even if he did hide it, at least he didn't throw your phone into a marina. Dylan tossed my sister's phone when she tried to pay for something. Jason's tried a few times but failed."

I quickly change the subject away from money and discarded belongings and ask Charlotte, "If you don't mind me asking, how long have you had your service animal?"

"Feels like ages." She reaches down to pet the dog. "Besvär's getting old but she's such a good girl. I can't bear to part with her."

"I've been thinking a lot about accessibility—making affordable prosthetics, wheelchairs and mobility options, as well as service animals, available to people when their insurance is unable to subsidize the majority of the cost."

"Ben! Since when?" Layla asks.

I reply with a shrug. "The last few days."

"That would be incredible," Jason chimes in. "Charlotte and I covered the difference when she got Besvär. My son is also autistic and, in order for him to live more independently, we will be getting him one as well, when he's ready."

I don't want to pry further, but I'm gathering from his phrasing that Charlotte is neurodivergent. If I can help men and women like her have a fuller, more independent life, why shouldn't I throw my money at accessibility options for people who need them?

"So, what spurred this on?" Charlotte asks curiously. "You said the last few days, but supporting charities for people with disabilities isn't the kind of thing that just magically comes to someone. Do you have friends who are wheelchair users or are neurospicy?"

"No, actually, I was in a motorbike accident when I was younger and lost half my leg." Layla holds my hand tight. While this conversation typically makes me uncomfortable, with Charlotte and Jason, I don't feel judged. "I started a prosthetic company but sold it and invested in publishing when I saw a greater opportunity for growth."

"Oh my gosh, can I see it?" Charlotte asks excitedly.

"Sweetheart," Jason warns, shaking his head.

"It's fine, really." I stand and lift my trousers to expose my leg to mid-calf.

"Shit, that has to be the coolest thing I've ever seen!" I can't help but laugh at her response; Charlotte's enthusiasm is a breath of fresh air, reminding me of Layla's positivity. I pull down the leg of my trousers and take a seat.

Halfway into a sip of my rum, she asks, "So, when are you two tying the knot?"

I'm not sure if she meant to shock me, but I don't flinch. "Whenever she wants. I would marry her today, if she'd have me." Layla, on the other hand, is in a choking fit at my words. "Are you all right, love?" I rub her back as she holds her hand to her chest, catching her breath. I hand her a glass of water and she finishes it in one go. "I'm glad to see you're drinking more water." She chuckles through her coughs and I pull her close.

The wedding announcer asks all the single women to join him on the dance floor for the bouquet toss. Layla doesn't get up, so I whisper, "That includes you, sunshine. Unless you intend to marry me right now, you're technically single."

"Will you stop joking about that?" She laughs and kisses me cheek.

As Layla stands, I grip her wrist and tug her down until our faces are an inch apart. "Not a joke, darling." She gives me a chaste kiss and makes her way to the dance floor.

The bouquet is tossed and Amanda lets it fall on the ground in front of her while she stands there unamused and stoic. The majority of those in attendance laugh, but to save face with those who didn't, she snatches it off the ground with a smirk and walks over to my table.

Amanda leans in and pierces me with her murderous gaze as she hands it to me. "Go marry my friend, but if you do something stupid, you know what will happen." She glances briefly to my lap. Without a doubt, she would make good on her promise. Charlotte overheard and is giggling to herself as Amanda rights her posture and heads back to her table.

Layla joins us a moment later and asks, "What was that about?"

"I don't know," I lie. "She handed me the bouquet and went back to her table. She must've thought I was the next to get married." She eyes me suspiciously.

The rest of the reception is uneventful. With it being the last dance of the evening, I stand and offer my hand. "May I have this dance, sunshine?"

Layla has spent the evening sitting and talking with the attendees at the table or dancing with her friends. Her smile is wide as she whispers, "You hate dancing."

"Oh, I'm aware, but this one is slow enough. Come on." I nod to the centre of the room.

Layla takes my hand and I guide her to the dance floor. As I keep our interlaced fingers tucked against my chest, I splay my free hand on her lower back, pulling her close to me. She typically shies away from eye contact but right now, she doesn't look away. I lean in and kiss her softly, keeping it respectable for a wedding reception even though I miss the taste of her.

"We don't have to leave for England, love. No one can hurt you here. But I still want to take you home, if only for a few weeks."

"And you won't propose a dozen times?"

"No, I'll propose two dozen."

"Well, if that's the case, how can I refuse?" She lifts onto her toes and kisses my cheek. "Or we can just stay there?"

I huff a laugh. "And you tell *me* not to joke."

"Not a joke. I love you and if you want to go back home, then I'll come."

"To be clear, I want you to move in with me."

"All right, book *daddy*, you twisted my arm. I'll move in with you." Her mischievous smile reaches her eyes.

"I warned you, sunshine." I reach into my pocket to turn on her vibrator and lean in, nipping at her ear. She whimpers. "I'll make good on my promise. I don't care who sees."

"Then, let's go home."

Oh, sunshine, with you, I already am.

40

LAYLA

ONE MONTH LATER

"I told you, they're in bedroom four!" I shout down the hall.

"Like I know which one bedroom four is! There are no numbers on them!" Ben yells back.

"It's your house! You should know where your suits are hanging!"

"*Our* house, sunshine!"

Sitting on the bed with my laptop, my back against the headboard, I'm wrapping up a round of edits on my book. It was supposed to be a contemporary billionaire romance, but turned into a fantasy pirate romance instead. Ben hates the premise, despite admitting it's some of my best work.

I groan, rolling my eyes. "It's not *my* fault that *you* have eight bedrooms. I had to make sense of it somehow! One through four on the left, five through eight on the right." I should've just spray painted the doors.

We have the same conversation once or twice a week. I hate that the house is so large. If it wasn't for all of the staff he employs guiding me when I need them, I would be one lost girl.

Roger's trial is today. 'Trial of the century,' as they're calling it. Ben has to testify and, with the whirlwind of Harriet's wedding, we didn't have a chance to really process what happened that day. When I envisioned Roger losing his company, I figured we would run it into the ground, destroying its profitability by stealing all of the authors from Kipling. Ben didn't allow any of my plans to come to fruition, which I'm grateful for. It was impulsive and would've only hurt the authors and support staff who stayed behind, not Roger.

Ben hired a few investigators to look into the company's profits, as well as Roger's personal accounts. There was a paper-trail a mile long of him tipping off people about when specific books were being released, which in turn gave them an edge when it came to investments. I still don't quite understand how the stock market or portfolios work—that's what I pay Dylan for. On top of it all, Roger's sexytime video went viral. I have to admit, I was impressed at his agility.

Even through it all, it's no surprise I've been pseudo-proposed to eighteen times in the past month. Eighteen. Fucking. Times. If I thought he was serious, I might actually say yes. It's usually a heat of the moment conversation after a little primal play or when he's trying to knock me up. He hasn't but there's no harm in him fantasizing he did.

I pause for a moment from my editing to do a little mental math, thinking back to when my last period was. I haven't had one since a few weeks before we came here and we've been here...

One month.

Fuck.

"Ben! Get in here!"

"If you're not tied up and naked in our bed, I'm not coming!" He yells back.

"Now is not the time! This is serious!" I should probably get dressed soon but wearing panties and his old oversized tee is far more conducive to my writing experience and productivity.

I've been on the pill since I got here but with how much we have sex, there is a very real possibility it was completely useless. I was warned to wait at least two weeks to have sex without protection, which we did, but it's still not one-hundred percent effective. And there's the matter of all the broken condoms.

Ben comes in, wearing his dark blue suit and light blue collared shirt underneath. He hasn't trimmed his beard in a few days; it's fuller than normal. The contrast between polished attire and his sexy pirate look he has going on is doing things for me. I'm pretty sure everyone is going to figure out he was the inspiration for my character.

I shouldn't be thinking about my book. I could be pregnant!

"Yes, love?"

"When was I supposed to start my period?"

He looks off to the side with pinched brows for a moment.

When realization finally hits him I'm a week late, his brows shoot up and his eyes darken.

"Ben," I warn as he stalks toward me.

"Sunshine," he purrs back.

"Don't get excited."

"Oh, it's a little late for that." He slips off his jacket and tosses it onto the chair, unbuttoning his shirt.

"You have to get to the courthouse."

"Unless the court you're referring to offers a marriage certificate, I'm not going. I have more important things to tend to."

Ben tosses my laptop to the side, grabs my ankles, and pulls me to the edge of the bed, making me yelp. "You need to stop with the fake engagement thing. Find a new hobby."

He braces himself with a hand on either side of my head. "Do you think you're actually pregnant?"

"I don't know, but it's possible. It could be my hormones being weird, or stress, but I'm late."

"Fuck, Layla, you're serious? There's a possibility I could be a father?"

"You never call me Layla," I whisper. He shakes his head and kisses me. I mutter against his lips, "I told you, don't get excited. I have to take a test."

"Today, of all days, you have to tell me this?"

"I know, I know! The trial is a big deal. Your testimony—"

"No, love. Reach in my pocket," he commands.

"I swear, if it's a vibrator and remote…"

Ben hangs his head forward and laughs, "No, love." He meets my gaze again. "Take it out."

I reach in and feel something soft but almost prickly, like velvet, the shape of a…

"Ben," I breathe.

"Take it out, sunshine, so I can ask you properly. Even if you're still in my old uni shirt and knickers. I wouldn't have it any other way."

I open the box to find what looks to be an orange sapphire, emerald-cut ring, with diamond trillions on either side. "Ben, this isn't a…"

"Sunshine, for the thousandth time, will you marry me? I was going to ask you at dinner tonight, but I don't want to wait another moment without being able to call you my fiancée, even if I'd rather call you my wife."

All I can do is nod. He's serious this time. There's a ring. A rock the size of Texas.

"Is that a yes, darling?"

"You really want to marry me? What if I'm not—"

"Yes, I want to marry you more than anything. I don't care if you're pregnant or not, love, I want you to be my wife. My intentions have always been clear. I'd rather fight with you every day about too many bedrooms, than spend a single day without you."

"And if I'm not pregnant?"

"Then you're not," he replies confidently. "I want to marry my first and only love."

"Okay," I breathe, my heart leaping into my throat.

Ben smiles and chuckles, "That's all I get? An 'okay?'"

"Yes, *Benedict*, I'll marry you."

Ben is about to kiss me when there's a faint knock at the open bedroom door. "So, did she say yes? Can I smother you in confetti yet? I have to pick up Jennifer from the airport in fifteen, can I use one of your fancy drivers?"

"Amanda, what the fuck are you doing here?" I shriek.

"So help me, if you walk in on me and my future-wife one more time, you can fuck right off and never be invited back here," he growls.

Amanda raises her hands in surrender. "Fair enough, my timing is shit. Everyone will be here this evening, but Ben's A Dick decided to move up the timeline. Congrats on the maybe baby, by the way."

"Did you listen to our whole conversation?" Ben asks and Amanda leaves without answering.

I can't help the laugh that escapes me. This whole thing is so surreal. I pause for a moment, my laughter ceasing as I ask, "Did she say my mom was at the airport?"

He kisses me again and chuckles against my lips, "Get ready, sunshine. As soon as the trial is over, I have a surprise for you."

41

BEN

"You know I hate surprises," Layla grumbles, arms folded over her chest.

After my testimony, I messaged Julian to ensure our guests are scarce. Layla is already aware her mum arrived, which I was able to cover and tell her I invited her for an engagement celebration in a few days.

I don't want to wait another moment without her being completely mine. What I have planned can go either way, and the pressure of everything could have her retreating from me. It's a risk worth taking if it means I get to spend the rest of my life with someone who makes me want to be a better man and loves me with my flaws.

I'm fully aware I've gone from corporate pirate to the male equivalent of a "live, laugh, love" cliché poster, but I couldn't care less. There isn't another woman on earth who sees me like she does. There will *never* be anyone but Layla.

Once everything is in place, I remove Layla's blindfold in our library filled with all of our friends and family. She gasps and I wrap her in my arms, kissing the top of her head, as I whisper, "Will you marry me today, right now?"

"Today?" she squeaks

"They think this is an engagement party. Say no, and I call off the pastor. It's soon, but——"

"Yes, I want to marry you." Her smile is wide and my heart skips a beat at her words. "But are you sure about this? I'm a pain in the ass."

The room grows quiet, only a faint murmur; not enough to drown out what I want to tell her. I take a deep breath and speak quietly enough only Layla can hear, though I'm sure Amanda is lip-reading. "Darling, I wanted to marry you our first night together at your flat. You're the love of my life and I want to wake up tomorrow with a ring on my finger that shows we belong to each other."

Without hesitation, she counters, "Tomorrow is Sunday. If you promise me mimosas with bagels smothered in avocado and gruyere, then I will absolutely marry you today."

"I love you so fucking much, sunshine. I promise bagels whenever you like, but no mimosas until you take a test," I insist. Unable to resist, I kiss her. While it's less fire than I'm used to with her—likely due to her mother being in attendance—I hold back. Perhaps I've figured out the whole 'meet the parents' thing, after all? Probably not, but I'm a step closer.

"We have an announcement," she says loud enough for everyone to hear, with a beaming smile. "Apparently, my fiancé planned an engagement party that is doubling as a wedding." While there are gasps and cheers, Layla glances down at her clothes and whispers to me, "I didn't dress for a wedding, Ben."

"Do you think I care what you're wearing? It's not as if you'll be wearing it for long, love," I smugly reply with my hand resting on her belly. I dare to hope, but even if she isn't, I'm the happiest man alive that she said yes to spending the rest of her life with me.

Edmund ushers us out of the room, where we meet Ethan, Sage, and a staff of no less than seven other event planners. "All right, so that didn't go entirely as planned," Ethan jests, "but we've dealt with worse. At least your emergency venue licence came through in time or we'd be having a wedding in a fucking barn."

"It's a stable," I retort.

Edmund laughs. "Ethan, you're running in-room interference while the couple gets ready. Sage, my love, you're in charge of our bride. Everyone else? Buckle up, it's going to be a fun hour and a half."

For the next half an hour, Edmund—or Tyler, as Layla knows him—and his team transform our library into the perfect ceremony space. The two-story, floor to ceiling bookshelves provide the perfect backdrop, and there are details of red, yellow, and orange throughout.

I stand at the end of the aisle with the pastor as music begins to play. For years, I thought I would be nervous to take this final step, but with Layla, every moment of this feels right. My only anxiousness comes from excitement that I'll get to spend the rest of my life with the most incredible woman I've ever known. She's changed me for the better.

The doors open and Layla is breathtaking. She's wearing a champagne satin gown that's form-fitting to her knees, trumpeting to the floor. Her hair is pinned in soft curls and she's wearing my favourite red lipstick. I can't wait to kiss it away.

Layla's mum finally came around and was fitted for a new prosthetic a few weeks back. It's comfortable enough that she can walk twenty paces without pain or risk of falling. While she prefers her wheelchair most days, today she's walking her daughter down the aisle. A tear escapes my eye and I brush it away, schooling my expression. Layla smiles, shaking her head. She caught me and will tease me mercilessly later about how I dare to show emotion and will lose my citizenship here. Worth it to see Jennifer happy.

When they reach the end of the aisle, her mum places Layla's hand in mine and whispers to me, "Take care of my girl." She sits in her wheelchair in the front row, next to Amanda, Becca, and Julian.

I look out to the rest of the seats and my mum is a blubbering mess. Like me, she honestly never expected me to ever get married, let alone marry someone for love. The two seats next to her are vacant; Jack must be running behind and didn't make it in time. Cameron, my other cousin, is stuck on an archaeological dig involving bridges or something equally boring, and wasn't able to attend last minute.

As I take Layla's hands in mine, I brush a kiss to her cheek. "I love you, sunshine, but I don't deserve you."

"Yes, you do. You always have," she whispers back, and my heart swells. She's wrong, but I'll spend the rest of my life proving her right.

The pastor keeps the ceremony short, as requested. When we finally say our 'I dos' I don't wait another moment, taking her face in my hands and kissing her. I can't help the growl that escapes me, she tastes like lime and orange—the remnants of a margarita.

"Did you have a quick drink, love?" I whisper against her lips. The pastor clears his throat and we break apart. She mouths "virgin," and I breathe a sigh of relief. "My apologies, please continue." He finishes the ceremony with words I couldn't care less about until he says "man and wife," and I go straight back to kissing the hell out of my now-wife. There are cheers around us but it's muted; my only focus is her. She's everything and so much more.

We finally join our friends and family, who are offering their congratulations. While talking with Layla, my mum, and Amanda, a hand clamps on my shoulder. "Shite, I'm late."

I turn and hug my cousin, clapping his back twice before breaking apart. "You missed the wedding, but you made it in time for the reception. Where are my manners? Jack, you remember my wife, Layla, This is her friend, Amanda. Amanda, this is my cousin, Jack."

Amanda's eyes are wide, the blood has drained from her face. Jack chuckles, takes her hand, and kisses her knuckles. "My wee spitfire, what are you doing here?"

"Darling, I'm not going to ask you again. Sit on my fucking face."

"No! I'm the size of a small suburban city. I'll suffocate you and leave our unborn children fatherless. Hard pass." Layla continues her hovering, which will only last a few minutes; her thighs will give out and I'll win this round.

I don't wait, grabbing her thighs and pulling her onto my mouth. She cries out, eventually giving in as I swirl my tongue around her clit and take her piercing between my teeth. I savor my time teasing her, my hands roaming to appreciate every inch of her. Next spring, we'll have not one, but two little ones running around. Our alone time will be scarce.

With the pregnancy, she's so sensitive that the moment I drive two fingers inside and curl them twice, she comes hard on my tongue, screaming my name. This past month has become a fun game of 'how many times can I make my wife come?' So far, she can only handle five. I slow my pace as she comes down from her orgasm, then I slide out from under her.

"Stay right there, sunshine, you know I'm not done with you."

Layla's still catching her breath, fingers gripping on our headboard. Her swollen belly carrying our children only makes her more beautiful. I take out a small anal plug from our bedside table and a bottle of lube, adding a dollop to the tip and a little around the sides.

"You leave this in until I say you can take it out. Are we clear, love?" She nods and I slowly slide it into her tight hole. "Fuck, you're exquisite." I playfully bite one of her perfectly round arse cheeks and she yelps.

"Am I allowed to move yet?

"Not yet." I move further onto the bed and sit, resting my back against the headboard. "Come here." She climbs onto me, sinking onto my cock torturously slow. I grip her hips and rock her back and forth to help her adjust to me. "We're not going to play today, love."

"Why the hell not?" she pouts.

"I don't want to be rough with you right now. I want to worship this incredible body of yours."

She snort-laughs. "Yeah, okay. This incredible body that's the size of a blimp."

"You're hardly showing. But dare to talk about my beautiful wife that way again, and I won't let you come."

Layla kisses me, chuckling against my lips. "Can we play later?"

"It'll be late. We have your book release party, and tomorrow is the charity gala; you'll need your rest."

"Why must we do all the rich people things?" she groans.

"I know, the timing is shit. Tell you what, you're going to let me make love to my wife, then we can play," I offer.

She doesn't respond with words, instead sliding further onto my cock until she's taken all of me. I wrap my arms around her, not wanting a single inch of space between us but being mindful of her growing belly. I thrust up into her, matching the pace of her grinding on me. I love when she gives herself to me completely, tangling her fingers in my hair, her tongue teasing mine, begging for more. She wants me to lose control—mark her, claim her. I don't give in.

It feels too good having her ride me and I need to slow down but she's close. My balls tighten and she whispers, "Come for me," into my mouth, kissing me harder.

A growl erupts from my chest and I roll her onto her back. "My little siren, you think you're in charge here?"

"No... *Daddy.*" I spread her wide and thrust into her harder. "Right there, just like that," she moans, the delicious sound filling the room.

"Oh, I am absolutely your Daddy. I've warned you countless times, my love. Yet, you never heed my warning. I can't very well put another baby in you, now can I?" Her nails dig into my back, pulling me closer. "You'll have to settle for me coming over and over inside you until I'm dripping down your legs when you stand. I want you aching for me the rest of the night. And don't you dare think about cleaning up."

"I'm so close... *please.*"

"Darling, you know I love it when you beg." After a few more thrusts, she arches into me, her head hanging back as she screams out in pleasure. She pulses around me and it's enough to almost push me over the edge. I carefully remove the anal plug and toss it aside to clean later, then roll onto my side, still inside her, as our breathing slows.

"Do we have time for another?" she whimpers, biting her lip.

"You, my wife, are insatiable. But I haven't come yet. Where's your favourite yellow toy?"

Layla reaches over and takes out her vibrator from the bedside table, handing it to me. I pull out of her perfect cunt and turn her onto her side, then slowly push my cock into her arse. "You know what to do if it's too much." She nods, giving me the green light to edge her a little. I turn her vibrator on to the lowest setting and place it on her clit.

"Fuck, that feels good," she sighs as I press further in.

"You're doing so well, love, taking my cock like this." I kiss and graze my teeth on her shoulder, moving the vibrator up and down her pussy. "Pull on your nipples" She pinches them, tugging on her piercings. "Just like that." As she cups my neck, she clings to me like a lifeline. I fucking love when she gives in to me. When she stops, I purr, "I didn't say you could stop, darling." I drop the vibrator and move my hand to play with her nipple piercings, loving the feel of her full breasts in my hand.

"Touch me," she begs.

Continuing to thrust in and out of her, I reach between her legs and glide two fingers inside her. I curl my fingers at the same pace as I'm driving into her, kissing and sucking on her neck. While I hadn't planned on marking her anywhere someone might see, something feral in me takes over and I leave a deep pink bruise and teeth marks on her neck. She'll need to wear her hair down to hide it, but a dark part of me wants everyone we meet tonight to know what we've done.

Layla grips my wrist as her pussy clenches around my fingers. "I know you're close, but you're going to be my good girl and come when I tell you to." When I pull my fingers out, she whimpers as I suck them clean. I grab the vibrator again. "I want to hear you scream, love."

I turn it on to the highest setting and place it on her clit. She jolts at the sensation. "It's too much."

"You can take it. Say the word and we stop," I remind her.

Layla shakes her head but tenses. I turn the vibrator to the third setting and she gasps at the sudden increase of stimulation. "Not yet, sunshine." I slowly increase the vibration until it's at its max. Her breath quickens and I've tortured both of us enough. I thrust harder, but not faster as she tightens around me. "You did so well. Come for me, sunshine." I press the vibrator harder against her clit and she screams my name. Hearing her has me coming hard and fast, unable to catch my breath. I hold her tight, kissing every inch of her I have access to as I empty myself inside her.

She's a fucking goddess, and I worship at her altar. I love her more than words could ever express. While I still don't deserve this incredible woman in my arms, maybe one day I will.

The rest of the morning we spend in bed, the majority of it with me inside her. I honestly never intended to get her pregnant, but I'd be lying if I said it wasn't the biggest turn on of my life when we confirmed it the morning after the wedding. I took her home from the doctors and made love to my irresistible wife, then fucked her like I could breed her again. Every time I fill her, the same satisfaction washes over me.

If we didn't have to go out tonight, I'd insist on no shower or bath. I love the idea of her smelling like sex the rest of the day, especially since she looks so beautiful and well-fucked right now.

Unfortunately, tonight will require a bit of professionalism.

"No one will miss me if I don't show, right?" Layla asks between yawns.

I slide my hand into her hair and kiss her deeply, chuckling against her lips. "It's your book release party, they will absolutely miss you."

"I'm just so tired. Is there a nap room?"

"Nap room?"

"Yeah," she laughs. "A room where I can take a nap."

With our schedules these past few weeks, we were making up for lost time today. I fear I may have gone too far with her and she'll fall asleep during her reading. "I'm sorry, sunshine. I know today was a lot for you."

"So, I'm not allowed to apologise to you, but you're allowed to apologise to me?"

"Sounds perfectly fair to me. What do you say when we get home, I draw you a bath with your favourite orange and lavender bubble bath, and we can wear those hideous black and white plaid pyjamas you insisted I have my own pair of after Harriet's wedding. We'll spend the evening reading or watching whatever you like."

She sighs wistfully. "That sounds amazing."

"Consider it done." I bring our joined hands to my lips.

We arrive at the pub a little later than everyone else. Since Layla can't drink, I've opted for sobriety until the twins are born, and order two lemonades with lime garnishes from the bar—the closest thing to a margarita that she'll be having for a while. We take a seat near her podium, where she'll be doing her live reading later.

I leave Layla to chat with a few of the other local authors who came to support her tonight. After making my rounds, I ensure the signing table is set up with Layla's favourite orange pens and enough bookmarks for everyone in attendance. Everything seems in order. As I'm making my way back to her, I spot my cousin, Jack.

"How's married life treating you?" he asks, sipping his whisky and adjusting his glasses.

"How's Amanda?" I counter.

He sputters a cough mid-sip. "I don't know what you mean. I haven't seen her since the wedding." As much as he pretends I didn't hear him call her his 'wee spitfire,' there's no denying something happened between those two.

"Right. Well, I think I've solved your funding situation for the additional research you wanted to do. Can we chat after the gala?"

"Of course, I'll give you a ring." Jack claps me on the back and takes a seat. If everything goes to plan, he'll end up with more than the money he needs for his project.

Layla takes the podium and I find a seat in the front row. She talks for a few minutes about how her project began as a story about a morally grey billionaire, but telling one about a villain who becomes a hero to get the girl was far more interesting to write. While I don't enjoy that he's a pirate, it's inspired by our story. How could I not love it?

After her quick reading, she receives a standing ovation from the entire crowd. Joining her at the podium, I take her in my arms and whisper, "Darling, I'm so fucking proud of you."

Layla did all of this on her own, getting out from under Kipling—or what's left of it—and going independent. Julian helped her find a talented female narrator and he voiced the male main character in her book. It's due to come out in a few weeks. She organised all of it, including a small book tour. Layla couldn't wait to release her book, and now that she's an independent author, she can do whatever the fuck she wants—including releasing her paperback and e-book early for her readers.

"I love you," she whispers back.

"Not as much as I love you, sunshine."

BONUS EPILOGUE — AMANDA

Layla and Ben's wedding was beautiful. As much as I give him a hard time, he's not *actually* a bad guy. Sure, he's destroyed careers over the years, but he's obsessed with my friend and knows if he dares to hurt her, there's an entire village of people who will see to it that he's thrown out to sea for a proper pirate burial.

Between Becca and Layla, my friends all seem to be living their best married lives. While I'm happy for them, I'm still the quirky, single friend and the odd woman out. It didn't help seeing the one man I've been craving since he left New York.

After a quick trip to the gym—*okay, so I just used the sauna and hot tub*—I check the mail and head up to my apartment. Once inside, I toss down my keys and sift through bills and junk mail. There's a burnt-orange envelope with handwritten typography that appears to be an invitation. I check the back for a return address and can't help my smile; it's Ben and Julian's new charity providing accessibility options for various disabilities. It's the day after Layla's book release; I should be able to swing it.

Our morally gray hero took a sharp turn onto Good Guy Avenue and I couldn't be happier to see it.

I'm actually a little nervous for the gala tonight. I'm sad I missed Layla's release party, but with my flight delayed, the soonest I could get to London was this morning. My preggo friend is forgiving, I'm mostly worried about this fancy event where I won't know which fork to use when.

I arrive and walk up entirely too many steps to the library. I'm impressed it's even more beautiful than the libraries in New York. Distracted by the architecture, I miss a step and nearly fall, if it weren't for someone catching me.

"Are you okay, lass?" a familiar, sexy as fuck voice asks behind me.

Shit.

"Oh, yes, thank you. I'm fine." I right myself and dust off my dress to ensure there are no marks from my almost-tumble. I turn and glance up. With him being two steps below me, we're the same height. The moment our eyes meet, my breath is stolen from me. "Hi, Jack."

"You got my invitation, I see." His boyish grin with the little wrinkles at the edge of his eyes is making my stomach do funny things… almost like *butterflies*?

Gross.

"*Your* invitation?" My brows pinch. "Ben and Julian invited me."

"You didn't get my note?"

"What note?"

"On the back of the invitation?"

I pause for a moment, eyeing him curiously, but then take it out of my purse to see what the hell he's talking about. Sure enough, there's a handwritten note from him.

**IT MAY HAVE ONLY BEEN ONE NIGHT,
BUT I CAN'T STOP THINKING ABOUT YOU.
-JACK**

Oh no. Oh no no no. This can't be happening. My little cinnamon roll archaeologist has a crush. Shit.

My cheeks heat. "Sorry, I didn't see this before. We should… head inside."

"May I escort you?" Jack offers his arm and, after a shaky breath, I link mine in his.

"Sure." He leads us up the rest of the steps, attempting to steal glances. I refuse to give in, and once we reach the top, we check in at the door. "Well, thank you for the escort. I can take it from here."

His face falls and he looks like one of those dogs in an animal shelter donation video. And, now, I feel like an asshole. Before I can change my mind, I move through the crowd to find my table.

Checking the name plates, I breathe a sigh of relief; Jack is not seated with me. I take a seat and the waiter comes by for my drink order. I ask for my usual—a whiskey sour. I'll be throwing back quite a few of these tonight with the way things are going.

I'm seated next to Bartholomew Jackson, III. Pretentious as fuck name. I shake my head with a light scoff, feeling so incredibly out of place here.

My drink arrives and, moments later, Jack takes a seat to my left where this Bartholomew fellow is supposed to sit. "Sorry, I think that seat's taken." I gesture to the nametag.

"Aye, by me."

"Bartholomew? So, is Jack a nickname? Or a pseudonym?"

"Nickname. Would you rather call me Barty?" he asks playfully, wiggling his eyebrows.

"Absolutely not." I bark a laugh.

Layla takes a seat to my right with a huff. "Fuck, I'm tired."

"How are my favorite little friends doing in there?" I ask, rubbing her belly as if I'm summoning a genie.

"They're being little assholes, I still have at least six months before they decide to show their faces. Whoever said pregnancy is amazing is a fucking liar."

Ben sits next to Layla without his usual pirate rum. I find it endearing he's not drinking until their children are born. "Jack. Amanda, how was your trip?" He possessively splays his hand across her belly. I'm a thousand percent sure he has a breeding kink, no matter how much Layla denies it when I ask; he's entirely too excited she's knocked up.

"Oh, it was fine," I reply, finishing my drink quickly and signaling to the server for another.

After three more whiskey sours, I'm officially drunk and have bid on some sort of castle tour in Scotland, as well as a whiskey tasting in Ireland. At least they'll keep me busy while I'm here, and far away from the hot Scot who keeps trying to find subtle ways of touching me. Brush of a hand here, whisper or two there…

I attempt to order another but Jack stops me. "Easy there, sprite, I think you've had enough." Who does he think he is? I attempt to scowl at him, but my vision is a little blurred and I likely look like an abstract painting. "If you drink any more, you'll be leaving here broke with all that you've bid on."

I wake up hungover, not remembering much from last night, other than I bought some outlandish activities to do while I'm here. I'll never drink a whiskey sour again… *Or at least for the next week.* I turn over and find Jack on top of the duvet, wearing an undershirt and boxer briefs.

Jack. Is in my bed. Again.

"Jack!" I shriek.

His eyes flutter open. "Mornin'."

"Don't you *mornin'* me, mister. What are you doing here?"

"You asked me to stay and do… *other things*." He winks and I hate that it makes my stomach do that fluttery thing again. "But I'm a gentleman. Besides, I could never take advantage of the woman who is my new investor."

"I'm sorry, I must've misheard you. Your what?" My voice comes out shrill, but I can't wrap my mind around it.

"Go check the paperwork on the desk. I was honestly surprised you agreed."

"Agreed to what?"

I don't wait for an answer and throw back the duvet. As I rush to the desk, I couldn't care less that I'm only in my underwear; it's nothing he hasn't seen before. I sift through the papers and find verbiage that states Ben will give me two-point billion if I invest one billion in Jack's research.

It feels like a bad spam email or pyramid scheme. The only stipulation I'm finding—other than monetary—is I'm on site for the six month dig. The area he's researching will yield millions of dollars worth of lost artifacts recovered, critical to his research. I only now vaguely remember them mentioning something at the gala about another investor they want me to keep an eye on.

Why me?

A billion dollars. All I need to do is hang out with a sexy man who is digging up old pottery shards. It can't be that bad, right?

"So, I fund your quest for fortune and glory, and in six months, I'll be a billionaire?" I confirm.

Jack props himself on his elbows. "That's it. You can review the paperwork with your lawyers, but I was in as much shock as you when Ben presented it last night."

"And what of the note?"

"Ah, yes, well… that does complicate things, doesn't it? But what do you say, my wee spitfire, are you up for an adventure?"

Amanda and Jack's story continues in
Unexpectedly Ruined.
To see their one hot night together, start with the
prequel novella, Maybe in Fifty.

LOVED NOT HER VILLAIN?

I hope you loved reading Layla and Ben's story as much as I loved writing it!

Wherever you feel most comfortable, please consider leaving a review on Goodreads, Amazon, or social media! Your honest review means the world to me.

You may have noticed cameos from the Top Shelf Romances series. Keep reading for a chapter sneak peek of *Royally on the Rocks* to find out how Edmund and Sage met. Don't worry, you'll see Layla, Amanda, and Becca again in *Unexpectedly Ruined!*

To keep up with all of my upcoming releases, be sure to follow me over on Amazon!

xoxo,
Irene

ROYALLY ON THE ROCKS
SAGE

"You've got to be kidding me," I mutter under my breath. It's been a hellish day at work dealing with bridezillas, and *this* is what I come home to?

"It's not what it looks like, babe!"

Except, it's exactly what it looks like. Troy is playing video games with a topless blonde woman's head between his legs. Based on how toned she is, without a single stretch mark, I'm guessing she's half his age.

The fresh-faced girl pops up at hearing the sound of my keys aggressively thrown onto the table. Fantastic, it's the girl from two doors down, and now I have to move. "Troy, what was th— Oh." *Yeah. Oh.* "Sorry, Sage. I was looking for, uh, my earring."

"Trinity, get out of my house," I grumble, then gesture to Troy. "Take out the trash while you're at it." My voice is even, void of all emotion; I don't have the energy to fight anyone else today.

I walk to the kitchen and pull out my bottle of whiskey from the cabinet. After grabbing a glass and two frozen stone cubes, I pour myself three fingers. I take a sip, and when I look up, I find her face back between his legs again.

Oh, for fuck's sake.

"Get out! Both of you." She startles and glances around for her top before scurrying to the front door.

Troy returns to his video games, likely about to gaslight me about the whole thing. I honestly couldn't care less. I don't love him. We have a relationship of convenience—he pays half the rent and is amazing in bed. That's it.

Drink in hand, I stand in front of the TV, awaiting his response. "Babe, I'm almost done, can you move?" I turn around and unplug the gaming system. "What the hell, Sage!"

"Really? I walk in to find you getting a blowie from the neighbor, and this is the response I get?" I'm only annoyed he didn't even try to hide fucking around.

He shrugs. "You heard her, she was looking for her earring."

There it is.

I gulp down the rest of my drink, and pull out my phone to order a ride. "You know what? I'm done. Stay the night; I'm headed out. When I get back in the morning, you and your things better be gone."

———

The car pulls up to my favorite bar and I make sure to tip

the driver a little extra for his punctuality; I needed to get the hell out of my house.

As I walk in, I spot my favorite bartender. He's sweet and always makes sure the barflies don't hit on me, so I can drink in peace. I really should learn his name, but after all this time, it's a little awkward. He's actually quite attractive —all 6'4" of him, with sparkling green eyes and a chiseled jaw. If he wasn't nearly a decade younger than me, I might consider a rebound hook-up.

I sit on my usual stool and he brings me a whiskey on the rocks without me having to order it. "Oh no, I know that face. What happened, love?"

After I blow out a deep breath, I down half of my drink in one go. "Well, I just walked in on my boyfriend cheating on me, I had a shitty day at work, and… now I'm here."

He yells to someone further down the bar, "I'm taking ten," then looks back to me. "I'm all yours. So, tell me, why were you with this git in the first place?" He has a pretty thick accent, almost British, but not quite. It takes me a minute to understand what he's saying before I can respond. Also, I have a light whiskey buzz going on, which doesn't help.

I sit up and lean forward, as if I am about to dish out salacious gossip. "He was amazing in bed." Sitting back into my seat, I add, "But that's the problem, you see. I caught the neighbor sucking him off as I walked in the door." I finish my drink and he passes me another. "Guess I wasn't able to satisfy his sexual appetite. It's not like I love him, but it's fucking rude, you know?" I'm not sure why I'm sharing all this, but it's easier to vent to a stranger than my therapist sometimes.

I've been coming to this bar for about a year. I know the owner, Keith, and I usually get comped drinks when I come. Every time my hot bartender is working, he's always fun and flirty, and I always tip well for his trouble. Though, I'm not familiar with this scowl he's wearing right now.

"Are you fucking serious? Well, this won't do." He unties his half apron and tosses it on the counter, then walks over to the other bartender, tells him something, and returns to where I'm seated. "Is he at your place now?" I nod. "Let's go." He moves to the other side of the bar, now less than a foot from me.

"Go where?"

He takes my drink from my hand and places it on the bar. "You're place, love. Do you trust me?"

"No." I cross my arms over my chest, eyeing him suspiciously.

A smirk tilts up his lips. "Well, you shouldn't. But are you up for a little revenge?"

Yes. I absolutely am.

I lightly lick my lip. "What do you have in mind?"

"Come on, pretty girl. Let's go. It may take a little bit of acting, but if my boss can do it, so can I." I have no idea what he means, maybe Keith does improv?

He takes me by the hand to help me off my seat, interlacing our fingers as he guides me out front. As we leave, he grabs two helmets and hands one to me. "You're going to need this." Before I can respond, I'm led to a row of motorcycles where he stops beside one.

"No, absolutely not. I don't have a death wish."

"Come on, Cinnamon. Live a little."

Cinnamon? Who the hell is Cinnamon? I'm not drunk enough to be a stripper tonight.

We face off for a moment and his eyes darken. In a flash, he reaches for me, pulling me into him with his hand splayed on my lower back. My breath hitches being this close to him and I almost drop the helmet.

"Here's what's going to happen, love. You're going to get on my bike, and we're going to go back to your place. I'm guessing the wanker is still there?" I nod. "Good. As you open the front door, I'm going to kiss you harder than any man has ever kissed you. I'm not going to take my hands off you. And I may even take my shirt off, for good measure. He's going to get a taste of his own medicine."

I ponder it for a moment. It's not the worst idea, and I would love to see the look on Troy's face when I bring home a younger man. Also, the possibility of seeing my bartender half-naked is definitely a bonus. "Why didn't you just say that in the first place? I'm in."

"Then it's settled." He steps back, puts on his helmet, and gestures for me to do the same. I borrow a jacket from him and we get on his bike. While it's not my first time on a motorcycle, I am a little nervous about all of this, unsure why he wants to do this for me. Regardless, I'm here for it.

Fuck Troy.

When we arrive at my house, we dismount the bike, and I lead us up the pathway to my front door. As I'm about to insert my key, his hand covers mine. "Don't you think we should practice first?" He's not wrong, this is acting after all.

"Uh, su—" He slides his hand into my hair and pulls his lips to mine, and… *holy shit*. I didn't know what to expect, but I certainly didn't expect this. His lips are soft, and this isn't a "*I had a nice night*" kiss. He tilts me where he wants me, and when my lips part, his tongue teases mine. This is definitely a "*I want to get you naked*" kiss and none of it feels fake. As he pulls back, a whimper escapes me.

"You ready?"

How did that not affect him?

I nod and slide my key back into the lock and turn. The moment I open the door, he wraps his arms around me from behind, kissing my neck. My breath catches the moments his lips touch my skin. He groans loud enough for Troy to hear, "Where's your bedroom? I want you naked. Right. Now."

For a moment, I almost forget this isn't real; it feels too good to have his hands and mouth on me. Out of the corner of my eye, I spot Troy playing video games with his headset on, and I finally reply to my stranger, "Uh, down the hall, second door on the right." He takes the keys out of my hand and tosses them with force onto the table like I did earlier today, then turns me around and winks before his lips are back on mine.

If I thought him kissing me at the front door was hot, this is scorching. His hands are in my hair, our tongues and teeth clashing, fighting for dominance. He breaks away for only a moment to pull my legs around his waist.

With my arms wrapped around his neck, he whispers beside my ear, "Sorry, I got carried away there. It isn't every day a beautiful woman lets you kiss her like that." I bite my lip, and do the only thing I want to do right now: kiss him again. I'm no longer acting, I want to take what I can from this beautiful man, to see how far he will let me go with this charade before it's over.

He carries me to my bedroom, and once we close the door behind us, he sets me down. "You kiss like that, and he still cheated on you?" Shaking his head, he continues, "If you were mine, I wouldn't even look at another woman, let alone touch one." I'm taken aback by the compliment; it's definitely one of the hottest things I've ever heard.

"Yeah, well, I—" He cuts off my reply with another bruising kiss I feel all the way to my toes. I don't stop him, instead I try to take things further, my fingers fumbling to unbutton his shirt. At the second button, I ask into his mouth, "Is this okay?"

He smiles against my lips. "You weren't acting either?" I chuckle as I continue with his shirt. "Then you better not be acting as I make you come all over my face." He shrugs off his dress shirt and tosses it on the ground. "And when you're screaming my name, you better not be fucking acting, either. This is for you, not him."

Shit, I don't know his name!

"I promise." He reaches behind me and with one zip and tug, removes my skirt. I'm tossed onto my bed and he settles between my legs. As he cages me in, it isn't lost on me that this man is in incredible shape.

Maybe I should start dating younger men if they all look and feel like this…

As I wrap my legs around his waist, pulling him closer to me, he laughs, "Someone's feeling spicy tonight. Here I thought I was going home with this sweet unassuming girl who got her heart broken."

A frown furrows my brow. "Since when have I ever been sweet?"

He leans in and kisses me softly, unlike how he feverishly tried to dominate me earlier. When we both come up for air, he insists, "You have your moments, love. That's why you're Cinnamon. Sometimes you're sweet, sometimes you're spicy. Since you've refused to give me your actual name for the better part of the last year, I had to come up with my own for you."

A hearty laugh escapes me. "I have never in my life been called sweet."

"Let me be the judge of that." He moves down my body, until his face is lined up with my... *Oh no. Did I shave recently?*

He strips me out of my underwear, slowly and seductively. For a man who was in a rush moments ago, time seems to have come almost to a complete stop. He glances up through his lashes, and with absolute certainty sighs, "You're a fucking masterpiece." Just as he is about to touch me, there's pounding on the door.

"What the fuck, babe?" Troy screams through the bedroom door. Thankfully, I locked it behind me when we came in.

"Sorry, Troy! Busy looking for an earring."

My sexy bartender joins in, "Don't worry, mate, I'll help her find it." He lowers his voice, so only I can hear him.

"Now, where was I?" A devilish grin spreads across his face.

If we do this, I'm pretty sure he'll ruin me for every other man.

ACKNOWLEDGMENTS

First, I would like to thank my amazing friend and cheerleader, Jodi — I couldn't do this without you!

To my alpha readers Dani, Whisper, Lakshmi, Jamie, Eliza, Effie, Marianne, Florence, Ivy, Bella, and Amanda — You ladies are amazing! I'm so grateful for all of your help with this book.

Dani, this book wouldn't be the same without your British flair! Thank you all for helping make this book the best it could be. I still think some of the words and phrases you suggested are made up, though.

To my ARC readers — Thanks for taking a chance on me! I know my books are so different from other spicy romcoms, so thank you for jumping in with two feet. I am so blessed to have all of you reading and reviewing my work before launch.

To my incredible line editor H.M. Darling — Without you, my books would be trash! I can't thank you enough for helping make my book amazing! Sorry for the butt stuff in the epilogue, again!

To my BFD's — I love you!

Finally, thank you to all of my author friends for not letting my imposter syndrome take over, my "real life" friends for believing in me, and my family for putting up with my silly little dream of becoming a published author.

ABOUT IRENE

Irene Bahrd is a feisty Capricorn and one of the most avid readers you will ever meet. Her favorite genres to read or write include romantic comedies, political romance, romantasy, and the occasional contemporary or dark romance.

She started her writing journey as a dare from a friend, after recounting dating stories from her early twenties. They inspired her to write spicy romantic comedies and parodies that feature a variety of book boyfriends—though most are cinnamon roll golden retrievers. Many of her stories contain LGBTQIA+, disabled, and neurodivergent characters.

Irene can be found on most social media platforms under @irenebahrdauthor

ALSO BY IRENE BAHRD

Flexible Standards

Royally Cuffed

Hard to Swallow

Thirst Trap Book Boyfriends Satire Series

Trapp Temptations: Vol. 1

Trapp Temptations: Vol. 2